SYLVIA'S SECRET

A WORK OF LITERARY FICTION
BY SCOTT EVANS

And we, too, had a relationship—
          Tight wires between us,
          Pegs too deep to uproot, and a mind like a ring

          Sliding shut on some quick thing,
          The constriction killing me also.
               From *"The Rabbit Catcher"*
               by Sylvia Plath

Sylvia's Secret

Published by Port Yonder Press LLC

Shellsburg, Iowa

www.PortYonderPress.com

ISBN 9781935600312

Library of Congress Control Number 2012949674

Edited by Chila Woychik

Editorial assistance provided by Heidi Kortman

Book design by *behindthegift.com*

A Port Yonder Book: an imprint of Port Yonder Press

First paperback edition

Printed in the United States of America 2013

Dedicated to those who battle depression and other forms of mental illness.
Look to Sylvia's *life* for inspiration, not her death.
Her talent was taken far too soon.

Chapter 1

Cassandra shivered in London's early December air. Snow fell steadily from clouds packed over the city's rooftops like a dentist's wads of cotton. The sidewalk on Oxford Street was normally bustling with shoppers at noon, but was all but deserted now. Yet Cass knew someone was following her. She was wrapped in a wool scarf tucked inside her heavy hooded winter coat, and looked more like a mummy than Halle Berry, the actress to whom most people compared her, though she was taller and a little darker. She craned her head to search the sidewalk behind, turning her face out of the wind for a moment. Yes. She was sure a shadowy figure in the distance followed her, too far back to be recognized.

Was it Trevor? Not Trevor Thomas, Plath's downstairs neighbor at the time of her suicide, but a younger Trevor she'd met in Devon, a handsome Brit her age who didn't smoke—well, not often anyway and only at pubs, late, late—and who hadn't made fun of yet another American scholar come to pick through the bones of Sylvia Plath and Ted Hughes. Trevor Howard had proven to be a good fellow researcher, a warm friend and an even better lover. A Cambridge scholar, Trevor's focus on the psyche of Ted Hughes complemented Cass's work on the amazingly creative drive of

Sylvia Plath. That had drawn them together in the first place.

At first, Trevor shared all of his ideas with her. His insights into the fiercely competitive ego of Ted Hughes helped Cass herself better understand Sylvia's conflicted spirit. Trevor changed after they'd become intimate in early October. What had seemed like care and concern abruptly transmogrified into jealousy and suspicion.

Trevor proudly showed her off as Catwoman at the Halloween party he'd taken her to, introducing her to many of his friends from Cambridge. She was a great hit with especially the men. They had purred and growled at her, pretending to gobble her neck. True, she had lapped up the attention, energized by it, having the most guilt-free fun since arriving in England on her Fulbright.

But later that night in his apartment, Trevor had screamed at her, yelling about how inappropriate her behavior was, how embarrassed he was to have such a "vulgar slut" as a girlfriend.

In the morning, he had apologized, blaming the name-calling on the liquor he'd consumed. They'd spent less time together over the next few weeks, an uneasy ceasefire.

By mid-November, Trevor had soured bitterly when she told him she needed to return to London. She invented an excuse—she had to meet friends who were visiting for the Christmas holidays. Trevor had seen through her lies, she suspected, but hadn't put up much of a fight.

Not at the time. But now that she was in London, perhaps he'd found the separation unbearable. Maybe he was keeping his distance, but stalking her, ready to fly into a jealous rage the moment she showed any interest whatsoever in another man.

She could imagine it—Trevor wouldn't keep his distance for long. He'd charge her and try to kiss her. Even now she sensed his presence. If not him, *someone* was back there, hiding behind lace curtains of snow, keeping pace with her, just far enough back to be unseen.

An agent from Ted Hughes's estate perhaps, watching, making

sure she didn't get too close to the truth. She hadn't wanted to believe it at first. More and more she knew the truth of it, the horrible, ugly truth about Sylvia Plath's cheating spouse. Ted *had* murdered Sylvia after all. Not just emotionally and psychologically, but actually.

Sylvia and the children had been ill for so long, weeks and weeks with very little outside help. By the time Ted appeared, Sylvia was in a rage, furious and vengeful. She'd written her brother that she'd bitten off Ted's earlobes. She'd destroyed Ted's prized edition of the works of Shakespeare, a book they had spent hours reading together, amorously, reading aloud, over-acting the scenes. Ted had to know, if Sylvia could tear *that* book to shreds, she could have torn his beating heart from his chest and bitten it into squirming, slug-like pieces right in front of his eyes.

Cass had, through her readings of all she could lay her hands on, come to suspect that Ted might have been afraid of Sylvia, fearing she might kill him before killing herself. That Ted had wished her dead was certain—even if he himself hadn't been brave enough to admit it. All one had to do was listen to the play he'd written for the BBC's Third Programme, *Difficulties of a Bridegroom*, in which the main character, Sullivan, purposefully runs down a rabbit on his way to meet a seductive mistress. The driver stops for the dead hare and takes it with him to London where he sells it to buy flowers for his lover. The symbolism unmistakable—Sylvia as road kill, a fat dead thing that needed to be eliminated, but a thing that still rewarded even after its death.

Ted had profited from Sylvia's so-called suicide, hadn't he?

Anger welled up within Cass. She walked faster, leaning against the wind and snow. In contrast to the slow-moving traffic on the street, her mind raced with thoughts. She didn't want to hate men, she wanted to love and befriend them, as she had Trevor Howard in Devon and Joe Conrad in California. Trevor had betrayed her trust by turning against her when she needed to leave. Understandable.

Lovers whose only attraction was physical could not bear separation. Donne had taught her that in his poem "A Valediction: Forbidding Mourning."

Joe Conrad was a different story. Not a lover, no, not at all. But a friend. A colleague at Central Lutheran University in Stockton, California. She'd felt so sorry for him six years ago when he was about to lose everything—his job, his wife, his freedom, his reputation. Suspected of horrid crimes against women, Joe had crumbled at first, a stale gingerbread man. Her heart had ached for him. She had tried to comfort him strictly as a friend, keeping it all professional, aboveboard. He was married after all and if she felt even the slightest attraction to him, she'd kept it to herself. And somehow he had found the strength to fight back against the falsehoods and triumph, not once, but twice. Now he was something of a star at their campus, going for tenure.

Thank God she'd written a note of support via email. She hoped it wasn't too late. She'd become so preoccupied with London and her research—her discoveries, the lost notebook, the missing journal pages!—she just couldn't keep the ordinaries, as she liked to call the humdrum chores of life, she couldn't keep the ordinaries straight.

She'd emailed Dr. Thorne before leaving her flat on Fitzroy Road just a few houses down from the building where Sylvia had gassed herself. Or where, like a Jewess of the Holocaust, she'd been gassed by someone else, someone who'd staged her death, even with her children sleeping upstairs.

The snow covered Cass's shoulders. Lost in her thoughts, she almost missed the coffee shop where she had arranged to meet a solicitor. She needed to share her findings with someone in an official capacity. Just in case.

Catching sight of her face in the dark window of the coffee house, her eyes ablaze with worry, she halted.

In case of what, Cass? In case I'm not wrong about being

followed? In case someone IS trying to stop me? Trying to keep the truth locked up in one of those trunks in the office of Ted Hughes's attorney?

She pushed through the door, shook off the snow, tugged off her hood and scarf, revealing her full lips, striking quite the pose in the doorway, she could tell, since all eyes fell on her. She smiled bashfully and looked around the cozy, dark room, searching for someone who looked like what she imagined a London solicitor should look like. The room smelled heavenly of coffee, scented teas and pastries.

A dour little man in a tweed suit, more like T. S. Eliot than the Daniel Craig or Pierce Brosnan she'd hoped for, stood and approached her.

"Are you Miss Johnson, the American poet?" Even his voice was thin and high-pitched. He held out his hand limply.

This is J. Alfred Prufrock!

She was tempted to deny herself and pretend she was someone else. But no, she had called him after all so it would be terribly, terribly rude, as Trevor might say, to turn him away. Besides, if push came to shoveling dirt on a grave—an expression she'd coined for her students, eschewing clichés—she would need an ally.

"Yes," she admitted. "My chums call me Cass."

"Delighted. Am I to be a chum, then?" He produced a smirk that seemed to be an attempt at flirting. "Thought this was strictly business."

Cass laughed politely, and then followed him to a small table in the rear. Taking her seat, she held his gaze, saying, "Everyone's my friend, Mr. Middlebrook. My chum. Until they betray me."

CHAPTER 2

Rain fell steadily from low, dark clouds outside the tall windows of the old classroom. Inside Joseph Lawrence Conrad sat at a heavy wooden library table, waiting to hear the decision of the tenure and promotion committee. Dr. Thorne, the Chairman of the English Department at Central Lutheran University, his white hair framing his face squarely, stood with a piece of paper clenched in his fingers, looking like Robert Frost reading at John F. Kennedy's inauguration. Joe Conrad, having turned thirty-four two months earlier, anticipated good news from the committee. Despite the dreary rain slapping the windows, Joe was confident, but something in the room—an air of tension—wormed its way into his thoughts.

Thorne cleared his throat. "Before we get to the committee's decision, I wanted to read an email I received this morning from Cassandra Johnson who as most of you know is in London doing a Fulbright. Cass wrote, 'Although I'm not a tenured member of your faculty myself, I want to express my support for Joe, who has been an outstanding colleague of ours for many years. Since he and I joined your department at about the same time, we have formed a special bond and friendship. Moreover, Joe has been a very supportive mentor to me and has helped me grow in so many ways as a teacher. If I had a vote, I would use it to promote Joe Conrad to the rank of full professor and grant him tenure. CLU is a better college with Joe there."

"Here, here," Craig Richmond said, bringing looks of surprise from other faculty members at the oblong mahogany table. It was no secret that Craig had opposed hiring Joe years earlier, but even he had warmed to Joe, thanks to his charm and good luck.

Joe's face flushed. "Very nice of Cass," he managed.

Thorne placed the note on the table, glancing at it before looking back up to scan the room of tenured professors. He finally gave Joe a weak smile. "You should know that the committee received a similar letter of support from Smitty, which is remarkable, considering his wife's condition."

The others nodded. Joe had seen Smitty—Jonathan Smythe—only the week before at the hospital where his wife, Alicia, was dying of leukemia. The memory brought tears to Joe's eyes. Smitty, if not a father figure, was at least like an uncle to Joe, ever since their adventures with the Shakespeare papers several years before.

Joe had endured the entire tenure process and it had occupied most of his fall semester. He had gathered letters of support, student evaluations, published articles—doing it all happily, sure he simply had to leap through the academic hoops necessary to be rewarded with the formal affirmation of his colleagues. But now the tomb-like silence around the table made the wait unbearable.

Finally, Joe himself shattered the silence with a laugh and said, "Should I force the moment to its crisis?"

"I agree," Craig Richmond said. "You've kept poor Joe in suspense long enough."

Thorne nodded solemnly and placed his fingertips on the surface of the table as if needing support. "I've been in this department over twenty-five years and there was only one other time, many years ago, when the news from the tenure and promotion committee was not favorable—for very different reasons, I should add. Joe, I regret to inform you that you will not be granted tenure at this time."

Joe's chest tightened. He'd been a member of this faculty for almost nine years, and had assumed they'd finally accepted him. Now he could barely look around the room. The others—eight male and three female colleagues—stared ahead, not daring to meet Joe's eyes.

"I'm stunned," Craig Richmond said. "Granted, when Joe first joined us, I didn't think he was qualified. And he's certainly had his ups and downs, especially falsely accused of those horrible crimes. But he's more than proven himself as a great teacher."

"There's no question that Joe's an excellent teacher," Thorne responded.

"Not to mention his contributions to the college," Richmond added. "I for one would hate to see Joe pull those Shakespeare manuscripts out of the library."

"We all would hate to lose access to the Shakespeare papers, of course," Thorne replied. "And, Joe, the vote was close. In fact, among the faculty, it was a tie."

Joe sat silently and let the verdict sink in.

"Who cast the deciding vote?" Craig asked. "You?"

Thorne shook his head. "No. The Dean."

Joe nodded. He closed his calendar book and pushed back his chair forcefully. Its legs grated across the wooden floor.

"Joe," Thorne said, "the fact that you received so many votes in your favor, despite the fact that you don't hold a doctorate, well, that's quite an accomplishment. I hope you can appreciate that."

Joe stood, his face red and his eyes stinging. "Yes, I appreciate those who voted in my favor." He glanced around the room, trying to pick out the faces of sympathetic colleagues.

"Joe," Thorne continued, "we've never given tenure to someone who didn't have a Ph.D. The Dean argued that we'd set a bad precedent if we were to make an exception."

"I see," was all Joe could manage. He was sick to his stomach. The night before, he and Sara had gone out to dinner. To celebrate. How foolish it all seemed now.

"Don't leave quite yet," Thorne commanded. "The Dean did offer two consolations, which all of us on the committee support."

Joe was facing the door, but stopped and turned back toward the Chairman. "What's my consolation prize?"

"Well, first, we want to offer you a permanent instructorship. Normally, someone of your rank is required to move on after six years, but with a permanent position, you can stay here at CLU as long as you like."

"Yippee," Joe said flatly.

"It's something, Joe," Thorne said. "You won't be a full professor, but with what you've made from your books and the sale of the Shakespeare manuscripts, you really don't need the money."

"No," he admitted. "I don't need the money."

"If you earn your doctorate, then you can reapply. As long as your degree is from an accredited institution, tenure is virtually assured."

Joe nodded. "That's very generous."

"Joe, the college is going through re-accreditation next year. Granting tenure to someone who doesn't hold a terminal degree—it wouldn't look good."

"I understand," Joe said. He stepped closer to the door. "That's an odd expression, isn't it," he said, his back to them. "A *terminal* degree. Makes it sound like an unsurvivable illness."

Joe pulled the door open and stepped into the dim hallway where he stood for a moment trying to decide what he should do next. He had a class in an hour and another later in the day, but facing his students suddenly seemed unbearable. They all knew he was up for tenure. He'd have to tell them the news. It would be humiliating.

True, it wasn't their fault he hadn't been promoted. But how would they look at him? News was sure to get out right away, if it wasn't already travelling with electronic speed among the students via text messages. No. He couldn't face his students. This was the last meeting before finals, so he hadn't planned on doing much anyway. Answer a few questions, offer a few hints about what might be on the final exams, and give the course evaluations, as he always did on the last day of the classes.

What was the point? They were as ready as they'd ever be. Besides, he wasn't even sure he'd be back in the spring to teach. Hell, he might even cancel his final exams!

The door opened behind him and Craig Richmond stepped out.

"Sorry, Joe. I thought you deserved it."

"That means a lot coming from you."

Joe started down the hall toward the staircase, heading for his office, his only refuge in this storm.

"You should take the Dean's offer."

"The permanent instructorship?"

"Well, yes. That. But also, finish your doctorate and reapply for tenure. You live in Davis. UCD is, what, ten blocks from your house?"

Joe nodded. He'd started there once before. *Maybe I should go back, if they'd let me in now. Why wouldn't they?* He'd donated one of the handwritten plays of the author formerly known as Shakespeare to the University of California, Davis. They owed him, damn it. A lot of people owed him.

"I'll think about it."

Craig laid a hand on Joe's shoulder. "Don't let the bastards get you down."

"Thanks, Craig."

Joe turned and walked to the staircase. Someone's class had let out, so a stream of students washed down the stairs, some of them nodding at Joe, a few adding, "Hey, Professor," and "Hi, Mister Conrad," as they hurried to escape the suffocating grip of the building.

Upstairs, Joe sat in his office, staring at the phone. He was tempted to call Sara and give her the bad news, but she would still be in class. *Should I leave a message on her cell? No. News like this is best delivered in person.*

Dark, convoluted rain clouds hung outside his window, the rain pelting the remaining brown leaves that clung to the old oaks. The dreary weather made him shiver. He wasn't sure how he felt. Betrayed, certainly. Angry, yes. But sad too. Utterly sad, as though the gloomy clouds were an ocean wave, pressing, smothering.

"The hell with it," he said. Using a dry ink pen, he scratched out a note that said, *Conrad's classes canceled today. Prep for finals next week.* Then he turned off his computer, packed a few papers in his briefcase, turned out the light and locked his door. He used a thumbtack and posted the note outside his classroom across the hall.

As he walked across campus to his car, gripping his umbrella and fighting to hold it against the wind and rain, the bell tower chimed—two o'clock. It would take him an hour to drive back to Davis from Stockton. Maybe Sara would be home with the kids. They'd be surprised to see him home so early on a Wednesday. Normally, with his four o'clock class, which lasted until five-thirty, he didn't arrive home until half past six. Sara would show him sympathy. She could help him figure out what to do now, and they could share a bottle of wine and talk.

It wasn't the end of the world. But with all he'd been through during the past seven years, fighting accusations of rape and murder, then fighting to prove that the Shakespeare manuscripts were authentic, this *was* the end of something. Joe just wasn't sure what.

CHAPTER 3

Traffic on northbound I-5 was lighter than normal, probably due to the steady rain, Joe suspected. When he made the turn onto westbound Highway 50, climbing slowly over the bridge that crossed the Sacramento River, Joe looked toward the coastal range, hoping to see the edge of the rain clouds. Instead, the blanket of dark, billowing clouds thickened farther west; they were in for a cold, wet December night.

Maybe it'll get cold enough for snow. It snowed in the valley every ten years or so. If they awoke to a snow-covered wonderland, his children—Katie, at nine, and Brian, at six—would be thrilled.

Christmas was only three weeks away. He and Sara had put up the tree, and all of them had helped decorate the house over the weekend. If he could just get through the next week of finals, he'd have five weeks off before the spring semester started, plenty of time to sort out this mess.

Joe tried to keep his mind from replaying Thorne's words—*I regret to inform you....*

With the money he had made from his book, *Tragic Flaws*, which recounted his experience of being wrongly accused of several rapes and murders, and with money made from "donating" the Shakespeare manuscripts, Joe and Sara had finally bought a home, larger than the one they'd rented, but still on Tenth Street, just blocks from the school Brian and Katie attended and from the high school where Sara taught math. Their new two-story home had four bedrooms and a spacious living room, along with an enormous backyard where the kids could play safely and where Joe threatened to have a swimming pool put in. But Sara—still frugal and uncomfortable with the wealth Joe had accumulated—resisted such an indulgence, arguing that the city pool was within walking distance from their house.

As he turned from B Street onto Tenth, a car he didn't recognize was parked in front of his house. A black Saab convertible with vanity plates that read GO FIGR. Joe pulled slowly into the driveway and parked behind Sara's car.

"Go figure." *Some math geek's idea of clever. Sara must have another math teacher over.*

Joe slipped in through the kitchen door and hung up his raincoat on the coat rack. Sara's bright yellow coat was hanging next to someone else's black slicker. Both were dry.

Setting his briefcase on the counter, he walked through the dining room, expecting to see Sara sitting in the living room chatting with another woman from the high school math department. Instead, he found an open bottle of wine on the table—a special red wine, Holly's Hill Mouvedre—that he had bought for the two of them to share.

Joe walked up the carpeted stairs and expected to find Sara and another female teacher in the study looking up math stuff on the computer and laughing over their glasses of wine, surprised to see Joe home early. Later, when they were alone, he'd tell Sara that, for a fleeting moment, he'd thought she might be with another man, and they'd have a good laugh. Sara would probably slap his arm, as she often did when she was pleasantly annoyed by something he said.

The study was empty.

Joe walked down the hall to the master bedroom. The door was closed. He listened, and his heart beat so loudly he was sure someone else could hear it.

No sounds came from behind the door. He tested the handle. Locked.

Joe pulled the Swiss army knife out of his pocket and opened the Phillips head screwdriver. He inserted into the hole of the door handle. He eased the handle down and opened the door slowly, fearing what he would see.

The dim room smelled of perfume. Candles burned on the nightstand next to Sara's side of the bed. An empty wine glass stood on each nightstand. The blankets and comforter were pulled up, so from the doorway, Joe could see only the top of Sara's head nestled on the shoulder of a man whose sleeping features he didn't recognize. The man had wavy black hair, thick eyebrows and a black mustache, his breathing heavy and rhythmic. Joe stepped closer to Sara's side of the bed. She too slept deeply, peacefully.

The curtains were drawn, but there was enough light for Joe to study the faces of the two lovers in repose. He felt weak, as if he might faint, but also as if he wasn't there, as if he were watching an episode on television.

He didn't own a gun, but if he had, he'd be tempted to blow the guy's head off. He considered sneaking back down stairs to grab a very large knife, but then he looked at the Swiss army knife that was still in his hand. He closed the screwdriver and pushed the knife back into his pocket.

Then he noticed the top of the man's chest. Much hairier than his own. *Was that the attraction?* Maybe Sara liked resting her cheek on this bed of matted black hair.

The image of him on top of Sara was too much.

Joe reached over and turned on the lamp. "WHAT THE HELL?"

Sara lurched out of sleep and tugged the comforter up around her. The man threw off the covers and jumped to his feet. Before turning around, he pulled a pair of jeans up over his muscular haunches.

"Who the hell are YOU!" Joe screamed.

"I'm nobody." The man bent down and gathered up the rest of his clothes, then scrambled to the bathroom and slammed the door.

Sara sat with a stunned look on her face.

"Oh my God, Joe," she said. "Oh my God!"

"Where are the kids?"

"What?"

"The kids, Sara. Where the hell are our kids?"

"Still at daycare." She pushed the palms of her hands against her eyes and shook her head. "What are you doing home?" she asked.

"Well, I'm sure not sleeping with a stranger!"

"You're never home before six-thirty on Wednesdays."

"So just because I'm usually late on Wednesdays, *that* makes it okay to screw another man? Today *was* different. Do you remember what was special about today, Sara?"

She uncovered her eyes. "Oh, God. Your tenure meeting. Of course. How'd it go?"

"How'd it go?" Joe laughed. "You're really asking me that? Are you kidding?" He snickered. "Let's just say, I've been screwed twice today. Or, no. Not screwed. *You* got screwed. I got betrayed. Betrayed royally—twice in one day!"

"Oh, God, Joe, I'm sorry."

The man in the bathroom knocked on the door. "Is it safe to come out?" he called.

"I should kill you!" Joe yelled.

"Joe," Sara whispered, then started to cry. "Please go downstairs and let Nathan leave so we can talk."

"Nathan? The asshole's name is Nathan?"

Sylvia's Secret

"Please," Sara sobbed. "Let him leave so we can talk."

Joe's heart pounded and acid rose in his gut. He stomped out of the room and hurried downstairs. Seeing the wine bottle, he picked it up and swung it in the air. "Hurry down, Nathan! I've got another bottle of wine for you!"

"JOE! PLEASE LET HIM GO!"

Joe put the wine bottle down on the table, then pulled out his pocket knife. He opened the blade and waited at the foot of the stairs.

Wrapped in the comforter, Sara came to the railing.

"No, Joe! Don't hurt him. Let him leave."

"He can leave," Joe yelled. "After I cut off his—"

"Joe, I swear to God, I'll call the cops if you don't get out of the way."

"You want me to get out of the way? You want ME to get out of the way?" Joe jerked open the front door. "Tell the asshole to get out of MY way, Sara."

"Let him leave, please, Joe. I know you're upset, but let him leave."

"Sure, dear. Whatever you say."

He stormed out to the Saab and smiled. With several deft motions, he sliced the convertible top of the car, opening a gaping hole over the passenger's seat that allowed rain water to flood in on the leather upholstery. Then he rushed around to the driver's door and scratched FUCK YOU into the paint.

Joe finished his artwork, saw the man appear at the front door, then duck back inside. Joe ran around the car, up the walkway and back inside the house. The man—Nathan—was running through the dining room to the kitchen. Joe chased him, grabbing the empty wine bottle as he ran, and hurled it at him. The bottle slammed into his lower back just as he opened the door to the driveway.

"Damn it!" the man yelled. He ran through the doorway and slammed it shut behind him.

Joe rushed toward the kitchen door, but then stopped and turned, racing back to the front. He made it out onto the porch and halfway down the walk by the time the Saab fishtailed around the corner and disappeared.

Dripping wet, Joe walked back into the house and slammed the front door closed. Sara sat on the stairs in front of him, wrapped in the comforter, tears streaming down her face. Joe's chest heaved, and he could only stare at her.

Finally, she managed to say, "I'm sorry, Joe. I'm so sorry."

Joe took a step toward her, but his knees buckled and he dropped down, as if to pray. Then he vomited on the new beige carpet.

After cleaning up in the downstairs bathroom, Joe watched Sara—dressed in jeans and a sweatshirt now—clean the carpet where he'd gotten sick. She was still crying, but not as forcefully. Joe sat on a step, weak, his stomach still churning.

"God, Sara, how could you?" His tone was more quizzical than accusatory, as if he just didn't understand. "As many times as you've accused me of cheating, how could you be so hypocritical?"

She shook her head, still rubbing the spot on the carpet. "I don't know. It just kind of happened over the last few months."

Joe shook his head, trying to clear his mind. "Wait. This has been going on for months?"

Sara stopped rubbing the carpet and sat back on her heels. "It started in September, I guess. Nathan was the consultant from UCD I told you about, the one who designed the new Real World Math program we're trying out."

"So you've been screwing him since September?"

"No, no. He started consulting with the math department in September. Everyone in our department fell in love with him. He's brilliant and funny, and he teaches karate in the evenings."

Joe snorted. "A real renaissance man."

"You've been so busy with your tenure preparation, Joe, you haven't really been very involved with us, you know."

"What the hell are you talking about, Sara? You're blaming your affair on *me*?"

Sara closed her eyes and another tear rolled down her cheek. "No, I'm not blaming you. I'm just trying to explain it. There was this attraction. I mean, I felt this incredible attraction."

"So when did you actually start fucking?"

"Would you not say that, please. You know how I hate that word."

"Oh, excuse me, dear. I'd hate to offend your sensibilities. Let me put it another way. How long has the brilliant and funny Nathan been sticking it to my wife?"

"Joe, please. This is hard for me."

Joe snorted. "Was Nathan hard for you too? I'll bet he was very hard for you."

"I know you're hurt, Joe. You have every right to be. Like I was when you were going to those topless bars."

Joe leapt to his feet. "Are you serious? That was years ago, and I never actually slept with any of those girls."

"So you say."

Joe saw a certain strength in Sara that he hadn't noticed in years. *She never believed me. All these years later, she still thinks I've been with other women.*

Joe walked into the kitchen, grabbed a glass from the shelf, and filled it with ice from the refrigerator door. Then he poured scotch over the ice, looked down at the sweet brown liquid, the vapor rising from the glass, swirled the scotch a few times and downed it. After swallowing, he refilled the glass and added a few splashes of soda. Then he sat at the kitchen table and gazed out the window at the darkness of the winter evening.

He hadn't worried about losing Sara in years, not since she had been wounded in the leg when he had battled a killer who was after the Shakespeare manuscripts. After returning triumphantly from England with his two helpful colleagues, Joe was certain his troubles were behind him. The money he'd made, the new house, the easy comings and goings of family life—all those comfortable routines now felt like a charade.

Sara walked in and rinsed out the towel in the sink.

"Do you love this guy, Sara?"

Her back to Joe, she shrugged. "I might. I'm not sure."

"Does he love you?"

Sara turned around. "I don't know. He says he does, but he's married, too."

Joe shook his head, exhausted. "Do you want a divorce?"

Sara shrugged again, tears streaming down her cheek. "I'm not sure, Joe. Do you?"

Joe gulped some of his drink and shrugged. "I'm still so stunned, I don't know how to feel."

"I didn't mean for this to happen."

"That's such a cliché, Sara."

"I'm just trying to explain what happened. *How* it happened. Maybe I'm still trying to make sense of it myself."

Joe swallowed the rest of the scotch and refilled his glass, foregoing the soda this time.

"We worked together, Joe. We worked *closely* together, and there were times when the attraction was so strong, I thought I might pass out."

"Nice. That's real nice to know."

Sara swiped a tear from her cheek. "Well, I guess that's what it must have been like for you. Wasn't the sexual attraction you felt for those strippers so strong you just couldn't keep away?"

"Jesus. That was six or seven years ago. When do I get forgiven?"

"It always causes me pain, Joe. Even now. Whenever I think about it."

Sylvia's Secret

"I never had sex with any of those women."

"You mean, you never had sexual intercourse with them. But you had sex. Letting them rub their bodies all over you, letting them feel your crotch. That's sex, too, Joe."

Joe lowered his head. They'd gone over this before, years ago. He'd apologized. He'd come to understand what Sara meant. In the meantime, he'd tried to be more responsible, more mature. *Was it all for naught?*

"Sara, I thought you'd forgiven me. I thought we'd moved on with our lives."

She nodded. "In some ways, we have, But. . . ."

"But what? In some ways, we haven't? In some ways, you have *not* forgiven me? Even after I saved your life? Twice!"

Sara grunted. "True. After putting my life in danger, *twice,* you did save me."

"Really? *I* put your life in danger? Is that what you think?"

"Yes. *Your* actions, *your* decisions put me and the children in danger. Both times."

Joe drained his glass, anger swelling inside his chest. "So somehow it's my fault that you're having an affair. I drove you into the arms of another man. A *married* man, no less. All my fault."

Sara's head gave a slight nod. "I'm not saying that you're completely to blame, but, let's face it, our marriage *has* been kind of rocky."

Joe stood so forcefully that he knocked his chair over. Sara jumped back. "The hell with you, Sara. It is not my fault, not this time. I've paid for my sins. I've made amends for hurting you in the past. And I've been faithful to you, despite what you think."

Sara crossed her arms. "Oh, really?"

"YES! REALLY!" He stepped toward her, his fists clenched in rage, but he stopped himself, realizing he wanted to hit her and regretting the impulse the second it materialized. "I've got to get out of here. I'm going to pack up some clothes and go to a hotel or something."

Sara nodded. "Fine. Yes. I think that's a good idea."

Joe took the stairs two at a time and grabbed an overnight bag from the closet. He tossed in underwear, socks, a pair of jeans and a clean shirt, and a few things from the bathroom.

"I'm going to pick up the kids from daycare," yelled Sara from the bottom of the stairs. "Will you still be here when we get back?"

Joe zipped up his bag and strode to the landing. Sara's hand was on the doorknob, and her eyes were filled with something, fear, uncertainty.

"No," said Joe. "I'm leaving. You explain it to the kids. Tell your daughter how it's okay for you to cheat on her father."

Sara looked down, as if just now noticing the spot on the new carpet where she had cleaned Joe's vomit. She nodded and then went out, pulling the door closed behind her.

CHAPTER 4

While Cass ordered another espresso, Mr. Middlebrook listened to her story about finding Plath's lost notebook of poems, apparently very interested at first. Then, as she shared her concerns about the people from Ted Hughes's estate following her, he changed. She saw it in his eyes. His facial expression morphed from intrigue to sympathy to a condescending reluctance.

"I'm quite sure your suspicions are unfounded," Middlebrook announced. His arrogance infuriated her. "The firm that handles the Hughes estate is first rate."

"Really? Then why have they refused to look at the notebook? You'd think they'd want to check its authenticity, wouldn't you?"

She hated the way Middlebrook slurped his coffee. After dabbing his thin lower lip with his napkin, like an old lady would, he smirked. "Perhaps they don't need to examine it to be assured it's *not* authentic."

That's when Cass realized that somehow Middlebrook was working for them, the people who controlled the estate of Ted Hughes. The people who, by extension, had profited from Sylvia's death.

But how? How had they known she would contact Middlebrook? *She* had chosen his name from the phone directory.

"Mr. Middlebrook, do you know why I chose you?" She found his bemused expression maddening.

"Several other solicitors turned you down, I suspect."

"No. I called you first. A woman named Diane Middlebrook wrote a superb biography of Sylvia and Ted Hughes. Are you related to her, by any chance?"

He chuckled. "Not that I know of. Does it matter?"

Yes! To her, it *did* matter. His name, to her, at least, had suggested an immediate loyalty. "Would you like to represent me or not?"

"I'm not sure you can afford me. You're just a college student, aren't you?"

Cass cringed. "No, I am *not* a college student. I'm a full-time professor on leave of absence for a year with a Fullbright scholarship. Don't underestimate me, sir."

Still sneering, Middlebrook said, "I charge one hundred fifty pounds per hour, Ms. Johnson. That's nearly three hundred American dollars. A case like this will require ten hours at minimum. Can you afford three thousand dollars? Or more, if matters should become complicated?"

She gasped. She'd imagined it would take a couple hours of work, no more than a few hundred dollars.

"All I want you to do is set up a meeting with the people at the Hughes estate so I can show them the notebook. That will require a phone call."

"Do you have the notebook with you? May I see it?"

She shook her head. "Of course not. Do you think I'd be stupid enough to carry something that is potentially worth a million dollars—or a million pounds, as you might say—through the streets of London without someone to protect me?"

The frail little man smiled. "Am I to be your protector then?"

Sylvia's Secret

She nodded, realizing how absurd it seemed. She was taller and physically more powerful than Middlebrook. "I want someone in a position of authority to protect my interests. Someone who will make sure they don't steal these poems, the way Ted stole Sylvia's notebooks after her death."

"You would have me accompany you when you meet with the firm handling the Hughes estate?"

"Of course."

"And I am to support you in your claim that this notebook of alleged Plath poetry is authentic?"

She leaned toward the man's pasty face. "You would represent my interests, yes."

"Miss Johnson, I would need time to study the notebook myself, to consult scholars who are experts on Plath's writing, time to—"

"*I'm* an expert on Plath's writing, damn it!"

People at the surrounding tables quieted and stared.

"Please keep your voice down."

"I'm sorry, I'm sorry," she said, her voice rising again. "It's just, you don't seem to grasp who I am and what I'm telling you."

"Please," Middlebrook said, gesturing with his hands, "lower your voice."

"Look, I'm a Fullbright scholar, a poet in residence, and I'm writing a book about Sylvia Plath."

"Yes, I do grasp all that."

"In the course of my research, I discovered one of the lost notebooks of Sylvia's poetry. Poems she wrote shortly before her death."

"Where did you find this missing notebook?"

Something told Cass she shouldn't trust this man.

"I'm not going to say," she answered. "Not yet."

"Oh?" Middlebrook leaned away. "And why not?"

"Because there may be other notebooks."

The little man grinned again, a most condescending little smirk that further infuriated Cass.

"Miss-ter Middlebrook," she said slowly, "I'm not sure you appreciate how significant this find might be. Ted Hughes claimed he burned one of Sylvia's notebooks of poems immediately after her death. He claimed he simply lost another. And there is evidence that a third unpublished notebook is being held by Ted's lawyers, to be published years after his death."

"I am aware of some of those details," Middlebrook responded. "I did a little research of my own, after we spoke by phone."

"You *are* aware, are you not, that one of those notebooks became Sylvia Plath's signature work, her book of poems titled *Ariel?*"

"Yes, I know."

"Well, imagine that three more *Ariels* could be released to Plath's fans."

"I'm sure they'd do quite well, but I doubt they'd be worth anywhere close to a million pounds."

Now it was her turn to lean away and smirk at this small man's misjudgment. "Oh? What would *you* estimate their value to be?"

"Poetry doesn't really sell, you know. You don't find books of poetry on the list of bestsellers, do you?"

"So what's your estimate, Mr. Middlebrook?"

The man shrugged. "I don't know. Five thousand pounds. Perhaps ten."

Cass leaned closer again. "Why do you suppose Ted Hughes burned one of the notebooks? Or at least claimed he had?"

Middlebrook took off his glasses and cleaned them with the white linen napkin.

"Because they were not flattering, I imagine. They didn't paint a very nice picture of Mr. Hughes, I'm sure."

She snorted. "That's an understatement."

"Well, one can understand his wife's vindictiveness, can't one? He'd left her for another woman."

"Yes, he did, Mr. Middlebrook. Ted left Sylvia and their two small children to go shag another woman, with whom he had a child, you know."

"Yes, I did know that much." The little man carefully placed his wire-rim glasses back on his narrow nose. "You see, I've already done a spot of research, as I mentioned earlier. You do know, of course, that we in Great Britain regard Ted Hughes far differently than you American feminists do. Hughes was one of England's great Poet Laureates, wasn't he. Plath, on the other hand, was a possessive, mentally ill shrew."

Cass pounded the table, startling the timid man. "Please don't talk about her that way!" she yelled. Then, lowering her voice, she added, "At the time of her death, Sylvia was under a doctor's care for severe depression, caused by your great Poet Laureate's lies and infidelity."

"Alright," Middlebrook said in a low, soothing voice. "Technically, if I take you on as a client, you'll already owe me for two hours of billable time."

She quickly calculated the amount, almost six hundred dollars. She gulped. Middlebrook might have been right after all; she might not be able to afford him.

"What if..."

"Go on, Miss Johnson."

"What if the notebook of poems I have are worth considerably more than your estimate?"

"As I said, I'd have to bring in outside experts."

Cass shut her eyes against the sting of Middlebrook's insult, and reined in her rage.

"Do you know what happened to the great poet's second would-be wife, Assia Weavill?"

Middlebrook stared at her blankly.

"Apparently, you didn't do enough research then," Cass answered. "She murdered their daughter, a toddler at the time, and then killed herself, just like Sylvia. Your great Poet Laureate was having more affairs, you see."

Mr. Middlebrook's jaw literally dropped and he adjusted himself in his chair. "While that's quite shocking, I still don't see how it would affect the price people might be willing to pay for a new book of Plath's poems."

She grinned. "Murder, Mr. Middlebrook. What if the new poems prove that Ted Hughes murdered Sylvia Plath?"

Middlebrook blushed. "These poems *prove* murder?"

Cass nodded. "Beyond a shadow of a doubt."

This news could easily have been the worm dangling on the hook to finally reel in the London lawyer, but it had the opposite result. The little man pushed his chair away from the table, and stared at her with something like fear in his eyes.

"This consultation is free, Miss Johnson, but if you call on me again, I'll have to get a retainer from you."

With that, he gathered up his briefcase and turned toward the door.

After he'd left, Cass sat in the coffee shop for another hour or so, wondering who she could turn to. Middlebrook had proven to be a coward. *Should I try a different solicitor?* No, not if they all had the same blind admiration for Ted Hughes. *You're on your own, Cass.*

The following evening while pacing inside her apartment, Cass replayed the conversation in her mind, wondering if she'd revealed too much, worrying that Middlebrook had run straight to the firm that controlled the Hughes estate. How would they react? Would they send someone after her again, making sure they succeeded this time?

The telephone's shrill ring startled her.

"Hello?" Her voice wavered.

"Is this Cass?"

"Yes. Who's this?"

"This is Zenon."

Cass remembered him well. Zenon—or Z, as everyone called him—had been dressed like the old-fashioned Dracula at the Halloween party and had nibbled her neck playfully, one of the reasons Trevor had gotten so jealous.

"Oh, yes. How are you?"

"Not well, I'm afraid."

Cass's heart skipped a beat. "Why? What's happened?"

"Do you have someone there with you?"

"No," she answered. "What's going on?"

"It's about Trevor. He was hit by a car last night while leaving a pub."

"Is he hurt badly then?"

"I'm sorry to say, he died early this morning."

Trever dead? Oh, God, no! Her knees gave out and she collapsed to a sitting position on the floor, still clutching the telephone.

"I wasn't with him," Zenon continued, "so I don't have all the details, but it was a hit and run. The driver never slowed down, according to witnesses."

She tried to control the fear in her voice. "Did he...did he suffer?"

"Never regained consciousness. Little comfort, I know, but it's something."

Cass closed her eyes and tried to stop visualizing the accident. "They're trying to send me a message, Z."

"What?"

"Certain people are trying to shut me up."

"Who? What are you talking about?"

"My phone might be tapped," Cass said. "And not by one of Rupert Murdoch's so-called journalists."

There was silence at the other end of the telephone line. She listened carefully to see if she could detect any noise, like the clicking noise in movies when the FBI was doing a wire tap.

"It's just like Sylvia said. '*The black telephone's off at the root. The voices just can't worm through.*' Maybe *her* phone was being tapped, too."

"Cass, I'm not sure what you're talking about. You haven't seen Trevor in weeks, so I don't know how his death could be connected to you."

She chuckled, though she was beginning to cry. "That's how they want it to seem."

"Look, if you think you know something about Trevor's death, then you should call the police, shouldn't you?"

She nodded, wiping tears off her cheek with her free hand. "You seem like a good guy, not a vampire, sucking the life from people like Ted did."

"Cass, dear girl, are you all right?"

"Watch yourself, Z. You might be next."

After a few seconds of silence, he came back on the line, the tone of his voice much different. "Look, I called out of courtesy to inform you of our mutual friend's death. I do not appreciate being threatened."

"But you're in danger. Don't you see?"

"No, Cass, I don't understand a word you're saying."

"It's the work we were doing. Don't you get it? People are still trying to protect Ted Hughes's reputation. And they'll go to any lengths."

"That's absurd."

"Is it? Are you sure? Because Trevor is dead, isn't he?"

"Maybe I should ask where *you* were last night."

"What! You're going to accuse *me*? You're going to accuse me of murdering Trevor?" Her face burned again with anger. "How dare you!"

"It never occurred to me to accuse you, Cass. But the way

you're talking now, it makes me think you aren't very stable."

She swiped the final tears from her face. "The hell with you, Z."

"The hell with *me*? I'm going to tell the police about our conversation. I think they'll be interested to know how Trevor's ex-lover took the news of his death."

She held the phone away from her face, stared at it and screamed as loudly as she could before slamming the receiver down.

Cass began pacing the floor again, trying to quiet her rage. Then she went to the window and held back the curtain to see who might be watching her apartment. A few people were walking around, but there was a work truck parked across the lane too. She couldn't tell if the driver was inside or not; she had a strong suspicion he was keeping tabs on her comings and goings. She could feel it, like the hot bright light of a sunlamp on her skin.

What should I do? Who can I trust?

CHAPTER 5

After Joe checked into the Palm Court Hotel in downtown Davis, he went to the bar and ordered a double scotch and soda. An hour later, with several scotches in his gut, he stumbled upstairs to his room and collapsed on the bed. Just before dawn he awoke, still drunk, confused about where he was, his head pounding.

He staggered into the bathroom, turned on the light and examined his face in the mirror. Then he remembered Sara with the other man. The image bit into him, and the room swam.

After splashing cold water on his face, he stared at his own dark, drooping eyes again. He had probably lost Sara, this time for good. His stomach churned—he felt hollow and sad, and began to sob.

"Sara, how could you?" He buried his face in his hands and cried uncontrollably for several minutes, but then his jaws tingled. With nothing on his stomach but scotch, his throat burned as he did little more than dry heave.

Slurping cold water from his cupped hand, Joe began to recover. He splashed water on his face again, dried himself with a clean towel, undressed and climbed between the cool, crisp sheets. Pushing the vision of Sara asleep on the other man's shoulder from his mind, he fell into a deep slumber.

A tapping on the door awoke him several hours later. The maid popped her head in. "Excuse me. I'll come back later."

Joe woke slowly. Had Sara hired someone to clean the house? No, this wasn't home after all.

He lay in the dark while his life with Sara played through his head. They'd first met in September at a football game in the stands at LSU. Tiger Stadium. Sara was with her mother and father, and Joe was seated behind them. Sara's skin was tan and her light brown hair, clipped in a flattened pony tail, was still almost blond, bleached by the summer sun. It was a warm Saturday afternoon, and Sara had removed her tight yellow sweater, revealing a purple halter top. Glancing at her back and narrow waist, Joe had noticed the top of a purple thong showing above the rim of her low jeans. He'd leaned forward and whispered, "Glad you're wearing LSU colors." She had turned around, grinning seductively. In an exaggerated southern accent, she'd replied, "Thank you, kind sir, for noticing."

Other memories flooded Joe's mind. Making love on a blanket one afternoon under the shade of low-hanging willow trees in a nearly deserted state park. Holding Sara's hand as she delivered Katie, cutting the umbilical cord with the doctor's oddly shaped chrome scissors. Sara looking up and laughing as she changed Brian's diaper—what had they been talking about that was so funny?

Then came the image of Sara in bed with *him*, the brilliant math professor with the stupid license plate, GO FIGR. He threw back the covers and stormed into the bathroom.

After dressing, he went downstairs and ate. It was 9:30. Katie and Brian would be in school by now, and Sara would be at work. He didn't have to go to campus today, but he did have three stacks of research papers to grade.

Typically Joe worked at home, grading one set of papers each day and enjoying the Christmas decorations as he worked. Now, he took the last bite of English muffin with a small triangle of ham and some Hollandaise sauce, and contemplated what he should do. He couldn't go home yet. It would be too painful. It would be too much to wander through the house as though nothing had happened. That left his office at CLU. Joe didn't really want to face his colleagues, either. Their looks of sympathy about him not being granted tenure would make him sick. And if anyone asked him how he was doing, he might blurt out what had happened with Sara. Their pity would never end. Still, he could probably sneak into his office, lock the door, and work undisturbed for the rest of the day.

Driving south on Interstate 5 from Sacramento to Stockton under a ceiling of gray clouds, Joe saw Lost Slough where he had saved Sara's life. The dark water, surrounded by green marshy plants and a tangle of overgrown bushes, still looked mysterious and threatening. Twice he'd been in that freezing water, and the sight of it sent a shiver through him when he remembered running from the I-5 Strangler.

To have survived that experience and to have had the great fortune of receiving the Shakespeare papers was all now swept away by a torrent of sadness. Joe cranked the radio up and tried not to dwell on it.

The campus was dead. A light drizzle was keeping the students inside their dorm rooms either studying for finals or, more likely, sleeping off a hangover similar to Joe's. He made it to his office without encountering a soul.

Joe checked his emails. Seven of his colleagues had sent short notes of condolence. He read the first five. All urged him to stay at CLU, saying things like, "You would be sorely missed!" and "Tenured or not, CLU is a better school with you here." While Joe knew they meant those sentiments, something about reading the words had the opposite effect. It was as if everyone now expected him to quit.

Maybe I should. Financially, he'd be fine for a year or two without any income. But he enjoyed teaching. He liked his students, and in all modesty, they learned from him.

Still, it would be humiliating to stay. Even more so now that he and Sara were probably separating. People would think she'd left him because he hadn't been granted tenure.

Feeling a sudden surge of anger, Joe typed an email to Dr. Thorne, the department chair, and copied it to the Dean.

> **After careful consideration, I have decided to take a leave of absence in the spring, during which I will make a decision regarding whether or not to return next fall.**

Joe read the email over several times and then moved the mouse up to the SEND button, hesitating only a few seconds before clicking on it.

As soon as the words MESSAGE SENT appeared on the screen, Joe sighed with relief. It was the right decision. He needed time to think, to sort things out with Sara.

The next email he opened was another note of condolence, but after that was an email from Cass. *Man, I could sure use* her *sympathetic shoulder.*

Joe opened the email and read it with growing concern.

> **I'm in trouble, Joe, and not sure where to turn. I think someone might be after me, either to shut me up or steal a notebook of Plath poems I found. A friend of mine was killed the other night, maybe murdered.**

> **I might be next. I'm seeing men in black with the Mein Kampf**

SYLVIA'S SECRET

look everywhere I turn. You're the only person I know who has actually dealt with killers and cops. Not sure what to do. Can't leave yet—too close to a major breakthrough—but it might cost me my life. Is it possible for you to come to London and help me? Please. I'm desperate. If not, then tell the police to check into the law firm that handles the estate of Ted Hughes if something happens to me. Those are the folks I suspect.

Joe read the email a second time. Cassandra's fear seeped through the lines, re-igniting the same fear he himself had when he was being chased by Benedict, the mercenary hired to steal the Shakespeare manuscripts three years earlier.

London in winter, like something out of Dickens. Away from Sara and campus politics.

"Why not?" he said aloud. "Why the hell not?"

He did an online search and found a reasonable one-way ticket to London. The flight would leave Sacramento the next morning.

Joe booked the flight and then sent a reply to Cass.

On my way. Give me your phone number so I can reach you when I arrive. Taking a United flight out of Sac tomorrow morn.

Next Joe emailed his list of students, sending them the final exam topic and instructing them to email their responses to him, explaining that their research paper grades would be posted electronically within a week. Knowing that Sara would be in class and unable to answer her cell phone, he called and left a message.

"Sara, I'm leaving for London and will be gone two or three

weeks. Not sure if I'll return for Christmas. Please tell Brian and Katie I love them."

He did not want to tell her the reason he was going. She had already expressed jealousy toward Cass. Besides, if Cass really was in some kind of trouble, he didn't want Sara to know that he was putting himself in harm's way again. That had been a major source of their arguments in the past. She'd told him he was a magnet for trouble. No. It would be better not to tell Sara. Chances were Cass was being overly dramatic. She did have a tendency to blow things out of proportion at times. Her mood swings were notorious. Still, this would be a good excuse to get away—yes, run away—from all the turmoil in his life.

And maybe he could help a dear friend escape her own turmoil in return for the kindness and sympathy she'd shown him in the past.

CHAPTER 6

Cass couldn't sleep. She worked at her small desk under the light of a single small lamp, late into the night, writing at a fever pitch, words flowing from her mind like blood gushing from an arterial wound. It was as if some outside force guided her hand. Everything made sense now. All the research she'd done, reading all of Plath's letters and her unabridged journals, all her published poems—everything was finally coalescing into a comprehensible form.

At 2:00 A.M. she heard a creak outside her apartment door. She stopped writing, holding her Waterford pen over the paper like a surgeon holding a scalpel over a patient just before the first incision.

Another sound came from the window behind her. She peered over her shoulder. The heavy curtains were drawn. Whoever or whatever was hovering on the other side of the glass, two stories above the sidewalk, could not see in. *Is the window locked?* She couldn't recall locking it—she'd opened it several times, even with the cold, just to breathe the air of London—the same air Yeats and Plath had breathed.

Another sound—a scraping noise against the door—jerked her

attention from the window. *Is someone trying to pick the lock?*

She screamed, "GO AWAY! LEAVE ME ALONE!"

Then she waited.

A pounding noise made her jump. Someone pounded on the floor underneath her. *The downstairs neighbor? Did I wake him up? Good! Maybe he'll call the cops.*

Adrenaline surged through her as she clutched the curtains and yanked them open.

She screamed—a dark, haggard face staring back at her from the glass.

Cass leaned closer to see through the mirage of her own distorted face reflected back in the mirrored window. She would have laughed at herself, but the face was not hers—not the face she'd known. *Something's different. I'm changing.*

Darkness filled the lane between her building and the row houses on the opposite side of the street. The windows of those houses dark. *Families asleep, children dreaming of Old Saint Nick, no doubt.*

The fear finally receded, and Cass checked the lock on the window. It *was* unlatched. She pulled the window up and leaned out, looking down at the snow-covered sidewalk first, then from side to side to see if anyone was clinging to a ledge, waiting to pounce.

Her skin tingled. Someone—or some*thing*—was hovering just above her. Too frightened to look up, even acknowledging the existence of a creature hovering above would make it real.

She was quite certain there *was* a blade above her neck, as if she had poked her head through a guillotine.

Her heart pounded, and she couldn't muster the courage to look up, so she pulled her head in and slammed the window down with a crash, cracking the glass. After turning the latch, she tugged the curtains closed again and ran to the front door.

There wasn't a peep hole, so Cass put her ear against the

cold wooden door. No sounds came from the hall. She waited. *Is someone on the other side listening at the door?*

Calming herself, allowing her heart beats to slow, she stood with her ear against the door for several more long minutes.

The image of a knife piercing the door made her jerk her head away.

No, I refuse to give in to this, damn it!

"I know you're out there," she said. "I know who sent you! You'd better go. Just leave! Leave me in peace!"

Cass heard no reply, so she gripped the door handle with one hand, unlocked it with the other, and threw it open. The narrow, dimly lit hallway was empty. But someone *had* been there. She was sure of it.

After shutting and locking the door, she turned slowly to scan the dark little living room. The desk lamp, with its green glass shade, cast an eerie light on the walls and curtains, and bathed the surface of her desk in brilliant, glaring white light.

She stepped closer. The lines she'd written were the swirls of blue ink that seemed to dance and flow. Whatever spell had allowed her to write so freely was now broken. She closed the notebook and walked to the worn settee facing the little electric fireplace. It glowed with warmth. Cass pulled an afghan over her legs, and slid her laptop out from under the little couch, opened it and hit the ENTER button to bring it out of its sleep mode. Blue light further illuminated the room.

Two new emails from her stepmother. *God, how she nags!* Lately she was emailing almost every day. Cass had stopped replying, sometimes waiting over a week before answering, reminding them that she was an adult now and could take care of herself quite well, thank you very much.

But could she? She snorted and said, "Maybe I *do* need Daddy's help after all, Cassy."

She shook her head—disgusted with herself for her cowardice—and deleted the emails from her stepmother without reading them.

The next email was from Joe Conrad. Cass blushed with embarrassment, realizing she had probably sounded too needy, too frightened, when she wrote him earlier that day. She opened the email with some trepidation.

On my way. Give me your phone number so I can reach you when I arrive. Taking a United flight out of Sac tomorrow morn.

She laughed. "What?" She laughed again. "Are you kidding me?" Her laughter filled the flat. "Are you kidding me, Joe?"

Another thumping noise came from the floor.

She looked over her shoulder at the floor and yelled, "GO BACK TO BED AND LEAVE ME ALONE!"

More thumping. Cass stomped her foot five times. Five thumps came from the floor, so she stomped both feet as hard as she could.

"I WILL JUMP UP AND DOWN ON THIS FLOOR FOREVER IF YOU IDIOTS DON'T STOP!"

No more thumps. Cass smiled and turned her attention back to the computer screen. She wrote a reply, giving Joe her cell number, and then Googled United Airlines. Joe's flight was scheduled to arrive the day after tomorrow at 8:45 A.M.

"Hold it together, girl," she said aloud. "You only have to make it one more day."

SYLVIA'S SECRET

CHAPTER 7

The new terminal at Sacramento International Airport was packed with people dressed in holiday colors. Joe sat alone, surrounded by young couples trying to cope with rambunctious children reminiscent of Brian and Katie—had he done the right thing in leaving this close to Christmas? As much as he yearned to hug his kids, he also burned with anger every time he replayed the recent bedroom scene of Sara asleep on the other man's shoulder. Still, to miss his kids laughing and opening presents filled him with sadness. He took out his phone and texted a message to Sara:

In case I'm not back by Christmas, gifts for you and the kids are on the top shelf of my closet. Already wrapped.

His finger lingered over the SEND button, debating whether or not to add more. He'd gotten new iPads for the kids and a gold ankle bracelet for Sara to wear when she played tennis. She'd gotten back into playing it after Brian started kindergarten, and sometimes he played with her. But many times he did not. Now he wondered who she played with when he wasn't around. She'd always claimed she'd played with some of her girlfriends from the high school where she taught, fellow teachers. Now he felt humiliated, imagining Sara playing with *him*, laughing and joking with her lover in front of everyone who knew them on the Davis tennis courts.

Would it be vindictive to tell Sara *not* to open her gift? *To hell with it. Let her decide what to do.* He pushed the SEND button and put his phone away.

Once settled into his seat on the Boeing 777, Joe set to work reading his students' research papers—seventy-six mostly mediocre ten-page essays. After six hours, he swallowed two sleeping pills with a glass of scotch and leaned back, an inflated pillow cushioning his neck. Emotional exhaustion plunged him into a fitful slumber. When he finally awoke, the flight was only an hour from England.

Joe had landed at Heathrow three years earlier with Jonathan Smythe and Sylvia Williamson, the colleagues he'd turned to for help with the Shakespeare manuscripts, so going through customs was not as mind-numbing as it had been before. Still, he was glad to see Cassandra Johnson's beaming smile when he arrived with his luggage at the ground transportation lobby.

She walked briskly toward him, holding out her arms. "I'm so happy to see you."

They hugged each other warmly, and then Joe leaned away, still holding Cass in his arms. "You've lost weight."

"Have I?"

"Yes. You're downright skinny."

"British food, I guess. It doesn't agree with me. Even hamburgers taste different here. And how many bangers and warm beer can a person consume?"

Joe laughed. "Ugh. I hate warm beer. Give me a scotch and soda instead."

Cass chuckled. "It's ten a.m. You want a drink this early?"

"No, no, of course not."

SYLVIA'S SECRET

They let go of each other and Joe grabbed the handle of his suitcase.

"How do we get to London? Do you have a car?"

"No car, I'm afraid. We'll take the tube."

"You've also picked up a bit of British accent."

Cass laughed. Then with an exaggerated accent, she said, "Have I *really*?"

As they walked to the train station, Cass asked, "How's your family? Bet they're jealous you came to London without them."

Joe simply nodded. He didn't want to lose the joy of seeing Cass.

"The kids are great. Doing well in school. Especially Katie. I swear, that kid's a genius."

"And Sara? How's she doing?"

As they stood at the ticket kiosk, Joe debated whether or not to tell Cass what had happened. *Not yet. Cass doesn't need to hear about our dirty laundry.*

"She's fine," Joe lied. "Sends her love."

The train to London was packed with people in wool sweaters and heavy overcoats, lugging suitcases of various sizes. Cass found a seat, and Joe stood in front of her, holding his suitcase handle in one hand and clutching a metal bar tightly with the other. Every time the train slowed to a stop, Joe leaned in one direction, and each time the train accelerated, he leaned in the other. Cass giggled at his exaggerated efforts.

Outside the subway station, he found himself shivering in the cold morning air. Dirty snow lined the streets and the edges of the sidewalk. The sky was mostly clear, but a few burdened clouds drifted slowly overhead. He'd brought a ski jacket, but it was still packed.

"How far is your apartment?" Joe asked.

"Ten or eleven blocks. Why?" Cass laughed. "Are y freezing?"

"Yes." Joe stopped and opened his suitcase, pulling the compressed jacket out and slipping into it quickly.Cass put her hand to her mouth and snickered.

"You've got that thin California blood, Joe. Not used to the snow."

When they reached the flat, Joe followed Cass in and closed the door. In front of him was a desk with a window behind it. To his left was a small sofa that faced a fireplace, which held an old electric heater with fake logs that glowed orange. On the wall to his left stood a bookshelf filled with books and magazines, a vase of dried flowers and other knickknacks on top. To the right was a small kitchen behind a narrow bar, as well as a dim hallway.

"Bathroom?" Joe asked.

Cass pointed to the hallway. Peeling off his jacket, Joe scurried down the hall and stepped into the small restroom. He turned on the light and grimaced slightly. The room smelled lovely—of musky roses like Cass herself—but it looked terrible. The sink was dirty and the towels hanging on the rack outside the shower probably hadn't been washed in weeks. He had never visited Cass at her home in Stockton, but since she'd kept her office at CLU so clean and orderly, Joe had always assumed she was an impeccable housekeeper.

When it came time to wash his hands, Joe wiped everything down with a hand towel, including the mirror, and arranged some of Cass's perfume and makeup bottles against the splashboard. Satisfied that he had left the room better than he'd found it, Joe opened the door and stepped into the hall.

He could see into Cass's bedroom. The floor was littered with rumpled clothing and the queen-sized bed was in disarray, covers thrown back, books and papers scattered across it, pillows leaning against the mahogany headboard in every direction.

"Hungry?" Cass called from the other room.

Joe walked back into the little living room and saw Cass g dishes in the kitchen. Dirty dishes and cups cluttered the countertops.

"Sorry," she said. "I've been so preoccupied with my research that I've just let everything else go." She seemed to become aware of the mess and blushed. "I guess I've been a bit frazzled. Honestly, housework isn't my thing."

"Can I help?" He stepped around the counter and started drying the dishes with a mostly clean white dish towel.

They worked side by side—and Cass smelled so very good— her perfume perhaps overly strong. They had the dishes finished and put away in twenty minutes. Cass turned and looked up at Joe.

"So you didn't answer my question. Are you hungry?"

"I could eat."

They held each other's stare for a few seconds, until Joe stepped away and walked into the other room.

The counter extended into the living room like a bar, so Joe took a seat on one of the three barstools and watched Cass bend over as she took a carton of eggs out of the little refrigerator.

"How about a cheese omelet?"

"Sounds fine."

As Cass worked on cracking the eggs and grating cheddar cheese, she talked about the neighborhood, reminding him that Sylvia Plath had committed suicide only a few doors down. Joe relaxed as he watched her work—the awkward intimate moment had passed. She shook salt and pepper into the eggs and then added a little garlic salt and oregano, whipping the concoction together with a fork.

"So, Cass, tell me what's happened that has you so worried."

While the cheese melted into the cooking eggs, Cass pulled two thick slices of bread from an old-fashioned bread box and pushed them down into a red-enameled toaster. Then she set about making coffee in an aluminum percolator like one his mother had used.

"I'm not sure how much you know about the way Ted han Sylvia's notebooks and poems after her death, but he was le able to take control over all of it since they were technically still married when she died."

Joe nodded. "Yeah, I know that much."

"It was Ted who had *Ariel* published. First in England. Then Frances McCullough and Donald Hall convinced him to publish it in America with Harper. They paid him $750 against royalties."

"Is that all?"

"Before that deal, publishers were only paying $250 in advance for books of poetry. Ted had made a great deal for himself."

"Okay. But I'm confused. What does this have to do with the problems you're having now?"

"Well, I bring that up to illustrate what kind of person Ted Hughes seemed to be. Interested in money more than his dead wife's memory."

"Yeah, I think everyone knows how self-centered he was."

Cass poured coffee into a cup and handed it across the bar. "The point is, ever since Ted was put in control of Sylvia's work, he'd been like a vulture, picking at her bones for every dime, or shilling, he could eke out."

He took a sip of coffee. It was strong but good. He watched Cass flip half the eggs over on top of the other half, making a perfect semi-circle.

"The legal firm in charge of the Hughes estate now is just like Ted. Greedy money-grubbers who are out to make as much as they can make. It's sickening."

Cass poured herself a cup and set it aside as she slid the large omelet onto a plate. She cut it in half and pushed one half onto a second plate. The toast popped up right on time, so Cass spread some butter on both pieces and handed a plate across to Joe.

"Thanks. Smells delicious." He shoveled a piece into his ᴏuth. The Italian seasoning nicely complemented the sharp ᴅddar cheese.

ᴄass took a sip of coffee. "Through my research, I've learned that at least one of Sylvia's notebooks of poetry is still locked in a safe at Ted's law firm. A few days after I arrived in England, I went there and asked to see it. One of the junior solicitors met with me for half an hour. He was very polite, you know, very cordial at first. He told me he'd take up my request with his boss, the man in charge of the estate, and get back to me."

After another bite, Joe asked, "So? What happened?"

"Well, first of all, they never did get back to me. I called several times and they never returned my calls. In the meantime, I learned that there might be several notebooks of poetry. Ted claims he burned one and supposedly lost another. But a lot of people think she left behind six or seven notebooks filled with poems, starts of different novels, journal entries."

Joe was half finished eating his omelet and toast, but Cass hadn't taken a single bite of hers yet. "You'd better eat before your eggs get cold."

Cass took a small bite, chewed quickly, and then continued. "You know, Sylvia wrote hundreds and hundreds of pages in her journals. Her journal entries start in July of 1950 and the last entry that's been published was in July of 1962, months *before* she died. I mean, she didn't write in her journal every single day, but almost, right?"

Joe nodded, eating the last of his eggs.

"Have you *seen* the book *The Unabridged Journals of Sylvia Plath*? It's almost seven hundred pages. A woman named Karen Kukil edited it. Weird name, huh. Coo-kill or cuck-kill, whichever way you say it, it's weird, right? She was a curator of rare books at Smith College, where Sylvia went to school. Listen to this," Cass said.

She plopped her cup down on the counter and scurried to the bookshelf as Joe watched. She plucked a book from the shelf, then hurried back to stand beside him.

"Here it is. Listen to this from the Preface. 'The two boun-

journals that Plath wrote during the last three years of her life are not included in this publication. One of the journals "disappeared," according to Ted Hughes'"—Cass looked up at Joe, a sardonic grin tugging her lips—"'and the second "maroon-backed ledger," which contained entries to within three days of Plath's suicide, was destroyed by Hughes.' How suspicious is *that*?"

Joe nodded, saying, "Very. But again, what's going on now?"

"So I went back to the law offices and asked again if I could see the remaining notebook. They said no. I asked if I could just look at it without opening it up, you know? Just to see for myself that only one really existed."

"Let me guess. They turned you down."

Cass nodded.

"What'd you do then?"

Cass stepped back around the counter and finally ate a little more of her omelet. "What could I do? I was heading to Devon the next day anyway, so I just tried to put the whole frustrating matter out of my mind."

Joe drained his coffee cup. "What's in Devon?"

"The home called Court Green in Devon is where Sylvia and Ted lived together, happily at first. But then Ted started the affair with Assia, going to London to see her. Assia and her husband, David Wevill, had rented Ted and Sylvia's flat in Chalcot Square. That's how they met. I've come to believe that Ted was drawn to her immediately."

Joe recalled something about Ted's affair with the other woman. "Didn't this other woman, Assia, kill herself, too?"

"Yes, after being with Ted, she killed herself *and* the four-year-old daughter she'd had with him."

An image of Katie's face popped into his mind. "That's horrible."

"It really says something about Ted Hughes, doesn't it?"

Joe shrugged. "Well, I guess some might say that he was

attracted to mentally ill women."

Cass's eyes darkened. "Or that he exploited vulnerable women. But, Joe, both Sylvia and Assia were strong, independent women when Ted met them. No, there was something very destructive about Ted Hughes, very manipulative. It's only through their writing—Sylvia's and Assia's—that we can ever hope to learn just how vile this man was."

Joe could see Cass was in no mood to hear even the slightest defense of Ted or any criticism of Sylvia.

"I mean, consider the facts, Joe. Both women killed themselves after being with him for just a few years! And the second woman also killed their child. I mean, how disturbed do you have to be to kill your own child?"

"Truly horrible."

"And the fact that he destroyed that last journal of Sylvia's, too. Makes you wonder what was in it, right?"

Joe nodded.

Cass leaned across the counter. "But *Mister* Hughes wasn't as clever as he thought he was. Evidently, it never occurred to him that Sylvia might have hidden some of her journals." She smiled, holding Joe's stare.

"What?"

"I found one of Sylvia's lost journals!"

"Are you kidding?"

"It's powerful, Joe. What it reveals about Ted is amazing. Very incriminating."

Joe laughed. "You've just made your career, Cass!"

"I know, I know, but what's more important is getting the truth out, the truth about Ted and Sylvia."

Joe contemplated the implications. "What *is* the truth, Cass? Can you share it with me?"

Cass sipped her coffee. Joe took note of the fact that most her omelet was still untouched. *No wonder she's so skinny.*

"I can tell you this much. Sylvia makes it clear that she feared for her life. She hid that journal in case something happened to her. I guess she assumed someone would find it before now, before Ted Hughes himself was dead, so he'd be held responsible."

Joe was beginning to grasp the potential danger of possessing the journal. "So, you went back to the law firm and tried to make a deal? I'll show you mine, if you show me yours?"

Cass clapped her hands together and laughed. "*See?* You get it!"

"And they still refused?"

"They said that if I really was in possession of one of Plath's missing journals, I was required to turn it over to *them*."

"What did you say to that?"

Cass chuckled. "I said, 'Quid pro quo, suckers.'"

Joe shook his head, laughing. "And what? They threatened to sue you, right?"

Her expression grew dark. "Yes, but they also said they would make me sorry, very, very sorry, if I didn't cooperate. The way the guy said it creeped me out, like, you know, he was Hannibal Lector."

Joe touched Cass's hand. "Well, I won't let the bastards threaten you while I'm around."

"After that meeting, bad things started happening."

"What kinds of things?"

"Well, I'm sure I'm being followed. I think my flat has been searched more than once while I've been out."

Joe looked around. "This place? Did they find the journal?"

Cass snorted. "No, thank God. Fortunately, I kept it with me then."

"Is it here now? Can I see it?"

"No. I keep it hidden now. It's safe." Tears started to spill from her eyes. "The thing is, I'm scared, Joe. Really scared. I'm sure they're watching me."

Joe slid off the bar stool and met Cass on the other side. He put his arm around her and held her against his chest. "You don't think they'd really harm you, do you?"

She sobbed more forcefully as Joe held her. When she'd finally caught her breath, she spoke in broken phrases. "I was seeing a guy. In Devon. He was researching Ted Hughes. We kind of clicked. At first, anyway. His name was Trevor. I just found out something awful. He was killed a few nights ago. They said it was an accident. Hit and run."

She looked up into Joe's eyes, tears streaming down her cheeks. "I think he might have been murdered."

"Murdered? Are you sure?"

Cass nodded. "And I think—no, I'm quite certain—it was intended to send a message—a message to me."

CHAPTER 8

Joe's arms were warm and secure. It was such a relief to be able to tell someone else about her suspicions. She wanted to show him all of it—the journals and notebooks filled with poems—but it was too soon. He'd be overwhelmed. Joe was one of the good guys, and he'd handled himself well when he and his family had faced threats in the past. But this was different. She wasn't quite sure where the threat was coming from. She only knew that here in Joe's arms, she was safe for the first time in weeks. *Too bad he's married. What a wonderful partner he'd be.*

"I'm so glad you're here, Joe. I feel better already."

He had nice lips and a gentle smile. His eyes, looking almost green in the morning light, stared down at her kindly. *Does he want to kiss me?*

Cass leaned away. "I need a tissue." She side-stepped Joe and went into the bathroom, where she blew her nose and then inspected her face in the mirror. God, she hadn't put on any makeup! She went to work on her eyes, then rubbed cream into her cheeks and finally applied a glossy new red lipstick. Her hair was pulled back into a pony tail, but she checked each side to see if stray strands l come unleashed. A quick spritz of perfume, and she was ready for Joe to see her again.

She found him standing at the window behind her desk, looking down onto the street.

"Any suspicious characters out there?"

Joe laughed. "No. I was just thinking about how close together these houses are. People living side by side. Do you have any privacy here?"

Cass stepped closer. "I close those heavy drapes and the world goes away."

"What about the walls? Can you hear your neighbors?"

Where's he going with this? "No, the walls are thick. I mean, sometimes my downstairs neighbor pounds on the ceiling if I'm playing my music too loud. But otherwise, I have a lot of privacy. Why do you ask?"

"You said Plath feared for her life, right?"

She nodded.

"I'm wondering if someone might have heard something the morning she died, a scuffle or arguing, perhaps."

Cass sighed with relief. For some reason, she'd thought he was going to make a move on her and wanted to be sure no one could hear his attack. *He's just thinking about the case!*

"The flat where Sylvia died. Is the floor plan similar?"

"No, no. Hers was a two-story apartment. The kitchen and sitting room downstairs. The bedrooms upstairs."

"You've been inside?"

"Yes. The people who live there now are very tolerant about allowing visitors to look inside."

"Can you take me there?"

"Of course. Late afternoon is best. It's tea time and the old couple doesn't mind entertaining guests then."

She watched as Joe glanced down at her desk. He seemed to be ⁻pted to open the leather-bound notebook she'd left there.

SYLVIA'S SECRET

"Are these your notes?"

Cass's heart skipped a beat. *Why am I so nervous about letting him see my work?*

"Yes," Cass admitted, "but those are just journal entries and notes of my own Brainstorming, really. Nothing very cogent."

"Can you share some of it with me? I'd love to hear about your progress."

Cass stepped closer to the desk and grabbed the notebook. "Sure. Let's sit in front of the heater."

The sofa was little longer than a loveseat, so when they sat down, they almost touched. The electric fireplace was warm-- she'd started to shiver. She rested her right thigh on the cushion so she could face Joe, and he turned to face her.

"I've come to believe that Ted was more responsible for Sylvia's death than anyone thought. Her last poems contain a tremendous number of clues, too. When you read her last poems in the context of a woman worried that she might be murdered, they take on much more meaning."

She opened the notebook and flipped through it.

"Here, for example. A poem titled 'The Detective' was published in *Ariel*. I find it very revealing. In fact, I'm surprised Ted allowed it to be kept in the original. Let me read this stanza to you and you tell me what it means, okay?"

Joe nodded. She couldn't read his expression. Was he curious or suspicious?

"First of all, don't you think it's suspicious that Plath would write a poem titled 'The Detective'? I mean, I thought of you, Joe, when I read this. You and all your experiences with police detectives."

He chuckled and blushed a little. *That's so cute—he's st embarrassed about his notoriety.* "Listen to these lines, Joe—

That is the valley of death, though the cows thrive.

In her garden the lies were shaking out their moist silks
And the eyes of the killer moving slug-like and sidelong,
Unable to face the fingers, those egoists.
The fingers were tamping a woman into a wall,

A body into a pipe, and the smoke rising.
This is the smell of years burning, here in the kitchen,
These are the deceits, tacked up like family photographs,
And this is the man, look at his smile,
The death weapon?"

She glanced up from the page, a knowing look on her face. "Why would she write something like that if she wasn't at least contemplating the idea that Ted might kill her?"

Joe nodded. "It's disturbing, all right. Of course, Ted's defenders might respond by claiming that it's all just figurative language, the usual metaphors that Plath used in a lot of her poetry."

Her frustration building, Cass tapped the page with her finger and said, "But what about 'the eyes of the killer'? Maybe that's actual, not metaphorical."

Calm down, Cass. Joe's only trying to help.

"Listen to these lines—

Did it come like an arrow, did it come like a knife?
Which of the poisons is it?
Which of the nerve-curlers, the convulsors? Did it electrify?
This is a case without a body.
The body does not come into it at all."

Jow." Joe nodded. "Really disturbing imagery."

SYLVIA'S SECRET

She snorted. "I'd say it's quite a bit more than imagery. Sylvia was telling us how Ted was going to kill her. Maybe with a knife, maybe with poison? Well, gas from the stove is a poison, isn't it? And the lines about the body? When she says, 'The body does not come into it at all,' she could be telling us not to trust the way her death looks."

Joe rubbed the back of his neck. "I agree with you about one thing."

She smiled. *He's beginning to see.* "What's that?"

"What you've read to me does not sound like a suicidal poet. It does sound like someone who's worried that some harm might befall her, and she wants to leave some clues behind."

"Yes!" She leaned over and gave Joe a hug. "I knew you'd understand. If anyone could, you would be the one."

"It's like the photograph of herself that Nicole Simpson left in her safe deposit box."

She pulled away and looked into Joe's eyes. *Is he going where I think he's going?*

"What do you mean?"

"You know. The O. J. Simpson case. Nicole Brown Simpson put a photo of her bruised face into a safe deposit box in case something happened to her."

She pushed herself back into the far corner of the sofa, indignation rising in her chest. "Quite a few people think O. J. might have been framed for that murder, you know. Everyone knows that racist cop planted the bloody glove at O. J.'s house."

Joe squirmed. "Well, the point I was making is that she tried to leave some evidence behind. Regardless of who really killed her, Nicole did exactly what you think Plath did—she left behind some clues so the detectives might be able to figure out who killed her in fact she was murdered."

She shrugged and closed the notebook. "Would you like more coffee?"

"I didn't mean to offend you, Cass. Maybe the O. J. thing was a bad example."

"You didn't *offend* me. It's just that, well, in the black community, it's pretty disheartening to see an icon get taken down. It seems like a lot of people were out to get O. J., and they were downright gleeful when he got arrested the second time."

As she made the coffee, Cass glanced at Joe. He was not facing her. Instead, his head was down as he sat on the couch. *I've put him in an impossible spot, haven't I!*

She watched him stand up and walk over, his dejected expression softening her. She switched to a playful tone, asking again, "Cream and sugar, Sugar?"

Joe tried to grin. "Got any sweetener? I'm trying to watch my boyish figure."

She made herself laugh. "You prefer the blue stuff or the pink stuff?"

"Well, I'm suddenly feeling a little blue."

"Then pink it is. I want you to be in the pink, Joe. Not singing the Blues."

CHAPTER 9

Joe sat on the barstool again, and took a sip of the fresh coffee. It was stronger but sweeter—Cass had put four packets of sweetener in, to sweeten the mood between them, he suspected. *She's usually not so sensitive. Can she really believe that Ted Hughes is guilty of murder, but O. J. isn't?*

"How's your coffee?" she asked.

"Terrific. Thanks." He was reluctant to say more.

"Now don't get all morose on me, okay?"

"I won't." He tried to smile but was suddenly very tired. "You know, Cass, I'm feeling kind of grungy from the long flight. Mind if I take a hot shower?"

"Oh, of course."

He had an idea that might improve the mood. "Could we visit Sylvia's flat this afternoon?"

"I don't see why not. Let me pop over and ask while you're in the shower."

"That sounds great," Joe answered.

"There's something else I wanted to ask you."

"Oh?" Joe left the counter and walked over to open his suitca on the floor. He pulled out his shaving kit, clean underwear and a folded shirt. Cass came and stood over him as he worked.

"Trevor's funeral is in Devon tomorrow. I'm hoping you'll attend it with me."

"Is that a good idea? You said that he might have been killed to send you a message."

Cass shrugged as he stood and faced her. "I want to see who shows up for it. Maybe Trevor's killer will be there, or someone from Ted's law firm. In any case, I think we might be able to figure out who's behind all this by going to the funeral. You seem to have an instinct for that kind of thing, Joe. That's why I want you with me."

"Okay. Sure. If you think it will help, then by all means."

Cass hugged him again, but this time not as warmly. "Good. We'll get the train in the morning. Takes about two and a half hours to get there."

He went to the bathroom and undressed. The warm water beat against his forehead and helped clear his mind. So much had happened in the past few days; it was all a little overwhelming.

Clean and clad in fresh clothes, he found Cass sitting at her desk, pen in hand, deep in thought. She ignored him, writing intently, so he quietly put his dirty clothes into a section of his suitcase and went back to the kitchen for more coffee. Sipping the coffee, he watched as Cass furiously filled one side of the paper, then turned the page and filled another.

He felt uncomfortable watching her, as if he were watching through a one-way mirror where he could see her but she couldn't see him. *What can she be writing about so fiercely?*

Finally, she looked up, staring straight ahead at the wall opposite her desk. Then as if she suddenly lost her train of thought, the intensity went out of her eyes. She laid her pen down, closed the journal and slumped back in her chair.

"Get inspired?"

SYLVIA'S SECRET

Cass blinked, as if waking from a dream. "What?"

"You looked like you were in the throes of inspiration," he answered. "I didn't want to interrupt you."

She nodded. "Yes. You know what Wordsworth said about poetry?"

Joe slurped the last of the bitter coffee and shook his head.

"Wordsworth said, 'poetry is the spontaneous overflow of powerful emotion, recollected in tranquility.'"

"That's a nice quote."

She smiled. "Isn't it though?"

"He sure got his *word's worth* out of that!"

Cass groaned. "Oh, that was bad. Even for *you*, that was bad."

Joe smiled—he couldn't resist another pun. "Bet you're glad I'm *done*."

Cass shook her head. "How does Sara put up with your awful jokes?"

He tried not to let his emotion show, choosing to shrug and force a grin instead, but he had to turn away—the painful reminder about Sara too much.

"I still need to brush my teeth, so...."

"Okay," Cass called. "I never made it over to the flat next door, so I'd better go check on visiting number 23 this afternoon."

"Number 23?"

"That's the address of Sylvia's flat," she explained. "Will you be all right while I'm gone?"

"Of course," Joe called from the bathroom. But he looked at his face in the mirror and tried not to see Sara in bed again, her hair on the other man's bare chest.

While Cass was gone, Joe was tempted to read what she'd written, but changed his mind when he saw the notebook's close cover. Instead, he walked to the window. Clouds were build' overhead, casting a gray pall over the narrow lane and brown houses with white-framed windows, most of which had shades pulled down. He wondered what went on behind those window shades across the street. Were families decorating their flats for Christmas or arguing about some petty issue? Was a wife cheating on her husband while the husband worked overtime to buy her something special?

Though he'd slept during most of the flight, he suddenly felt exhausted. He had imagined that being in London at Christmastime would be cheerful, and Cass had always buoyed his spirits in the past. When he'd been accused of a series of rapes and murders years ago, Cass had been one of the few colleagues who'd stayed by his side. She'd helped him look for clues to the identity of the real killer. They had analyzed a poem written by Autumn Smith, one of the victims who'd been linked to him. The poem turned out to be a dead end, but Cass's assignment had been interesting— write a poem from the point of view of someone else, someone of a different race or gender.

The apartment door opened and Cass rushed in.

"It's getting colder outside." She hurried over to the heater and stood in front of it, bending to hold her hands closer to the orange glow on the fake logs. "The McKurneys will have us for tea at three."

"The McKurneys?"

"Tilda and Roger McKurney are the current occupants," Cass explained. "A nice old couple, very tolerant of people like me who want to see the scene of the crime, so to speak."

"You mentioned that," Joe replied. "What shall we do until then?"

"Well, if it weren't freezing outside, I'd take you on a walking tour of the neighborhood so you could get a feel for the place where Sylvia spent her last days."

He smiled, stepped away from the window and joined her by fireplace. He stood with his back to the heater and looked at

SYLVIA'S SECRET

"Tell me about Plath's last days."

"A major snowstorm started the day after Christmas. It practically paralyzed London. The Boxing Day Snowstorm, as it was called, heralded the coldest winter since 1740, according to my research. The first months of 1963 had been miserably cold as well. Sylvia and her babies had been ill for weeks with the flu and colds, and Ted rarely came around to help out. By most accounts, Sylvia's depression was bad that January. In fact, her doctor tried to find a bed for her in one of the psychiatric hospitals, but Sylvia was not the only depressed woman in London that year. The hospitals were full."

"She died right before Valentine's Day, didn't she?"

Cass nodded. "That's right. The morning of February eleventh. She took plates of bread and glasses of milk up to the children's room, opened the window, then according to the reports, closed the door and sealed it with packing tape. She went downstairs to the kitchen, closed the door, stuffed a towel underneath it and sealed it with tape, too, so the gas wouldn't float up and harm Frieda and Nicholas."

"Then she turned on the gas and stuck her head in the oven?"

Cass snorted. "That's what we're supposed to believe."

"But you don't think so? You don't think it was a suicide?"

"No. I think Ted staged it to look like a suicide."

Joe sat on the sofa, puzzlement etched on his face. "Don't you think the police would have investigated that?"

"No, I don't. The police were *men*, after all."

"Cass, not all men are out to hurt women."

"No, I know that. But it was a more chauvinistic time. It was before the women's lib movement. The Gender Gap was more like a gender *chasm*! And Ted was already well-known by then. The police would have trusted whatever the famous Ted Hughes told them. *You* of all people should know how stupid the police can be."

Joe chuckled. "They *can* be shortsighted at times."

"Shortsighted? That's putting it kindly." Cass paced in front of Joe as she spoke. "They assumed the poor, weak woman couldn't live without her big, strong, handsome man. It's a classic example of how gender bias caused the police to have tunnel vision. The death *looked* like a suicide, everyone *said* Sylvia was depressed, so it was the easiest conclusion to draw. Never once did they ask who stood to gain from Sylvia's death. Never once!"

"Cass," laughed Joe, "don't get so worked up. It was forty years ago. And, besides, Ted's dead."

"Huh! And burning in hell, I hope."

He chuckled again, adding, "I hope *I* never get on your bad side."

"Just don't cross me, Joe. Don't cross me and you'll always be on my good side."

The smile faded from his face. "I won't cross you, Cassandra. I'm your friend, remember?"

Cass tossed her head back and laughed. Then she leaned down and kissed Joe on the top of his head. "I know you're my pal, Joe. You flew all the way over here to be with me, didn't you?"

"Yes, I did."

"And I love you for that." Cass took his face in her hands and kissed him on the left cheek. "If you weren't married, I'd kiss you for real."

He squirmed and tried to smile, but having her lips so close to his made him uncomfortable. He imagined Sara kissing the other man. Though he wanted to tell Cass about it, he stayed stone-faced.

"I'm hungry," Cass said, letting go of his face. "Are you hungry?"

"Yeah, I could eat again."

She stepped around the sofa and walked to the kitchen.

Sylvia's Secret

"I've got some clam chowder. And I can make grilled cheese sandwiches. I found this really great sharp cheddar."

"Sounds great." Joe glanced at the window. Snow had started to fall. He shivered. *Why am I suddenly feeling trapped?*

CHAPTER 10

After lunch, the mood had returned to normal. Cass worked at her desk while Joe used her computer to check emails. Several students had requested their grades, and an email from Dr. Thorne told him he'd been granted a leave of absence for the spring. Thorne's communiqué ended with the line, "We all hope you will return in the fall."

When he scrolled down, he found several emails from Sara. He opened the earliest one.

> Where are you? Did you really fly to England? You're not answering your cell. Called the department. Secretary says you cancelled your finals and are taking a leave in the spring. I'm sorry I hurt you. Please come back so we can talk.

The next email was short.

> I know you're angry, but please call us. The kids are worried and so am I. At least let me know where you're staying.

His eyes teared up while he read the third message.

> Katie cried herself to sleep tonight. She's worried that
> something really bad has happened to you. I told her that we
> had an argument and that it was my fault. Don't think we
> should tell her the truth yet. But she knows something bad
> happened, so please call her. Brian seems worried too.

He knew one reason for not telling Sara where he was going was to hurt her, but he'd figured she would make up a story that would allay the kids' fears. The next email required a reply.

> I'm worried you hurt yourself. If I don't hear from you soon,
> I'm calling the police. I assume you're holed up in a hotel
> somewhere, but I'm sure you're checking email sometimes.
> Please respond. We can work this out.

Joe glanced back at Cass to make sure she hadn't been looking over his shoulder. She had three books opened and was jotting notes into her journal, so he started typing.

> I had to get away to think. I'm in London. Cassandra's
> having a little trouble and asked me to come. It's really
> painful, Sara. You have to tell the kids. I'm not going to
> have them think this is my fault. Not this time. I know I've
> put you and the kids in harm's way before, but I've owned
> up to it. Now it's your turn. I'll email you again in a few
> days. Meanwhile, you need to decide if you want a divorce
> or to work on repairing our marriage. Tell the kids I love

them with all my heart and I'll see them soon.

He read it over, hit the SEND button, and closed the lid. Shoving the laptop under the couch, he glanced back to see Cass still working studiously.

Joe curled up on the small sofa and faced the heater. Then he closed his eyes and thought about Sara's emails. The more he tried to sort it all out, the more muddled he became. His mind just would not work when it came to thinking about what had happened. Or what he should do next. When he tried to think it through, he could only see the man jumping naked out of *his* bed.

Someone was nudging his shoulder. He heard Sara's voice calling his name.

"Joe? Can you wake up?"

He opened his eyes. Cass, not Sara, stood over him, her warm hand on his shoulder.

She smiled. "You dozed off. Feeling better now?"

Joe sat up, groggy, feeling as though he could sleep for ten more hours.

"Yeah, I guess so." He sat up and stretched. "What time is it?"

"It's tea time!"

After he splashed some cold water on his face, Joe and Cass started down the street to the front door of 23 Fitzroy Road. Outside the door was a round blue ceramic plaque inscribed with the words, "The Irish poet and dramatist W.B. Yeats lived in this house as a boy."

Joe tapped the plaque. "This was the main attraction for Plath, wasn't it? That another poet had lived here?"

"That's right," Cass answered. She knocked on the door.

The door was narrow and dark, set in against the white st façade of the building. From inside, he heard a man's deep say, "Here come our guests, Tilda. Put the kettle on."

A slightly built, dignified old man opened the door

hello," he said, taking Cass by the arm. "Do come inside out of that blasted cold."

Cass gave the elderly man a gentle hug.

"This is my colleague from California, Joseph Conrad. Joe, this is Roger McKurney."

Joe took the man's frail hand. "Nice to meet you, Roger. Has anyone ever told you—"

"That I look like the actor, Peter Cushing? Yes, young man. A thousand times." He shook Joe's hand vigorously and smiled. "Joseph Conrad is it? Like the Polish writer?"

Joe nodded. "I'm afraid so. My mother was a fan."

"Well, we shan't hold that against you, I suppose."

Joe followed Cass into the front room. A dark green couch sat against the wall facing the front window. Over the couch hung a large oil painting of a sailing ship steering into a storm. In front of the couch was a large coffee table, magazines pushed to one side. Two overstuffed chairs sat in the middle of the room facing the sofa, on the other side of the coffee table. On a table under the front window stood a lamp on one end, leather-bound books in the middle, and at the other end, a vase filled with fake flowers. The far wall was taken up by the same sort of fireplace with an electric insert as the one in Cass's flat, the fake logs glowing warmly.

"No Christmas tree yet?" Joe asked as Roger McKurney tottered into the room.

"Lord, no. We usually don't decorate a tree until Christmas Eve. However, this year we're going down to Spain to spend the holidays with our son and his family."

"Oh, that'll be nice," Cass said. She took a seat in one of the overstuffed chairs and motioned for Joe to do so, too. "Will it be warm in Spain this time of year?"

"Well, let's put it this way. It won't be as bloody cold as it is "

equally frail and dignified woman strolled into the room

carrying a tray, carefully balancing a white flowered porcelain teapot and four cups and saucers to match. Joe noticed a plate with four scones sitting next to a small white sugar bowl and a little pitcher of cream.

"I'm Tilda, Mr. Conrad," she said. "I heard your introduction from the kitchen." She placed the tray down on the table in front of Cass, and then straightened up to take Joe's extended hand. "You have a rather famous name. How do you cope with being named after the author of *Heart of Darkness*?"

Joe smiled. "I've learned to live with it."

As Tilda let go of his hand, she reached down and poured tea into a cup, and then handed it to Cass.

"Is your heart filled with darkness, Joe?"

Cass chuckled. "No. Joe's heart is usually filled with light. That's why I like having him around."

The older couple laughed politely and the four of them settled into pleasant chitchat until all the tea and scones were consumed.

Roger cleared his throat during a lull in the conversation and said, "Well, I suspect you want to show Joe around."

"Yes, I would, if you don't mind?"

"No, no. Help yourself. You know the way."

Joe followed Cass upstairs, where she showed him the two bedrooms, average-sized, each with a double bed in the middle of one wall, the usual nightstands and lamps on each side. The larger room had a vanity table and an armoire. Both rooms had large windows, out of which Joe could see the steady snowfall.

"Take note of the windows," Cass whispered. "I have something I want to share with you." Then she led him downstairs to the kitchen.

"This morning when you were taking your shower, I was trying to work out how Ted did it. I think I know the answer."

The kitchen was small, the sink, stove and refrigerator on
wall, a small breakfast table shoved against the opposite

Muted yellow daisies and butterflies seemed to be the common motif.

Cass stood in the middle of the room and faced Joe, her eyes wide. "Imagine it happening this way," she said, her voice trembling as she spoke. "Ted comes to the house late that night just as Sylvia is preparing the children for bed. He implies that he might want to get back together after all. 'Let's have another go of it,' he says, knowing that Sylvia will assume he means the marriage, but he's suggesting a last tryst. In her confused, aroused state, she's susceptible. He suggests giving the children the light dose of sleeping medicine, as they had in the past when they wanted to make love undisturbed."

"Would Sylvia go for that?" asked Joe.

"She had before. Anyway, just hear me out," said Cass in an annoyed tone of voice. "They put the children down—or better yet, the children don't even know Daddy's in the house, and Sylvia puts them down with their special glass of warm milk. Meanwhile, Ted readies another dose of special warm milk for Sylvia."

"You mean, while Sylvia's upstairs with their children?"

"Yes, of course. 'Let's play at being children ourselves,' he tells Sylvia when she comes back down. She prepares another glass of milk and two plates of buttered bread, just as they found in the sealed room with the children the next day."

"That explains why the police found her fingerprints on the glasses."

"Yes, right," she snapped.

Joe could see that it was all so clear in her mind that she couldn't stand his interruptions.

"So she sips her milk, but Ted doesn't touch his. Instead, he encourages her to drink while he massages her neck or kisses her arlobe, or something else. She's soaking up his attention like the gry dry sponge she'd become by then."

"I don't know, Cass. It's one thing to argue that Ted's infidelity pushed Sylvia over the edge, but explain how Ted could have murdered Sylvia and made it look like suicide. After all, the door to the apartment was locked from the inside. How did Ted get out? How did he seal Sylvia in the kitchen without being in there himself and dying in the gas?"

"Suppose he drugged her as I suggested so that she was very sleepy. Maybe in seducing her, he pulls her down to the floor in the kitchen. They roll around and she admits to feeling sleepy. Ever the loving husband, he offers to hold her in his arms while they sleep together on the floor. How romantic, right? *RIGHT!* I mean, think about how Ted is pitching this shit to her. They can do it later, consummate their rekindled love in the morning. She drifts off into a deep sleep in his arms, secure in the knowledge that she has her husband back, that the children have Daddy back."

"Okay, but how does he seal her in the room and leave? And remember, the children's door was taped shut, too."

"I'm getting to that."

The irritation in her voice concerned him, so he listened without speaking.

"Once Sylvia is passed out on the kitchen floor, Ted puts the masking tape around the edge of the door to the kitchen, with the door standing open. He also puts a dish rag under the door, taping it in place so that when he pulls the door closed upon leaving the kitchen, the sticky tape adheres to the door frame and the dish rag is dragged along under the door."

Standing in the very room, inspecting the door frame around the kitchen door, Joe could see Cass imagining it. The door frame did stick out, like most door frames, so upon closing the door, if masking tape were around the edge of it, the tape would stick to the frame.

"Brilliant!" said Cass. "Everyone assumes that Sylvia stuff the dish rag under the closed door and then taped herself insid

"You're saying Ted tugged her sleeping body closer

stove, opened the door, turned on all the gas, and taped the door himself, pulling it shut as he left?"

"Yes. Then he went upstairs with the same roll of masking tape and sealed the door to the children's room."

"But how did he get out, Cass? The apartment was locked from the inside, wasn't it?"

"Yes, but think. Wasn't there one opening through which he could have escaped?"

Joe shrugged and shook his head.

"Think, Joe. With sleeping beauty downstairs filling her lungs with gas, how could Ted escape?"

He glanced up at the ceiling. "Through the open window in the children's room?"

"Yes!"

"But how?" asked Joe. Yet he was beginning to think Cass might be on to something. Still, to test Cass's logic, he offered a problem. "The apartment was too high up for him to jump from the window, and there wasn't a fire escape outside that window."

"True," Cass admitted, her brow furrowed, "but after sealing himself inside the children's room in much the same way he had sealed Sylvia inside the kitchen, he could have used a rope to climb out of the window in the dark. Remember, it was a cold, quiet night in a quiet neighborhood. No one was out that night."

"But the police would have found the rope Ted used to climb down, wouldn't they?"

Cass grinned. "Not if he took the rope with him."

"But how?"

"If the rope was long enough to loop through the children's bedpost, then Ted would have both ends of the rope down on the sidewalk. Once he climbed down, all he had to do was pull one nd of the rope. With the children drugged and covered up by their vy quilts, they wouldn't hear the rope being pulled through the ost. And assuming Ted pulled the rope slowly and gently, it wouldn't leave a rub mark on the post to raise the suspicion of the police."

Joe closed his eyes to imagine it. He could visualize it happening just as Cass had explained it. But he could also imagine Sylvia Plath's suicide happening just the way it had always been explained, too. Just as it had been dramatized in the film with Gwyneth Paltrow.

"One loose end, Cass. You forgot that the police found the roll of masking tape inside the sealed kitchen with Sylvia."

Cass smiled. "They found *a* roll of masking tape, Joe. Ted could have used a second roll for the children's room. Or he could have used the same roll for both doors and then left the roll in the kitchen before closing either door."

"It's possible, I suppose," admitted Joe. "But I always go back to something you reminded me of years ago."

"What's that?"

"Occam's Razor. The simplest explanation is usually the right one."

"Usually. But consider something else."

"What?"

"Consider the version of Sylvia's last book of poems, *Ariel*, the way Ted edited it. Then consider the way the restored edition is organized."

"Okay," said Joe. "What do you mean? Where's the clue?"

Cass smiled, as if she had the final piece of the puzzle.

"The last poem in Ted's version of *Ariel* is a poem titled 'Edge,' which is a poem about a dead woman. It wasn't supposed to be in that book, but Ted added it as the ending. That depressing poem helped to cement everyone's view of Sylvia as the dead woman. As if she meant it as a suicide note."

"Go on."

"Well, without realizing that she might be implicating her fa Frieda Hughes might have provided the best evidence again when she put her mother's book of last poems together in their original order, the way Sylvia herself wanted them."

"I don't understand," said Joe.

"The restored edition of *Ariel* ends with a poem titled 'Wintering,' which is about surviving the dark, cold winter in preparation for a new life in the spring. There are references in that poem to getting away from men and storing six jars of honey, which could refer to her notebooks of poems. The poem ends with this line: 'The bees are flying. They taste the spring.' I think Sylvia had finally found her voice. In her bitterness and anger toward Ted, she had allowed herself to feel all the emotions she needed to produce the kind of work she ultimately wanted to share with the world. Why, in God's name, when she was finally writing what she really wanted to write, why would she kill herself?"

"Because of the breakup with Ted, of course."

"But don't you see? She could have a much sweeter revenge by publishing her poems, poems people would know were about him, poems that might destroy him."

"And so Ted destroyed her?"

"Well, we know Ted destroyed at least one of her notebooks. He admitted to burning one. Maybe there were six, like the six jars of honey mentioned in the last poem. One of those jars of honey turned out to be *Ariel*. Another went missing, until now, when I found it."

"And Ted burned a third notebook."

"Sylvia Plath *was* her poetry," Cass said, sounding too passionate now. "Ted Hughes was able to destroy part of the poet by burning some of her poems, just to make himself look better in the eyes of the public. Why not also destroy the poet?"

SYLVIA'S SECRET

CHAPTER 11

After saying their goodbyes to the McKurneys, Joe and Cass stepped out into the quiet air. Snow fell steadily, obscuring their view. On the sidewalk, he turned left, assuming they would head back to Cass's flat, but Cass grabbed his arm.

"There's a nice little pub down the street. Let's go there for dinner, shall we?"

"Oh, of course."

They trudged through the snow, Cass slipping her arm into his. With each step, the fresh snow crunched under foot. Joe had done a little snow skiing in the Sierras near Lake Tahoe, but being from Louisiana, he didn't have much experience with the cold and he wasn't sure he liked it.

"Everything's so quiet," he noted.

"Yes. Isn't it lovely? Peaceful?"

"It makes me think of that Frost poem. 'Whose woods these are I think I know / his house is in the village though; / he will not mind me stopping here / to watch his woods fill up with snow.'"

Looking down at their feet as they walked, Cass quoted the next stanza: "'My little horse must think it queer / to stop without a farmhouse near / between the woods and frozen lake / the darkest evening of the year.'"

He shook his head from side to side and whinnied like a horse. Cass laughed but then fell silent as Joe provided the next lines. "'He gives his harness bells a shake, / to ask if there is some mistake. / The only sound's the sweep / of easy wind and downy flake.'"

Cass quoted the final stanza, speaking softly: "'The woods are lovely, dark and deep, / but I have promises to keep, / and miles to go before I sleep, / and miles to go before I sleep.'"

They walked on for another block, the snow crunching under their feet and an occasional car rolling slowly down the lane.

Finally, he couldn't stand the quiet. "So, tell me. Do we have miles to go before we eat?"

"No, no. Another block and around the corner," said Cass. "You'll love this place. But I need to stop at a little bank next door before we go inside."

"Oh, I'll be happy to pay for dinner, Cass."

She grinned. "I don't need any money. I want to get something out of a safe deposit box."

"What?"

She smiled a devilish grin. "You know what."

"One of the missing notebooks of Plath's poetry?"

Cass nodded. "Yes, the one I discovered at Court Green in Devon."

Joe's heart raced with excitement. Unlike his last experience when he simply hadn't understood the worth or importance of the Shakespeare manuscripts, this time he realized how significant Cass's discovery could be. *The missing poems of Sylvia Plath, long presumed destroyed by Ted Hughes!* He quickened his pace, happy for the first time in days.

"I'm beginning to feel a little like Indiana Jones," Joe said, grinning.

"Yes, exciting, isn't it?"

SYLVIA'S SECRET

Cass pushed into the bank, and Joe was struck by the smallness of the place. Only two teller windows, one manager's desk, and a hallway entrance.

Cass marched straight to the manager's desk. The bespectacled banker raised his head. His dark features suggested he was East Indian, and his accent confirmed it.

"May I help you?"

"Yes. I'd like to get into my safety deposit box, please."

The balding banker took a set of keys from his pocket, and Cass followed him into the hallway. Joe waited in the small lobby. Soon after, an elderly woman dressed in a heavy coat pushed against the door and Joe hastened to open it for her.

She smiled up at Joe—she could have been the Queen's double—and said, "Thank you, young man."

Ten minutes later, Cass appeared, clutching an old-fashioned hard-bound journal in her arms, her face drawn and her mouth taut.

Joe held the door and then rushed after Cass as she ran around the corner and down the street. The sign in front of the restaurant said, Goose on the Lamb, Pub and Eatery, and the colorful image on the oval wooden sign showed a goose with his head down, riding a sheep like a jockey across the finish line.

Joe chuckled. "How in the world did you find this place?"

"Roger recommended it to me during my first visit to Sylvia's flat."

As austere as the little bank had been, the pub was just the opposite. Warm wood-paneled walls, cozy wooden booths filled with smiling people likely glad to be in from the cold, waitresses in Levis and tight sweaters holding trays over their heads, weaving between tables.

"There's one," Cass said, and led the way to a booth in the back. When they got to the table, Cass placed the notebook down and tugged off her coat, tossing it into the seat. Joe did the sa with his jacket and slid in across from Cass.

"May I see it?"

Cass took a quick glance around. "Yes, but please be careful."

He pulled the notebook closer, saying, "Trust me—I handled four-hundred-year-old documents in the Folger Shakespeare Library, Cass, so I have a little experience with old manuscripts."

Joe opened the journal carefully. It opened all the way and lay flat on the table, making the black ink on the pages easy to read.

"Wow. The handwriting is different from what I expected. More printing than cursive. Her capital *G*'s look like *6*'s and her lower-case *g*'s look like fish hooks. It looks...."

"Angry?" she asked.

"Yes. Not flowing and looping, like a cheerleader's penmanship. You know, where they draw little hearts instead of periods or dots over the *i*'s. And her capital *I*'s look like *F*'s."

Cass snorted. "As if she's saying 'Fuck' every time she writes 'I'."

Joe read one of the poems aloud:

"Paralysis again. How I waste my days.

I feel a terrific blocking and chilling

Go through me like anesthesia.

I wonder, will I ever be rid of Johnny Panic?

Ten years from my successful seventeen,

And a cold voice says,

What have you done? What have you done?"

"This is great," Joe said. Does it go on like this all the way through?"

A waitress scurried up to the table, and Cass suddenly closed the notebook and pulled it closer to herself.

"Can I get you something to drink?"

"A drink sounds good to me," he said. "How about you, Cass?"

SYLVIA'S SECRET

"Yeah, sure. I'll have a Bloody Mary."

"Scotch and soda. Make it a double, please."

"Any particular kind of scotch, sir?"

"No. I mean, what's the point if you're going to pollute it with soda?"

"My feeling exactly," chimed the waitress. "Back in a flash."

Once the attractive young woman had gone, Cass opened the notebook again.

"I want you to read as much of this as you can tonight and we can talk about it on the train tomorrow."

"Sure, Cass. It will be an honor."

She shook her head, and frowned at the comment. "I want to pick your brain, Joe. See if you read these pages the way I do." She opened the notebook to one of the last pages. "The poems and passages in this notebook, which everyone—I mean, EVERYONE!—thought was missing, prove that Sylvia was suspicious of Ted, not just about having affairs, but of him wanting her out of his life for good. She as much says, 'My husband will murder me,' in these lines. Listen to this." Cass scanned the page until she found the line. "It's a poem describing her husband as a vampire. She writes that it's 'draining me, draining me / till I turn into air.' And what about these lines?"

He took the notebook from her and read part of a scratched out stanza:

"If he were as clever with deeds as words
They'd find my body in a fat black sack
And think I tied the rope
Around my own pretty red throat."

He shrugged. "Some will simply say these are the parano ramblings of a depressed, angry, jilted woman."

Cass pounded the table with her fist. "No! Don't go there. Don't reduce this to nothing more than the rant of a jilted lover."

Joe flinched, but Cass's outburst didn't attract much attention in the noisy pub. "I didn't mean that *I* see it that way. I'm just telling you what others might say."

"It just sounds so demeaning—*jilted*. So damn condescending."

The waitress came back and placed their drinks in front of them. "Are you two ready to order dinner, or do you need more time?"

Cass took a sip of her drink, shrugging.

"Give us some time," Joe told the waitress.

"Sure thing, Honey."

Cass rolled her eyes as the girl walked away. "My God, is she flirting with you?"

He laughed. "I don't think so. She's just being nice."

"And she assumes you'll pay the bill, so she'd better butter *you* up, so you give her your big tip!"

"Jeez, Cass, lighten up."

She took another sip of her drink and closed her eyes as she swallowed.

"I'm sorry. It's just, when I think about what Ted did to Sylvia, it just infuriates me. He used her and used her, then left her for another woman. She was the better talent. *She* should have jilted *him*!"

Joe took a long pull from his glass and let the scotch warm his throat.

Cass drained her glass and held it up, catching the eye of the waitress. "I'll have another, please!"

Joe took another sip of his drink, then pulled a menu out of the rack and opened it. "So, what's good here?"

"The roast beef has a good flavor, but it's usually kind of dry. They do an excellent roasted half chicken with thyme and rosemary. I get the baked pork chop. It's breaded with a sweet sort of cornbread coating, and it's nice and moist inside."

"You're making my mouth water."

When the waitress returned with Cass's drink, they ordered—both getting the pork chop—and soon settled into an easy conversation about how well Joe's daughter Katie was doing in school.

"And how's Brian doing? He's in the second grade now, right?"

"He's struggling a bit. Like most boys, he has trouble sitting still for very long, or paying attention, so his teachers have had their hands full."

"'Like *most* boys?' Joe, really. See how easily we fall back to stereotypes? What's Sara think?"

Joe shrugged. "She thinks we should have Brian tested for a learning disability, but I think he's just a typical boy. And sorry if that sounds sexist to you, but boys are typically pretty rambunctious."

Cass chuckled. "That's *exactly* the kind of thing a *typical* man would say!"

Joe, taking a drink, almost spit it out. "Cass made a joke! I'm impressed."

She dipped her finger into her drink and flicked a drop in Joe's direction.

"Maybe Sara's right."

Joe shrugged. "I think she just feels guilty."

"Guilty? Why would she feel guilty?"

"Well, if Brian does have a learning disability, I think she believes it was her fault. You see, when she was pregnant with Brian—that was when I was being accused of all those crimes—she had planned to terminate the pregnancy."

"Yeah. So?"

"So she had a few drinks and smoked a few times while she was pregnant. It was a very stressful time in our marriage."

"I remember."

The waitress returned with their plates. Steam rose from the crisp, brown coating of the pork chops, and the fragrance put a smile on Joe's face. He cut a generous piece and put it in his mouth, savoring the moist, salty meat.

"You were right. This is delicious."

Cass nodded and took a small bite. "So tell me more about Sara and the kids."

"Anyway, I think she blames herself, which is why I try to play it down and tell her Brian's just being a kid. Katie was so exceptional, Sara assumes all kids should be that bright."

"Well, if smoking and drinking when you're pregnant was a guarantee that your kid would have a disability, then I should be really screwed up. My mom smoked her whole life and self-medicated with wine all during the time she was carrying me."

"Self-medicated?" Joe asked. "What do you mean?"

"My mom was mentally ill. It went undiagnosed most of her life. She was finally starting to get treatment, but then she killed herself."

Joe reached over and touched her hand. "Jesus, Cass, I didn't know about any of that."

"It's not the sort of information one puts on a curriculum vitae, is it?" She looked into Joe's eyes for another second before pulling her hand away and cutting another bite of meat. "I have my mother to thank for my interest in literature. Lydia was very much into the arts. She painted a little, took me to see plays and musicals, and she was always tossing a book in my direction. Usually one from Oprah's book club. When I learned that Sylvia Plath had killed herself just like my mother, that's when I really fell in love with her. She and my mother would have been about the same age. It's eerie."

Cass shoveled a piece of meat into her mouth and chewed it vigorously.

"How did your mother...die?"

"You mean, how'd she off herself? Pills. She was taking meds for her illness and had just gotten the prescription refilled. I guess sometime after she dropped me off at the middle school, she went home and took all those pills and some others with a whole bottle of wine."

Joe was at a loss. "Well, that's more peaceful than sticking your head in an oven."

Cass nodded. "I knew something was wrong. When she didn't pick me up from school, I just knew she'd done something really bad. The principal called my father and he picked me up. We both found mom on the couch. There was a stupid soap opera on TV. Can you believe it? My mom checks out while watching *Days of Our Lives*."

CHAPTER 12

Cass's anxiety grew—what Sylvia would call "Johnny Panic"—as she told Joe about her mother. She'd never quite fit into the English Department at CLU—most of the faculty being male and white—so she had not wanted to stand out any more than she already did. Now that Joe knew the truth about her past, the others were bound to learn about it, too. She needed to change the subject—she didn't want Joe to ask about the dirty details of Lydia's insanity.

"Oh my God, Joe. I haven't even asked yet. Are you tenured?"

The sympathetic look on Joe's face turned to embarrassment, so even before he shook his head, a wave of pity swept through Cass's heart. She reached across the table and took his hand.

"Oh, I'm so sorry. What happened? I mean, what reason did they give you?"

Joe sipped his drink, as if needing to wet his lips. "I don't have a Ph.D."

"What? But you've given so much to that damn school. The Shakespeare papers. And you've published."

Joe huffed. "One autobiography explaining why I'm *not*

serial killer is hardly a *valid* work of scholarship."

"But the book debunking Shakespeare that you wrote with Smitty and Sylvia Williamson—doesn't *that* count?"

He shrugged. "I don't know. A lot of the faculty thought I didn't have much to do with that book."

"Still, you have two books out there with your name on the cover, and you've donated or loaned several of the Shakespeare manuscripts—all that should count for something. Not to mention all the notoriety you've brought to CLU."

"Some of that notoriety was pretty bad, Cass."

She squeezed his hand and then let go. "So what are you going to do? Look for another job?"

"Maybe. I'm not sure. I've taken a leave of absence for the spring so I can think about my options."

"Wow. I can't believe it. CLU won't be the same without *you* there. How'd Sara take the news?"

Tears welled up in Joe's eyes, and he finished his drink. "She was sympathetic, of course. Our marriage is a little strained right now, so that didn't help."

Even in the dim light of the pub, Cass could see the blood drain from Joe's face. Joe and Sara's marriage had always been rocky, but Joe was committed to his family. "You want to talk about it?"

He smiled and put on a brave face. "No, not really. We're going through a rough patch, so I think this time away will be good for both of us. Let's just leave it at that, okay?"

Could Sara be that shallow? To leave him just because he didn't get tenure?

"Sure, Joe," she said.

They finished eating in silence, and when the waitress returned to clear their plates, Joe ordered coffee.

"Coffee? Really? This late?"

"Well, if I'm going to stay up reading this journal...."

Cass nodded.

SYLVIA'S SECRET

Fewer people were seated at the tables eating, but more had gathered at the bar. A cute tall guy with wavy black hair and thick black eyebrows, probably in his mid-twenties, smiled at her. She smiled back and then turned away. She was in a good place now, feeling the alcohol but also energized.

"Man, I'd like to go dancing."

Joe laughed. "Dancing?"

"Yeah. Do you dance?"

"I haven't been in years. It's hard to get out when you've got young kids."

"Maybe that's part of the problem with you and Sara. Take her out dancing more often." He nodded, but his expression crumbled. *Jesus, is he going to cry?* "Hell, then again, what do *I* know? I'm not married. I don't know what goes on behind closed doors."

Joe nodded again and turned away.

Cass drained her glass and watched the waitress sidle between people with Joe's coffee.

"Excuse me," he said, standing up. "Gotta use the restroom."

Joe disappeared from view just as the waitress stepped to their table.

"Here's your boyfriend's coffee. Does he want cream and sugar?"

"First," she said, leveling a stare at the other woman, "he's not my boyfriend. We're just friends and colleagues. Got it? We work together."

The woman tried to keep that oh-so-innocent smile plastered on her face. "Oh, sorry, dear," she said, her voice an octave above syrup. "Will he be needing cream and sugar, do you know?"

"I suppose if he wanted it, he would have asked, don't you think?"

Cass grinned inside, and the waitress tightened her smile.

"I suppose so," the waitress said, then put the bill on the table and strode away.

Cass followed her movement until she saw the cute guy looking her way again. He smiled, nodded, then turned back toward the bar. She checked out his jeans. *Nice butt. I bet* he *can dance!*

Joe returned, refreshed.

"Feeling better?"

"Yeah, much. Guess I'm still a little jet lagged. Is there any cream or sugar?"

Cass chuckled. "The waitress asked me if you wanted some, but I wasn't sure if you did, so…."

"It doesn't matter."

He sipped the coffee, and his grimace told Cass it was bitter.

"Not so good, huh?"

"No," he said. But he took another sip before pushing the cup away. "Do you really want to go dancing?"

She was having trouble reading his expression. He seemed to be feigning enthusiasm.

"Maybe another time."

She glanced toward the bar. Cute guy was talking to a chap standing next to him. He said something that caused both men to look at Cass and smile. Cass smiled in response, but then looked away.

"What's wrong?" Joe asked.

"Are those guys at the bar still looking this way?"

Joe leaned out of the booth. "I guess so. You know them?"

Cass nodded. "I think the one guy works at the lawyers' office. You know, Ted's firm—the one that's got Sylvia's other journals."

Joe strained to look back over his shoulder. "Are you sure?"

"No, but he looks like someone I saw there. It's hard to say for sure because he's dressed so differently."

"Want to confront him? I'll go with you."

An almost uncontrollable sense of panic swept over Cass. The notebook—the one *she* had found—was right here on the table! She slid the notebook off the table top and placed it on her lap.

SYLVIA'S SECRET

"No," she whispered. "I don't want them finding out about *this*."

"You want me to talk to them?"

She imagined Joe walking over and confronting the two men. She visualized fists flying, a knife plunging into Joe's gut, herself running out clutching the notebook.

"No, no. I might be wrong," she admitted.

She kept her eyes on the men as other people crowded behind them, blocking her view. "Come on," she told Joe. "Let's get out of here."

Cass picked up the bill, then pulled two twenty pound notes from her wallet and left them on the table.

"Thanks, Cass," Joe said. "I'll get the next one."

After tugging on her coat and pulling up the hood, she followed closely behind Joe, hoping the men wouldn't see her leave. The notebook was firmly in her grip. The rush of cold air against her face revived her, as if the demons inside had evaporated. *Jesus, I'm seeing enemies everywhere I look!*

"Still snowing," Joe said. "Can you believe it?"

"Yeah," Cass answered. "A blanket of purity covering this befouled little town."

CHAPTER 13

The trudge back to Cass's apartment over the snow-covered sidewalks in darkness interrupted by occasional lamplight should have imbued Joe with the holiday spirit, but the claustrophobic cold sent waves of apprehension through him. Cass clutched his arm in the familiar way Sara often did, but he still felt alone and lost.

Is it just homesickness?

No, it was something much greater. Cass's discovery—while not nearly as valuable as the Shakespeare manuscripts he'd been given—could actually be putting her, and now Joe himself, in danger. Last time, perhaps stupidly, he'd been up to the challenge. Maybe it was just Smitty's contagious enthusiasm and Dr. Williamson's extraordinary competence that had buoyed his confidence three years ago. Parts of that adventure—especially his first trip to England—had been thrilling.

Now, however, he waffled, weak and vulnerable. *And what else? Anchorless?* Sara's betrayal had set him adrift, disconnecting him from the family he'd thought was his.

A wave of sadness washed through him. *Sara's leaving me for another guy!* He wanted to tell Cass about it but fought the impulse. She had enough to worry about.

Cass stayed quiet, too, her profile barely visible inside the hood of her coat. Maybe she was lost in memories about her mother. To get his mind off his own thoughts, Joe would talk to her.

"So what did you and your father do after your mom's death?"

Cass didn't answer for a few seconds, as if debating within herself how much to reveal. "Well, we held a nice funeral that was pretty well attended. And then we planted her in the ground and moved on with life."

"That must have been hard for you. A girl needs her mother."

"Yes. Yes, it was very difficult. For the first few weeks, I cried myself to sleep almost every night. My dad was great, though. He'd come into my room and rub my back and say encouraging things, like, 'Mommy's up in heaven, watching over you now.' But even then, I didn't believe it."

"Did your dad remarry?"

"Eventually. About three years after Mom died, he met a nice woman at church, a widow. They dated for a couple of years, and after I graduated from high school, they tied the knot. Had a quiet little ceremony at the church and then one helluva party in the rec hall. I'd never seen my dad drunk until that party."

"What's her name? Do you like her?"

"Samantha? Yeah, she's wonderful. In many ways, better than my real mom. Certainly more stable. She emails me every other day or so, checking up on me. Kind of annoying, if you want to know the truth. But I know she does it out of concern. She really adores my dad, so naturally she's overly protective of me."

Joe imagined his own children saying something similar about a new stepfather in their lives, years from now, after he and Sara were divorced. He cringed.

"Your dad's in medicine, isn't he?"

"He's a biomedical engineer at a company that makes heart

stents, catheters, shunts—you know, all those glamorous products used in gory operations."

"Sounds interesting."

"He loves it."

They had reached the doorway to Cass's apartment, so she unlocked the door and they climbed the stairs. Once inside the flat, Cass shed her heavy coat and scurried to stand in front of the heater.

"I need another drink," Cass announced. "You?"

"Why not?" He removed his ski jacket and hung it on the back of the closest barstool. "Let me visit the restroom first."

While Joe washed his hands at the sink, the full weight of Sara's infidelity finally hit him. Part of him wanted to return to her and beg her to stay faithful, to love him as she had when they were first dating. Another part of him was glad he was now so far away that he couldn't make a fool of himself by begging her to stay. *I'm not even sure I still love her.*

Was it just the comfortable habit of married life that he craved? He loved his children, and thinking about Brian and Katie—about not living with them and not seeing them every day—distressed him. *Maybe a trial separation? Spend the spring apart and sort out our feelings?*

He'd find an apartment near their house, spend as much time with the kids as possible. And if he and Sara decided to get divorced after all, he'd move to Stockton to be closer to CLU. *Assuming I return. Hell, they don't want me either.*

Feeling utterly lost and disconnected, he wondered if he could find the courage to face this new untethered life that awaited him.

Cass was standing by the fireplace holding a wineglass.

"I poured us some sherry. That should warm us up." She took a second glass from the mantle and handed it to Joe.

"Cheers," he said, clinking her glass. He sipped the sweet, thick wine. "Mmm. This is very nice."

Cass took another sip, smiling up at him. "One of my few

indulgences."

He realized then that if he were truly free, he'd lean down and kiss Cassandra—she was certainly flirting—but, no, they were only friends, and he would keep it that way. What he really wanted was to kiss Sara, despite the pain she'd caused.

He took another sip of the sherry and set the glass down on the coffee table.

"So let me see that journal. I'm ready to read."

Cass grinned, but Joe noted a wince of disappointment. She walked over to her desk and grabbed the notebook she'd taken with them to dinner. "Please be careful."

He sat on the sofa and opened the journal, while Cass stood next to him. The handwriting was almost masculine.

> I shall perish if I can write
> About no one but myself.
> Where is my old bawdy vigor
> And interest in the world around me?
> I am not meant for this monastery living—
> Finding always traces of passive dependence,
> A desire to have someone decide my life,
> Like some Nazi General.

Joe scratched his head. "Wow. This is pretty good. Not as much imagery as in a lot of her poetry, but clearly confessional."

Cass nodded. "Read on. I'll be interested in your assessment."

She strolled over to her desk and sat down, opening her notebook. Joe went back to reading.

> My poems pall.
> A jay swallows my crumbs on the wet porch.
> My head is a battalion of fixes.
> I don't even dare open Yeats, Eliot...

Sylvia's Secret

The old fresh joys, for the pain
I have remembering my first bright encounters.

"I see why you told me to read on," Joe called to Cass. "The imagery certainly picks up."

Cass nodded again, entranced by her own work now, so Joe returned to reading. In a few hours, he'd read the entire journal and closed the cover, contemplating how to phrase his critique. Some of the fragments of poetry were superb, but many sections read like a diary, musings of a mind warming up to write.

He was ready to tell Cass what he thought, but she was no longer at her desk. He put the notebook on the sofa and walked down the hall. The bathroom was empty, so he checked the bedroom. Cass had climbed into bed and covered herself with the comforter. Her breathing was rhythmic and serene, reminding Joe of his daughter. He smiled and pulled the door closed.

The sofa was not long enough for him to stretch out, but he found that if he curled up on his side, as he had that afternoon, it was quite comfortable. He pulled the afghan off the back of the couch and covered himself. Then he laid his head on the pillow, and gazed at the orange glow of the fake logs.

Sara kissing his cheek, her musky fragrance arousing him, her warm breath on his face, a husky voice whispering his name… "Joe? Joe?" *Sara's voice?* No. Someone's voice…but whose? Someone nudging his shoulder, rocking him…"Joe? Wake up."

Joe opened his eyes to someone kneeling in front of him. *Where am I?* He didn't recognize the dark silhouette, the strong fragrance. A woman, not Sara, not her shape, but a warm body, close, so very close.

"Joe, it's Cass. Can you wake up?"

Joe sat up, his clarity returning. "Cass? Why's it so cold?"

Cass's body was blocking the heater. "The electricity went out," Cass whispered. "I'm frightened. I think someone's in the hallway."

Joe rubbed his eyes, trying to fully awaken, and he was shivering "What? Why is it so cold? I'm freezing."

"I told you. Someone cut our electricity. The heater's been out for over an hour, I think."

Finally awake enough to realize just how cold he was, he clutched Cass's shoulders and they stood up together.

"Let me get my jacket." He rushed over to the bar and threw on his coat. "What time is it?"

"About three. I'm scared. There were footsteps in the hall and then I heard voices."

Nothing was really visible in the utter blackness, only the vague outlines of furniture. He felt his way to Cass's desk, found the curtains, and tugged them open. No street lights or light from neighboring row houses illuminated the night.

"I think the electricity is out on the entire street, Cass."

She stepped over and stood next to him. "I was too afraid to open the drapes."

Joe laughed. "Why?"

"I don't know. I could just imagine someone or something right outside, ready to break through the glass and tackle me."

He was unable to see her expression in the darkness. "Let's check with your neighbors."

"I, I don't want to open the front door."

He put his arm around her. "It'll be okay. I won't let anything happen." She trembled like a child, and her fear seeped into him, raising the hairs on the back of his neck.

"Tell you what, you light some candles and we'll make sure we can see our hands in front of our faces before we open the door."

She didn't move, except to shiver in his grip. He remembered seeing a scented candle on the bar and another in the bathroom.

SYLVIA'S SECRET

"You have some candles, don't you? And some matches? Cass?"

"Yes," she whispered. "Okay."

She pulled away and her silhouette moved slowly toward the kitchen. In a few seconds, Joe heard the strike of a match and Cass's face was illuminated by its orange glow. She lowered the match into the glass that held the candle, and soon the wick was aflame, casting a flickering light onto her body. She was wearing a sheer white, low-cut negligee, her skin glowing like honey in the dim light. This was exactly like a scene out of a slasher film—a pseudo-hero showing bravado moments before a butcher knife is plunged into his heart. Joe could almost hear the "*sh, sh, sh, uh, uh, uh,*" of a *Friday the 13th* movie.

He tried to hide his apprehension, revealed in his clammy palms. "You have another candle in the bathroom, don't you?"

Cass's eyes widening with fear. "I'll get it."

She disappeared down the hall and Joe unlocked the front door before Cass reappeared holding the other candle. She'd put on a robe, but it hung open in the front, revealing her cleavage.

The sound of a creaking floorboard startled them. Then another. Someone *was* creeping down the hall. He reached for the door handle.

"Please," she whispered, "please don't open that door."

He shot her a reassuring smile, still trying to mask his own fear. "I'm sure it's nothing." He wanted to grab a knife from the kitchen, but that would only be admitting that he, too, believed the threat from the hall was real. Joe tried not to let his hand tremble, but turned the handle and tugged the door open.

A beam of light hit his face, sending a shrill scream from Cass's lungs. Joe stumbled backward, nearly tripping.

"Oh, I'm terribly sorry," a man's voice called. "You startled me!"

Joe watched Cass retreat into the bathroom. He grabbed the

candle from the bar and stepped into the hall. The man held the flashlight under his chin to illuminate his face. It was a smooth, pasty white face of a small man probably in his forties, dark circles under the eyes.

"Who are you?"

The other man held out his hand. "Nolan Anderson. I live next door."

Joe shook the man's bony hand. "Is the electricity out in the whole building?

"Yes. You're American?"

"That's right. I'm a friend of Miss Johnson."

"Oh, I see." The man nodded in the dim light, smiling faintly. "As far as I can tell, the electricity is out for blocks and blocks. The damn snow, I suspect, has brought down the power lines."

"Does this happen often?" Joe was beginning to feel the cold again.

"Rarely. Last time was ten years ago, I think. Should be on again sometime tomorrow."

Cass peeked around the door. "Oh," she said, sighing with relief. "It's only you, Mr. Anderson."

"Yes," he said, shrugging. "Only me. Please, call me Nolan."

"Did I hear you correctly?" Cass asked him. "The power lines are down?"

"Well, dear, I chatted up the landlord. That's what *we* suspect. But no one seems to have a battery-powered radio, so we don't know with any certainty."

"The cell phones should still work, shouldn't they?" asked Joe.

"Oh, I suppose so," said the petite man. "I don't keep one myself."

"Well," Joe said to Cass, "why don't you call 9-1-1, or whatever, and see what they say?"

"Alright."

Sylvia's Secret

Joe addressed Mr. Anderson then. "Would you like to come in and wait until we've learned something more?"

Anderson raised an eyebrow. "You know," he said, "I'm so cold, I think I'll just climb back into bed, but if the situation is other than we thought, please stop over and knock me up."

Joe chuckled. "Knock you up?"

"Oh, yes. You're American. Knock on my door, is what I meant."

"I shall," said Joe.

The little man shuffled down the hall, and Joe closed the door. Cass was standing by the bar just pulling the phone from her ear.

"Yes, just as he said. Snow brought down the lines."

"Any estimate on when they'll be repaired?"

"They said mid-morning."

"Good," said Joe. "I'm freezing."

"So am I. Let's go back to bed."

"Do you have any extra blankets?"

"Oh, dear, I don't. I'm sorry."

Joe zipped up his ski jacket. "Can I borrow your coat then?"

"Sure, of course." Cass took it from the stand and handed it to him. "Will that be enough?"

He nodded. "I think so."

"No, wait. This is silly. I've got a big down comforter on my bed. You can sleep with me."

He smiled in the candlelight. "I don't think that would be a good idea, Cass."

She chuckled. "I'm not going to jump your bones, Joe."

He stepped closer to the sofa. "I'm not sure Sara would approve."

Cass came closer. "Our bodies won't even have to touch."

"It's a nice gesture, but I should be okay." He took another step toward the couch.

"Well, I can't have you freezing to death on me, Joe."

He imagined his frozen blue body resting on top of hers. The image reminded him of the body he'd found six years ago in Lost Slough.

"With my jacket and your big coat over me, I should be fine."

"Are you sure?"

Joe nodded.

"Well, promise me that if you get too cold, you'll come in and get under my comforter." Cass smiled a smile that almost made Joe change his mind. "I'm a heavy sleeper, so I won't even know you're there."

"Okay. If I get too cold, I'll sneak in."

Her smile was sweet, innocent, seductive. "Promise?"

"Yes, I promise."

She slowly retreated down the hallway, taking one of the candles with her. The other she left burning on the bar, its dim orange glow casting shadows against the walls.

Joe settled on his side on the little sofa and tugged Cass's heavy coat up to his chin. Her musky rose-scented perfume filled his nostrils. Maybe in time if he and Sara really did get divorced he would sleep with Cass, but now it wasn't right, no matter how sweet she smelled or how seductively she smiled.

Chapter 14

The morning sunlight shone through the crack in the heavy curtains, and just as Joe was opening his eyes to the bright line of light cast on the wall opposite him, the little electric heater hummed back to life. Stretching, he climbed off the couch and ambled down the hall to the bathroom.

"Coffee," he said to his reflection. "Must have coffee."

In the kitchen, he found Cass's cache of ground coffee—an Ethiopian blend—and set about making a fresh pot. He turned on the gas burner expecting the "click, click, click" of the electric igniter but only getting the hissing of gas, so he turned it off and searched for matches. A box was on the shelf over his head, so he tried again with success—a circular blue flame whooshed to life.

A few minutes later, Cass wandered in, sleepily rubbing her eyes. A white terrycloth robe was loosely tied, exposing her sheer negligee of the night before.

"Morning," she mumbled. "You started the coffee?"

"Yeah. Hope you don't mind."

"Mind? Oh, *hell*, no." She forced her eyes open. "So the electricity's back on, right?"

Joe chuckled. "*Yeah.* That's why the light is on."

She slapped Joe's shoulder playfully, the way Sara used to do.

"Don't be a smart ass. I'm still asleep."

Cass shuffled to the window and pulled open the drapes, letting in a stream of bright sunshine that immediately warmed the room.

"Oh, it's so beautiful outside," she gushed. "Come to the window. See for yourself."

The streets and sidewalks were covered with fresh white snow, and the rooftops of the row houses across the street were glistening like tiny diamonds had been strewn across the white surfaces. Above the rooftops, the azure sky was clear and bright.

"Like Christmas morning in the movies!"

Joe nodded. "I'm from Louisiana, so we never—I mean *never*—woke up to snow on Christmas."

"Me neither. Living in southern California."

They stood together, Cass in her robe and Joe in his ski jacket, lost in the view.

Cass suddenly grabbed his wrist. "Oh, my God. What time is it?"

"A little after eight. Why?"

"We've got to get the ten o'clock train."

She raced to the coffee pot and poured herself a cup. Joe was still in a daze at the window. "Mind if I shower first?"

"No, go ahead."

Cass disappeared, so Joe stepped to the kitchen and poured himself a cup of coffee, which he took back to the window. A few cars inched through the snow and a few brave souls, bundled in stylish winter coats, wandered down their steps to the sidewalk.

Joe sipped the rich dark brew. *Off to work, no doubt.* His awakening mind turned to Sara and the kids. *Brian and Katie would love seeing this snow. They'd go crazy.* He thought about the times during winter break when he and Sara had taken them up Highway 50 to Suzie's cabin behind Strawberry Lodge. They'd gone sledding on the nearby hill where all the winter vacationers played, and Katie had even started snowboarding the past two winters at Sierra Ski Resort. They had laughed while they rode the saucer sleds down the hill over and over again.. Joe's heart ached at the memories.

Then there were the times he and Sara had made love in front of the fireplace after the kids were asleep upstairs. Thinking of that brought the recent fiasco to mind, and Joe wanted to hurl his coffee cup at the window, as if shattering it would somehow shatter the unforgettable image.

"It's all yours."

Joe turned to see Cass leaning around the corner, a towel wrapped over her steamy skin.

"The shower—-it's all yours."

"Oh, okay."

She disappeared again, and Joe grabbed fresh clothes from his suitcase.

An hour later, they were dressed and packed and, after eating a quick breakfast, headed to the subway that would take them to Paddington Train Station. Once they'd cleared the suburbs and were out in the country, Joe was awestruck by the beauty of the wintry rolling hills. Stone walls outlined patches of land like giant jigsaw pieces, and occasional thickets of trees, their tops powered with white, stood like clusters of dark soldiers huddled around a fire, backs to the train windows. Sitting across from him, Cass stared out the window smiling, apparently lost in thought. After a few moments, she suddenly turned and said, "I've got to warn you about some of Trevor's friends."

"Oh?"

"They were very protective of him. I think they saw me as a complete outsider, which of course I am, but Diane in particular seemed—jealous, I guess."

"Who's Diane?"

"Diane Mousalinas, Trevor's old girl friend."

"Mousalinas? Sounds like the female version of Mussolini, the Italian dictator."

"No, her father's from Greece. He's rich. Made his money importing goat cheese and olives. And she's a bit spoiled, if you ask me."

"Okay, so I need to be careful around Diane. She saw you as a rival."

"I guess so, which doesn't make sense, since Trevor told me she broke it off with him."

"Who else?" asked Joe.

"Well, then there's Zenon Castillo."

He chuckled. "*Zenon?* Sounds like a character from *Doctor Who.*"

"I know, right? Everyone calls him Z."

"Just Z? That's weird."

"Not really. I have a friend named Xavier, but everyone calls him X."

Joe smiled and said, "Why? Get it? X,*Y,* Z?"

Cass shook her head. "Do people actually laugh at your jokes?"

"My students usually do."

"They're just sucking up for a better grade. Anyway, Zenon's grandparents fled Spain after Franco came to power. He's gorgeous. He's got those Spanish good looks—dark complexion, bushy black eyebrows, a great head of glossy black hair. Diane's with him now, I think."

"So why do we need to worry about Z?"

Cass shook her head. "Somehow he got the idea that I had something to do with Trevor's death. At least, that's the impression I got from his phone call a few days ago."

"I don't understand. He died in Devon, right?"

"Right."

"And you were in London, so how could you have caused his

death?"

"I'm not sure what Z's thinking, but I told you what I think. Maybe Z's right. If someone killed Trevor to send me a message, then…" She started to tear up, and Joe took her hand.

"Let's not get ahead of ourselves. We'll look into Trevor's death and figure this out for ourselves, okay?"

"Okay." Then she wiped her eyes and turned away. She seemed to need silence, so Joe said nothing more.

He reviewed the train car's passengers, some dressed in business clothes, reading the newspaper, some dressed for holiday, chatting cheerily. Everyone seemed to be in a good mood, their spirits buoyed by the sunshine and the beauty of the dazzling winter landscape.

Two hours later, they arrived in North Tawton, the small town in Devon where Plath and Hughes had lived. Cass led Joe to the Lamplighter Hotel where she had stayed with Trevor. The hotel clerk informed them that only one room was available.

"Should we try someplace else?" asked Joe.

Cass glanced at the clerk, who said, "You can check, if you like, but there are quite a few people in town. Some poor guy's funeral has brought a lot of strangers to town."

"That poor guy was my friend Trevor," Cass said, obviously annoyed.

"Does the room have two beds?" Joe asked.

The clerk checked her computer screen and nodded. "Yes, as a matter of fact. Two doubles."

Cass spoke first. "I don't mind sharing the room, if you don't."

If Sara found out, she wouldn't be happy, but Sara was one of the reasons he was here in England. *The hell with it.*

"Yeah, of course, if that's all you have," Joe said.

Cass slapped her credit card on the counter and filled out the paper work.

"It's almost one," she said. "The service for Trevor's in two hours, so we'd better get ready."

They rode the small elevator up to their floor, dropped off their suitcases in the room, freshened up and went back down to the lobby.

"There's a pub around the corner," Cass said. "Let's get some lunch."

By then, the snow on the streets had turned into a muddy slush and the sidewalks were almost clear. The sun had warmed the air, and little streams flowed across streets and in the gutters.

The pub in Devon was larger than the one they'd eaten at the night before and more brightly lit, with sunlight streaming in through the windows.

"Oh," Cass said, leaning close to Joe's ear, "there are Trevor's friends."

A table in the back was encircled by seven people, four guys and three women. All were dressed in dark clothes, as were Joe and Cass. He followed Cass to the table, unsure what to expect from the somber group.

"May we join you?" Cass asked, her voice filled with sincere sympathy.

One of the guys raised his head. Must be Zenon, the one Cass described on the train. He resembled a bullfighter—tall, muscular, with jet black hair and thick eyebrows. He leveled his eyes at Cass in a cold unwelcoming way.

"Oh, hi, Cassandra. Sorry, we don't really have room at our table for more."

"Nonsense. We can squeeze in."

There were no empty chairs at the nearby tables, and the group exchanged glances like they didn't really want company.

Joe put a hand on Cass's shoulder and nodded to the right.

"Come on, Cass. There's an open booth down there."

Cass stood her ground. "You blokes don't seem very happy to see me. What's up with that?"

One of the women's eyes lit up. Joe was surprised by her appearance——she could have been Cassandra's half sister, though pale with straight dark hair that hung down to her shoulders.

"It's just, we're all feeling a bit sad over Trevor."

"So am I, Diane," said Cass.

"Well, of course," Diane replied. "But we didn't expect to see *you* here."

Cass knit her brows. "But why not?"

"It's just, you left Trevor, Cass," Diane explained. "He took it pretty hard."

"He became too possessive," Cass answered. "Even a little abusive."

"So *you* say," said the man who'd first spoken.

Cass put her hand on the Spaniard's shoulder. "What's *that* supposed to mean, Z?"

Diane raised a hand. "We don't want any trouble. It's nice that you came to pay your respects."

"You're acting as though I had something to do with Trevor's death."

Zenon pushed Cass's hand away and turned in his chair to face her more directly. "Didn't you admit as much to me on the phone the other night?"

"What?" said Cass. "No, I don't think so."

"You said someone may have killed Trevor to send you a message. Isn't that right?"

Cass nodded. "That's a possibility, yes."

Joe tugged Cass's arm. "Maybe we should go sit down."

She jerked her arm away. "No! Hey, I cared for Trevor, I really did, but it just wasn't working."

Diane took Cass by the hand. "Trevor took the break-up pretty hard. He couldn't understand how you could accuse *him* of being violent, when really...."

"When really *what?*"

Z stood up. "Oh, for God's sakes. *You* were the one who struck *him*, not the other way round."

Cass laughed. "Is *that* what he told you?"

"We saw the bruise on his cheek, Cass," said Diane softly.

"Listen," Cass said, her voice louder than before, "Trevor got really jealous after that party at Halloween. He called me a slut and all sorts of other names."

One of the guys sitting farthest away snorted. "Well, if the shoe fits."

Cass stormed toward the man, but Joe blocked her.

"Let's sit down, Cass, please," he pleaded.

Joe grabbed Cass in his arms and held her. She pushed against him in an effort to reach the offender, but Joe held tight, surprised by her strength.

"Cass, please," he whispered. "Let's leave these people alone. They're obviously confused and upset."

"Yeah," she yelled, "they're confused all right. Real fucking confused."

She wriggled out of Joe's grip and stomped away.

The group's intense stares reminded Joe of the alien children in *Village of the Damned*—any second they'd likely shoot rays of hot light from their eyes and incinerate him.

"I just arrived yesterday from the States," he explained. "Cass and I teach together at CLU in California. I've known her for years. If she says Trevor was abusive, then I believe her."

Zenon, still standing, held out his hand. "What's your name, Yank?"

"Joe Conrad." He took the Spaniard's hand, but the handshake turned into a contest to see who could squeeze the tightest.

"Listen, Mr. Joe Conrad. All of us have known Trevor for years. We never knew him to be violent toward a woman. *Any* woman."

Joe applied as much pressure to Z's hand as Z was applying to his.

"Well, there's a first time for everything, isn't there?"

The guy across the table stood. "You don't really want to take on all of us, do you, Yank?"

Joe grinned sadistically, vowing to himself that he would not be the first to release his grip.

"I've been outmatched before," Joe said, "but I'm still standing."

Diane reached over and yanked Z's fist away from Joe's.

"This is a terrible day for all of us," she said calmly. "Let's not make it any worse than it needs to be."

Below Diane's thin dark eyebrows shone glistening brown eyes filled with sadness. Her soft and sympathetic air reminded him of Sara.

"Okay," he answered. "But at some point, I'd like to be filled in on what actually happened. I'm here to help Cass get through this, so maybe one of you"—he stared into the woman's eyes—"one of you will tell me what's going on."

Diane nodded as though she understood and then turned away.

Joe was again struck by how much she looked like Cass's white twin. He moved to the table by the window where Cass was sitting with her back to the crowd. Tears were streaming down her cheeks.

"Don't cry. It's not worth it."

She dabbed her eyes with a paper napkin.

"I cared for Trevor, Joe. I really cared for him."

Joe put his arm around her. "I know you did."

"I can't believe what his friends are saying about me! How dare they!"

"Everyone's upset. Let's eat and we'll feel better."

She blew her nose into the napkin. "I'm going to the bathroom. Please order me a Bloody Mary. And a roast beef sandwich."

On the train, Cass had told him there would probably be a wake after the funeral. She'd said it would be good to drink with Trevor's friends and share memories. Now, attending Trevor's wake seemed like a bad idea.

CHAPTER 15

During lunch, Joe stayed quiet, waiting for Cass to talk but reluctant to prod her, so they ate in silence. When the waitress came to take their plates, Cass ordered another Bloody Mary while Joe stuck with coffee.

"Diane sure looks like you."

Cass rolled her eyes. "Yeah, if I were a pasty white Goth bitch."

"She seems okay. Trying to keep the peace."

"I don't understand it. Those guys were all over me at that party and *I'm* the slut?"

The people at the next table fell quiet and glanced over. "Maybe you should keep your voice down."

She shot them an angry look before continuing. "I wish you'd been there. Every single one of those guys danced with me. And half the women were grabbing me, too. I mean, it was practically an orgy."

Joe tried not to imagine it.

"That guy Zenon? He was dressed like Count Dracula, you know, the old one from the black and white movies."

"Bela Lugosi," said Joe. The group was still sitting together, drinking stout, ignoring him and Cass.

"Whatever. Anyway, he was pretending to bite my neck so much, he gave me a hickey. Trevor was furious. I thought it was all in fun, you know? Their usual style of partying, and I usually don't get that crazy but I was trying to fit in. I thought we'd had a great time."

The waitress came back with a fresh Bloody Mary and the coffee pot. She placed the cocktail in front of Cass before refilling Joe's cup. When she left, Joe patted Cass's hand.

"They're just upset, Cass. Maybe looking for a scapegoat."

"A *scapegoat*? What do you mean?"

He shrugged. "Well, you were in London when the accident happened, right?"

She nodded. "I'd been gone for weeks."

"But they were here with Trevor, drinking with him the night he died, right? So if they can't point the finger of blame at you, they have to point it at themselves."

Cass nodded again. "Right. *They* should have taken better care of him the night he was hit by that car. I mean, what the hell could *I* have done?"

"Exactly."

She smiled that great smile of hers. "Thanks. I knew you'd be good for me."

"Of course, the real person to blame is the driver of that car, whoever he is."

Cass sipped her drink. "I'll bet you he was from the law firm that watches over the Ted Hughes estate. Or maybe someone they hired."

"Do you really think a law firm could be mixed up with murder?"

She rolled her eyes. "You of all people should know how corrupt some so-called authority figures can be. I mean, look who tried to frame you for those rapes and murders."

Sylvia's Secret

"Right. Still, what makes you so sure someone from Ted's law firm might be involved?"

Cass scowled. "The way they treated me! When I started asking about the missing journals and whether or not Ted really burned one, they got really defensive." She took a long pull from her drink before continuing her rant. "I mean, they threatened to call the police—the POLICE—and then they threatened to have me thrown out of their offices. Who in the HELL do they think they are!"

"Calm down," Joe said. "I believe you."

"I've got a feeling they'll send someone to Trevor's funeral. That's one of the reasons I wanted to come here today, to see if someone tries to intimidate me. You got my back, right?"

Joe nodded. "Sure, of course."

They both turned toward the window. Clouds had started to roll in and the sky was darkening. Another snowstorm was likely.

"Is the church far from here?" he asked.

"No, not really. Within walking distance."

"Maybe we should leave before they do so we don't have another confrontation here. I doubt they'd cause a scene inside a church."

"Good idea."

Cass drained her glass and they stood to leave. She opened her purse and pulled out some ten-pound notes.

"Sorry, Cass. I didn't get a chance to get money."

"That's okay. I got this."

"How much is it?"

"Twenty pounds."

"What's that in U.S. currency?"

"Almost forty bucks."

He'd forgotten how expensive things were in England.

"I should have changed money when we were at the bank yesterday. It just completely slipped my mind."

She smiled, pulling on her heavy coat. "C'mon. There's a bank on the way."

Joe used an ATM to get eight hundred pounds and some change, and then handed Cass two ten-pound notes for lunch as they walked up the hill to the church. The gutter's ugly brown slush reminded him of bulldozed dirt along the edge of a mass grave like one he'd seen in a newsreel from the concentration camps in Germany.

The old church on Essington Road was small, its walls made of stone rubble and granite, with wood shingles on the roof and gables finished in gray slate. A squat tower stood at the west end of the oddly restored structure. The inside was small and dim, and the plastered walls and few windows gave the interior an austere feeling.

At the front, candles were already lit on the altar and two small-framed elderly women dressed in heavy dark clothes seemed to be readying stacks of Bibles or song books. Besides the women, Joe and Cass were the only people in attendance.

"Guess we're way early," Cass said.

"Should we hang out or go somewhere?"

Cass looked around and sighed. "Stay, I guess." She slid into the last pew, and scooted over away from the aisle. Joe slid in beside her. "I never met Trevor's parents, so I hope to pay my respects to them, at least."

A white-haired priest dressed in a black robe came in through a side door at the front and spoke quietly to the women. They nodded and distributed the stacks of books to the rows of pews, placing a few in each.

It was the only action going on. Joe may as well have been twiddling his thumbs. Despite Cass's concern that some hired gun from the Hughes estate would show up, he wanted to take a nap. Sitting in the church reminded him of his childhood in Baton Rouge when his mother would take him to mass at St. Jude's on Sunday mornings. Though raised Catholic, his father usually stayed home and read the paper. The picture of his father sitting in his easy chair, in his pajamas and bathrobe, holding the newspaper open, a lit cigarette between his fingers, filled Joe's thoughts. Sometimes when he and his mother returned from church, Joe would climb into his father's lap and they'd read the comics together while his mother cooked. He could almost smell the bacon.

Then he recalled another image—one from years later while he was a senior in high school. It was the image of his parents' caskets side by side at their funeral. That opened a flood of memories—police officers, neighbors crying, trying to comfort him, someone in a business suit at the funeral parlor showing him pictures of coffins, someone else in a business suit who said he was the family attorney there to help guide Joe through the process. *The process!* He'd always remember those words. The process of filing the insurance claim, paying off the house, declaring Joe an emancipated youth under Louisiana law. It was a process, the lawyer said, *like making sausage*, thought Joe, and his parents' corpses were going through the grinder. The end result was two shiny cheap caskets side by side in a place named for the saint of lost causes.

He'd stopped going to church after that.

Joe wondered if Cass had sensed his sudden fall into sadness, but she stared straight ahead, eyes glazed over. He closed his eyes and for the first time in years, said a prayer inside a church. *Dear God, please help me do what's best for my family. Please help Sara figure out what's in her heart. Please watch over my children while I'm away and keep them safe.*

Suddenly, the overhead lights came on and the room seemed cheerier. Then the doors behind them opened and people began filing in. First a middle-aged couple—Trevor's parents, guessed Joe—followed by a steady stream of other middle-aged folks. A crowd of younger people pushed in, including Julia and the other women from the pub. All bore solemn expressions and spoke only in whispers.

No one sat in the same pew with Joe and Cass, even though seating was growing scarcer.

When all the pews had filled, some of the folks in the front turned to look over their shoulders, as if expecting a bride to walk down the aisle. Instead, after a few moments of dead silence, the main doors opened and an oak casket was wheeled in, guarded on each side by Zenon and the other three men from the pub. All but one—the outspoken guy from the pub—ignored them as they walked by. That one glowered at Joe and Cass before turning his attention back to his chore.

That's when Cass started to cry. She'd taken several tissues from her purse and was struggling to control her sobs. Joe put his arm around her, hoping it would help.

The priest entered carrying a crucifix on a tall staff, attended by an altar boy on each side, their red and white garments reminding Joe of his brief time as altar boy when his parents were still alive in Baton Rouge. The service began with the Lord's prayer. Joe mumbled along, repeating, "Our Father, who art in heaven, hallowed be thy name...."

After repeating several more lines softly, Cass spoke the next line loudly enough that people sitting in front of them turned to look: "Forgive us our trespasses as we forgive those around us...."

Joe blushed.

The rest of the service was a tense, uncomfortable blur, but at the end the priest mentioned that there would be a brief reception in the hall next door.

"Maybe we should skip that," Joe said.

Cass had stopped crying but her gloomy expression lingered.

"No, I want to meet his folks."

"Are you sure that's wise?"

She gave Joe a quizzical look. "Why wouldn't it be?"

SYLVIA'S SECRET

People were rising to leave, so Joe leaned over and whispered, "What if they feel the same way Trevor's friends do?"

"Don't be ridiculous." She dabbed her eyes once more before nudging Joe. "I'm sure they'll want to know how much I cared for their son."

Joe was confused by her answer. He'd gotten the impression that Cass really had *not* cared that much for Trevor once he'd become abusive, but now she was acting as if she'd lost her one true love. *Maybe she's feeling the strain of the last few days, or maybe alcohol makes her more sentimental.*

Outside, quilted gray clouds covered the sky and it was growing darker, but the air was not nearly as cold as it had been the day before. Blotches of snow looked like white scabs on the lawn between the two buildings.

The reception hall was a small building adjacent to the church. Cass held onto Joe's arm as they walked down the path to join the others.

"Be sure to search the crowd for anyone who looks suspicious," she whispered in a voice loud enough for others to hear.

"Okay, but I'm not sure what to look for."

Cass snorted. "Well, look for someone like that mercenary who was after the Shakespeare papers. You must have an instinct for those types by now, after everything you've been through."

Joe chuckled nervously. Being reminded of his previous misadventures raised his anxiety. The last thing he wanted was to be shot at again.

Inside the dim hall, people were filing by the older couple, whispering their condolences. Trevor's mother was completely crestfallen and his father seemed to be struggling to hold back tears by blinking his eyes and twitching the left side of his mouth.

No one in the little hall reminded Joe of the killers he'd encountered before—the mercenary Benedict or the I-5 Strangler. His mind ranged in all directions as the line inched forward with glacial slowness. *Maybe a British mercenary would have a different appearance and give off a different vibe.* He recalled the young Asian woman who had attacked him and Smitty on the London Eye three years earlier. He hadn't seen *her* coming until it was almost too late.

There was a well-built man in a dark suit standing alone in a corner. Ex-military, maybe. Intent and serious—not mournful. And he was staring at Cass, following her progress in the receiving line. The closer Cass got to Trevor's folks, the angrier the man seemed.

Joe wasn't sure what to do. His first instinct was to step out of the line and confront him. But how? What would he say? *Are you a paid assassin, here to kill my friend?*

He considered pulling Cass out of line and herding her outside. But if they left the crowd, would the man follow them? No. Better to stay put. *Safety in numbers.*

Suddenly, Cass was embracing Trevor's mom and shaking hands with his father, saying, "I'm so sorry about your son."

Joe moved forward and shook the woman's graceful hand, repeating Cass's sentiment.

Then Cass said, "Trevor and I dated for a while before I moved back to London."

The expression on the older man's face changed from sadness to suspicion and then to red hot anger. Still holding his hand, Cass seemed oblivious.

Releasing his grip, the man said, "You're the American slut that drove Trevor bonkers?"

"Excuse me?" Cass said. "No one calls *me* a slut!"

"Well, our Trevor did, didn't he?"

"Don't go there," replied Cass.

Joe clutched Cass's arm. "Let's leave," he whispered.

She jerked her arm away. "Your son and I had a good thing at first. Then he went crazy, crazy with jealousy."

The woman began to sob uncontrollably.

Sylvia's Secret

"Look what you've done," said the man. "Upset Trevor's mum."

Joe finally took Cass by the wrist and shuffled her out of line. "Let's get out of here. We're not helping anyone."

Cass's face went blank as if she'd forgotten who he was. Then she nodded and allowed Joe to lead her to the door.

When they got outside in the chilly air, she said, "That whole family's crazy."

The winter day had grown dark, and Joe guided Cass down the pavement toward the town, ever vigilant to see if anyone was following. The angry-looking man in the dark suit stepped out of the church, his body silhouetted in the light of the doorway.

"Do you recognize the man standing there?" Joe asked.

Cass turned her head but kept walking. "Can't see his face."

"He was watching you when we were in line."

She stopped and turned fully then.

"What are you doing?" Joe asked.

"I want to go back up there and ask that guy what he's staring at."

"That's not a good idea, Cass. Let's go back to the hotel."

"I'll bet anything he's connected to the Hughes estate somehow."

"If he is, then we'd better get the hell out of here."

Cass tugged her arm away. "Why? I'm not afraid of that creep."

"He has the advantage. We're out here in the dark alone."

"But I'm so angry I could probably take him on my own."

"Not if he has a gun or a knife, Cass."

She stared at the man in the doorway for a few seconds before turning and walking toward the sleepy little village and the hotel. Joe glanced back a few times until the man stepped back inside the reception hall and closed the door behind him.

A few street lights lit the way, and some of the storefronts had meager Christmas lights on display. The colorful lights struggled in vain to fill Joe's heart with holiday joy. He was thousands of miles from his children, surrounded by hostile people, all because of his friendship with a woman he clearly did not know as well as he thought he did.

Joe turned to his old friend Hamlet, recalling the lines, *The time is out of joint: O cursed spite, That ever I was born to set it right!*

But could I really set things right?

CHAPTER 16

"I'm too wound up to go to the hotel," Cass said. "Let's go back to the pub."

"What if that guy shows up?"

"We'll call the police. He wouldn't do anything in a public setting, would he?"

Joe chuckled. "Probably not, but who knows? If someone wants you dead, they can find a way. Put poison in your food or—"

"Run you over in their car."

"Right. Which is why going to the hotel is a wiser thing to do."

Cass shook her head. "The idea of being cooped up in a hotel room for the rest of the night drives me crazy. I'll feel safer surrounded by people."

Joe shrugged. "Whatever you want."

Back in the pub, Cass said, "I need a cigarette." She went to a vending machine before they found an empty table.

The room was nearly empty, but a few locals, Joe guessed, were seated at the bar, talking to the bartender. Two waitresses stood the end of the bar, talking and smoking.

When Cass returned, she was already opening a pack of Salems.

"Want to sit by the window?" he asked.

"Sure, that's fine."

After they'd sat down, Cass fished a cigarette out of the pack with trembling fingers. She put the filtered end between her lips and picked up the little red candle on the table. Once she had it lit, Cass inhaled deeply and then blew a stream of smoke over her head.

"I didn't know you smoked."

"Sometimes. Not often." She took another long drag and exhaled with a satisfied sigh. "Only if I'm upset or if I've got to finish a lot of work before a deadline."

The same waitress who'd served them before came back and stood next to Joe.

"Would you like something from the bar?"

He nodded, the tension tightening the ropes in his neck and shoulders. "Scotch and soda, please. Make it a double."

"And you, miss? Same as before?"

Cass eyed the waitress curiously, as if surprised she remembered her drink. "No, I'll have a white Russian now. And make it a double, like my friend's."

After the waitress left, Cass took another deep drag on her cigarette and then blew the smoke toward the ceiling, as if exhaling the very tension she'd been feeling.

Joe searched her eyes. *What's going on in that mind of hers?* "Do you want to talk about what happened?"

She shook her head and wrinkled her brow. "I don't know what those people told Trevor's folks, but I'm mad as hell."

"I can tell."

"Trevor and I worked really well together. He shared my view of Ted, but he still wanted to explore Ted's psyche and how his ╴oism influenced his writing."

"That actually sounds fascinating."

Sylvia's Secret

"It was. Trevor was really digging into Ted's mind, doing what might be called a Freudian analysis. His research complemented mine perfectly. He even shared some pages from one of Ted's little known notebooks, drafts of a poem Ted wrote about the night Sylvia supposedly killed herself. It was so relevant to what I was working on that I begged Trevor to let me use it, too. And he agreed."

"That was generous." Joe fondly recalled how well he had worked with Smitty and Sylvia Williamson on the Shakespeare manuscripts.

Cass nodded. "Exactly! I mean, what scholar shares something so significant with you? That's how closely we were working together. Share and share alike." She took a last drag on her cigarette and then crushed it out in the ashtray. "It wasn't a competition. We were cooperating, damn it!"

"Sounds like it."

"I brought those notes with me and the photocopies of Ted's drafts. I'll show you when we get back to the hotel. You'll be able to see for yourself that Trevor would never have shared a find that important if he didn't trust me."

The waitress returned with their drinks and placed them on the table.

"Shall I open a tab?"

Joe looked at Cass. "Want to head back to the hotel after we finish these drinks?"

She shook her head, digging another cigarette from the pack. "No, I'm gonna need a few more."

Cass was preoccupied with the cigarettes but Joe was trying to signal his discomfort about staying. "Sure," he said, "open a tab."

After the waitress walked away, Cass lit the cigarette, blowing a stream of gray smoke over Joe's head. Then with the cigarette between her fingers, she held out her glass. "Cheers," she said. "Here's to friendship."

He picked up his glass. "To friendship."

She took a long drink and put the glass down before sucking on the cigarette again. "Friendship is really important, don't you agree?"

He nodded.

"And loyalty, right?"

He nodded again, Sara's betrayal stabbing his heart.

"I love that you're here for me, Joe. Thank you."

They touched their glasses together again and drank. Over the rim of her glass, Cass smiled that warm, wonderful smile of hers, her eyes going soft and sleepy.

The scotch warmed and loosened Joe. A few more customers had come in, but the man from the reception hall wasn't among them. *The hell with it,. Cass needs me here. Sara doesn't.* He took a long pull from his drink, draining the glass, and then held it up so the waitress would see.

An hour later, Trevor's gang of friends filed into the pub, Zenon with his arm over Diane's shoulders and the others laughing, until they spotted Joe and Cass. They grew sullen and worked their way to a table in the rear.

The pub had grown all but full with people—natives and tourists alike—who'd come for dinner. Joe was sipping his third double, and Cass had switched to soda, but she was working on her sixth or seventh cigarette.

"Well, the pallbearers are back." Joe didn't think he was slurring his words.

Cass nodded. "If their eyes could shoot daggers, we'd be dead."

"Haven't seen any mercenaries yet," he added. He was joking, but he also wanted Cass to know he was still on the job, so to speak. He scanned the room for unsavory types. No one looked suspicious. "I don't see that creep from the funeral, do you?"

"No. I think we're safe for now."

"Safe and snug, like two rugs in a bug."

Cass smiled. "You're getting drunk."

"Am I?" He inspected his glass. "How's it possible my glass is empty?"

"Are you hungry?"

Joe leaned over to whisper into Cass's ear. "I could eat a banger or two." He leaned away and laughed.

"I don't even know what that means," Cass said, laughing. She waved at the waitress. "What do you want, Joe?"

"Banger," Joe said. "Bang her." He laughed. "Isn't that an English sausage or something?"

The waitress stepped over. "Another round?"

"No, my friend needs some food. What's good?"

"Our roast beef with mashed potatoes is pretty good. Fish and chips, 'course."

Joe smiled at her. "Got any banger sausages?"

"Got a fair Polish sausage dish, love."

"Nope," he answered. "If I can't bang her, I don't want sausage."

Cass patted his arm. "Let's have two orders of the roast beef."

"Sorry. Was I being crass, Cass?" He chuckled. "Hey, that rhymes."

"Yes, a little."

The darkened window was now a mirror, and Joe could see the lights of the stores across the street, but also his own face.

"Do I need a shave?"

"You *are* getting quite a five o'clock shadow."

"What time is it?"

Cass chuckled. "Almost seven."

"Did I tell you about Sara?"

Cass pulled a cigarette out and lit it.

"No, not really. Is something going on with Sara?" Cass exhaled.

"Sara used to smoke, too, sometimes. Did you know that?"

Cass shook her head.

"I don't like kissing her when she's been smoking."

"Oh?" Cass grinned. "Well, you probably wouldn't want to kiss me then."

"No, I would. I would love to kiss you, Cass, if I weren't married."

She raised an eyebrow, grinning. "My smoking wouldn't bother you?"

"'Course it would." He reached for her cigarettes. "Maybe I'll smoke, too."

Cass slid the pack away, saying, "No, you don't want to do that."

"You're right. I don't." Joe glanced back to where Trevor's friends were gathered. They were swapping stories and laughing. A wave of sadness swept over him because he and Cass hadn't been able to join them. "I'm going to the john."

He stood slowly, grabbing the back of Cass's chair for balance and then straightened himself before attempting to walk.

"Are you okay? Need my help getting there?"

Joe patted her shoulder and took a deep breath. "I'm fine."

Walking between the tables proved a bit more challenging, but he navigated his way to the restroom and into a stall. The graffiti kept him amused as he finished his business.

Reading one, he said aloud, "*Dyslexics untie!* That's not nice. Funny. But not cool."

At the sink, he washed and splashed his face with cold water. When he opened the door to leave, he surprised Zenon, who was poised to step inside.

"Asshole," Joe said before he could stop himself.

Zenon pushed his face against Joe's nose. "What?"

"You're such an asshole for treating Cass that way."

"You're drunk."

"I might be drunk, but at least I'm not an asshole."

SYLVIA'S SECRET

The tall Spaniard shoved Joe against the doorframe and stepped around him. "You and your girlfriend should leave here before you get really wasted."

Joe nearly followed Zenon back inside, but someone yanked him away. It was Zenon's girlfriend, Diane. She pulled Joe into the dark hallway and pinned him against the wall.

"Are you crazy? Z and his chums are footballers. They'll stomp the shit out of you and your girlfriend."

"Cass isn't my girlfriend. I'm married."

"Then why are you sticking up for her? She's bonkers."

"What the hell are you talking about?"

"Look, at first, Trevor was really into her. You know, they were both into that suicidal American poet and Ted Hughes. We all thought they were amazing, the way they worked together so well. But then, at that party, Cass was all over every guy there."

"So you say," was all Joe could manage.

"Ask the others. It was like she had something to prove. She was trying to get every guy to join her and Trevor in a threesome. I don't know if she was drunk or high, but she was acting like a crazy whore that night. It destroyed Trevor. Just ruined him."

"That just doesn't sound like Cassandra Johnson. Not the woman I know."

"I'm telling you the truth. Trevor was going to propose to her that night. Maybe she knew and *that's* why she flipped out."

Joe let the information sink in. Diane's description of Cass's behavior sounded nothing like the sympathetic, professional colleague he knew back at the CLU campus in California.

"How'd Trevor die? What really happened that night?"

Diane's eyes flitted back and forth. "Not here," she said. "Follow me."

She led him to a door that opened to the back alley, and they stepped into the cold night air. Joe began to sober. Diane held the door slightly ajar so they'd be able to get back inside.

"Trevor had been talking about going to London to find Cass. He said she was ill and needed his help."

"Ill? How?"

"Like mental. He said something about her needing medicine, a prescription or something, but she'd run out."

Joe took a deep breath, letting the cold air fill his lungs.

"That night—the night Trevor died—we all went out for drinks after dinner. The goal was sort of an intervention, to talk Trevor out of going to London. He had an engagement ring and everything."

Diane seemed to be telling the truth.

"So what happened?" Joe asked.

"We failed. The more we tried to convince him not to go, the more determined he became. Said he was going to hop a train in the morning. We got fed up and left him. He was pretty drunk by then, and even though he seemed determined to go to London, he was also very hurt that we weren't supporting him."

"So you left him?"

Tears welled up in her eyes, and she nodded. "Yes. We left him because we knew how wrong that woman was for him."

"Nice friends *you* are."

Diane burst into tears, and after a moment of watching, he couldn't stand it any longer. He held out his arms and she fell into his embrace.

"Yes, we abandoned him. Her pull was too strong."

"I have to ask," Joe said. "His death. Are you sure it was an accident?"

Diane wiped at her stream of tears. "What else could it have been?"

"Cass thinks someone might have killed him on purpose, to scare her."

She pulled away. "Scare her? What for?"

"She found something, one of Plath's notebooks of poems, and Cass thinks the lawyers from the Hughes estate want it."

Sylvia's Secret

Diane cocked her head to one side. "Wait. She thinks some solicitor ran down Trevor? That's insane."

"No, not a lawyer. But maybe someone they hired."

"But why? I don't understand."

"It's complicated. First of all, the journal itself could be worth a lot of money, so it's only natural that the people looking after the Hughes estate would want it. Also, the writing makes it pretty clear that Sylvia was worried Ted might kill her. That could really damage the Hughes legacy."

"Sounds pretty farfetched."

Joe shrugged. "Maybe not as farfetched as you think. I had a similar experience a few years ago when I was given the handwritten plays of Shakespeare. Except they weren't written by Shakespeare."

Diane's eyes widened. "Oh, so you're the bloke who ruined Shakespeare."

"Not ruined," Joe corrected. "I prefer to think we unmasked a fraud."

"I thought you looked familiar. That stuff was all over the news a few years ago."

"Tell me about it. I was questioned by Scotland Yard when some hired gun tried to kill me to get the manuscripts."

"That's right. Someone fell off the London Eye, right?"

A bullet had exploded through the glass wall of the carriage on the huge Ferris wheel. He and his pal Smitty had almost been killed that day.

"That's why Cass asked me here. She thinks someone might be trying to do to her what they tried to do to me. Steal the papers and shut her up."

"So you're here, why? As some sort of bodyguard or something?"

In the cold night air, Joe sobered quickly. It all sounded so silly now. "I'm just here to help a good friend. She stood by me when I was in trouble some years ago, so I'm returning the favor."

Diane turned to go back inside, but Joe stepped in front of her. "Are you sure Trevor wasn't being followed by someone, that his death was an accident?"

"Absolutely certain, yes. Trevor stayed until the bartender kicked him out. The bartender said he was really drunk by then. He saw Trevor stumble down the sidewalk. He swears Trevor saw the car coming but he stepped out in front of it anyway. Like he did it on purpose."

"But why?"

Diane shook her head, and a tear ran down her cheek. "Who knows? Maybe he felt torn, you know, between his feelings for her and his loyalty to his chums. Maybe it was all that dark shit he was reading about Ted Hughes. I don't know. All I know is, if Cassandra Johnson hadn't come into his life, Trevor would still be alive."

CHAPTER 17

Large flakes of heavy, wet snow began to drop from the darkness, illuminated in the dim light spilling from the windows of the pub. One flake after another landed and melted on Diane's shoulders. Something about the dampness on his cheeks made him think of Sara. *What the hell am I doing here? I've got my own problems.*

Diane spoke softly. "You're not a bad bloke, for an American."

"Thanks, I guess. Maybe we'd better get back inside."

She took a step back. "Right, certainly. Only, if you're around tomorrow, maybe we could break away from our friends and chat a bit. I want to tell you more about your pal, Cass."

Joe held the door and they walked back inside the dim hallway and past the restrooms. When they turned the corner and stepped into the lighted bar, Cass was arguing with Zenon, her face inches from his and her fists clenched. Her violent arm gestures stunned him.

Diane raced over and tried to tug Zenon away, but he held his ground, a grim smile on his face.

Joe tried to step between them. Cass shoved him aside.

"You're all ASSHOLES!" she yelled.

Z shot an angry look at Joe. "Get your girl away from me before I go off on her."

Joe wrapped his arms around Cass and tried to pull her back, but she fought like a wild woman.

"Is it that I'm BLACK? You're a bunch of British BIGOTS!"

"GET HER OUT!" screamed the Spaniard.

Someone else yelled, "GET THAT CRAZY BITCH OUT OF HERE."

That was it. Cass broke Joe's grip and threw herself across the table at the skinny loud mouth. He flew backward in his chair with Cass on top of him, punching him in the face. Joe pushed around the table but wasn't able to get close.

Someone grabbed him by the shoulder and swung him around, landing a punch on his temple. Lights exploded in his brain, but he threw up his arms and flailed about madly, landing a few punches on whoever stood nearby.

One of the other guys had an arm around Cass's neck and was dragging her off the fallen man, whose face was now covered with blood. Cass scratched at the man's arms with both hands, and Joe could tell she was being choked to death.

"LET HER GO!" he yelled.

He managed to break away from the people who were trying to hold him and he pounced on the guy who was choking Cass, knocking both of them onto their sides.

Cold water splashed over them as they rolled on the floor, and Joe gasped. The bartender stood with an empty pitcher in his hand.

"Stop it now, or I'll have you all arrested."

The others had moved away. Only Joe, Cass and her choker were on the floor, Cass still squirming to get free.

Joe slipped his arm around the neck of Cass's attacker and squeezed. "Let go of her now or I'll choke you out." He squeezed harder. "NOW!"

SYLVIA'S SECRET

The man opened his arms and Cass crawled away, clutching her throat and coughing. She stood slowly while Joe held the man on the floor.

Still clutching her throat, Cass kicked the man in the stomach, and he went limp. Joe released him and scooted away.

The bartender hoisted Joe to his feet and then spun him around. "You and your girlfriend get the bloody hell out of my bar and never come back!"

Joe nodded, his heart pounding. Cass's messy hair and flashing eyes made her look like someone he didn't know. Did she even know what she was doing?

"Cass, let's go, before we both get arrested.

She nodded and slowly took Joe's arm.

He led her back to their table, grabbed their coats and rushed her out the door.

Once back inside the hotel room, Cass disappeared into the bathroom and washed her face. Joe examined himself in the mirror over the dresser and sized up the lump on his temple. No bruise.

Cass appeared in the mirror behind him, confused. "I haven't been in a fight like that since junior high."

Joe couldn't see a mark on her. "That was pretty crazy."

"Thank you for getting that guy off me. I thought he was going to kill me."

"I think he was just trying to choke you out so you'd stop."

"*Me* stop?" Anger flashed in her eyes again. "What about *them*?"

Joe put his hands on Cass's shoulders. "Why'd you go over to their table, Cass?"

She shook her head. "I don't know. I guess I was just trying to reconnect with them. I mean, we all used to be friends."

"What set you off?"

"Huh?"

"When I came back, you were in Zenon's face and acting prett mad."

Cass shook her head again. "I don't know. He said something that really pushed a button."

"What exactly?"

"Something to the effect that I was just using Trevor to help my own research. He said Trevor was too good for me. It seemed racist."

Joe took her in his arms and held her. She soon relaxed in his grip.

"They're sad about their friend. And maybe a little jealous."

"*Jealous?* Why?"

"Maybe they thought you were taking Trevor away from them."

She took a deep breath and put her arms around Joe. "I just don't get where all that hostility came from," she said.

"It's hard to let a new person into your inner circle, Cass."

"I know."

"Maybe they felt threatened by you."

"Why?"

"Diane said Trevor was going to propose to you."

Cass's eyes widened. "What?"

"The night of the Halloween party. She told me Trevor had bought an engagement ring."

Her eyes filled with tears. "I had no idea."

"Really? Diane thought you knew."

She shook her head. "No. I didn't even suspect." She let go of Joe and turned toward the window. "I had no idea he was *that* serious. I mean, I thought it was all light and breezy, you know, just having fun."

"I guess you made quite an impression, Cass. That's why his friends are so...angry. Diane made it sound like his death was a suicide."

She turned back to Joe. "A suicide?"

"That's what it sounds like. According to Diane, he got drunk and started walking home. The bartender saw him step in front of an on-coming car."

"When did you talk to Diane?"

"She was leaving the restroom at the same time I was and I asked her to tell me what happened. We went outside and she told me what she knew. Based on her story, it doesn't sound like a murder to me, Cass. It sounds like a stupid, sad, drunken accident."

Tears were streaming down Cass's cheeks now. She nodded and stepped closer to the window. Her intense gaze bore into a darkness filled with far too much heartache and loss.

"Are you all right?"

"I had no idea he was actually in love with me. I mean, he said it all the time. 'Cass, I love you. You're the best.' I'd say it back to him, too, but I didn't know he really meant it. Not like that."

"You're not a mind reader."

"I know, but still…. I'm usually more astute." She took a deep breath and sighed. "Sometimes I feel like I'm so in the dark that I can't see my hand in front of my eyes."

"We all seem to be blind sometimes." He thought of Sara. "We're only human, Cass."

She nodded. "It's still snowing. I can't decide if I love the snow or hate it. When it's new and fresh, it hides all the ugliness of the world, but that's just an illusion, isn't it? The ugliness is still there, buried under frozen, empty ice and air. Then when it melts, it turns to sludge, as thick and ugly as pus. Anyway, it's beginning to snow."

Joe wanted to say something more, but he was completely drained and suspected Cass needed to be alone with her emotions.

"If you don't mind," he said, "I'm going to take a hot shower and get ready for bed. I'm exhausted."

Cass nodded again, her back to him.

Joe went to the suitcase on his bed and grabbed a t-shirt and pajama bottoms. In the bathroom, he undressed and stepped into the tiny shower stall. The water got good and hot, and he allowed it to beat against his neck and shoulders. After the shower, he wiped steam off the mirror and checked his temple. A lump, but still no bruising. He brushed his teeth and turned out the light.

The bedroom was dark, but he could tell Cass had climbed into her bed. She wasn't stirring, so he didn't break the silence but eased into his own bed instead.

Lying on his back, he fell asleep almost immediately.

Sara is being strangled by the lover she called Nathan. Joe can only watch. She calls out to him, pleads for him, Joe? Joe? But Joe can't move. He has his arm around Sara's throat; he's choking her. But he doesn't want to kill her, only stop her, stop her, stop her from going to the other man. She's struggling to get free. The other man, the one she calls Nathan, is standing in a corner, leaning against the wall as though he doesn't have a care in the world. He's smiling at Sara, waving her to join him. Joe must release her, or else he'll kill her. He begins to cry....

Emerging from his nightmare, Joe was on the verge of tears. It was only a dream, but the emotions were so real. Then someone climbed into his bed. *Where am I? Is Sara here?*

The woman's body moved closer to him under the sheets. Lips kissed his cheek and a hand slid down his chest and thigh.

"Sara?" he whispered.

A hushed voice whispered in reply, "Joe, it's me."

"Sara?" he asked again.

Coming out of the deep, dreamy sleep, something wasn't right. The smell. Stale cigarette smoke. Sara had stopped smoking. Or had she?

Joe reached over to the woman lying next to him. She took his hand and pulled it toward her breast.

He opened his eyes and pulled his hand away, reaching for the lamp on the nightstand. Finally finding the switch, he turned on the light. Cass peeked out sheepishly from under the covers.

"What are you doing, Cass?"

"I figured it out."

Joe sat up and slid far enough away that his body wasn't touching hers.

"Figured out what?"

"Trevor. I didn't get it with Trevor. My radar was off or something. That's when I realized I wasn't getting it about you either."

"About *me*?" Joe rubbed his eyes. "What about me?"

"You wouldn't be here if you didn't love me, Joe. I get it. I was clueless when you first showed up, but I get it now."

Joe shook his head. "No, Cass. I came because you were in trouble."

"But guys don't fly halfway around the world unless they love a woman."

He took a deep breath.

"I care for you, Cass. You're one of my closest friends. But I'm married."

Cass sat up, pulling the comforter around her shoulders. "Your and Sara's marriage is like a roller coaster. I mean, it's got to be one of the rockiest relationships I've ever seen."

He laughed. "You have no idea."

"You're here with me, Joe. You came to my rescue. I don't care if it's cliché, you're here for me. You fought for me."

Joe reached over and cupped Cass's cheek in his hand.

"I *do* care for you and I do want to help you, but…."

"But what?"

Joe shrugged. "I'm still married, Cass. You're right—our marriage is rocky. We're going through a really rough time right now, too, which is one of the reasons I felt I should get away and leave Sara to sort out a few things. But I still love my wife."

Cass searched his face, trying to detect the truth. Then she thre the covers off and stomped into the bathroom, slamming the door.

Joe climbed out of bed and tapped lightly on the bathroom door.

"Cass, please don't be angry."

"I'm not angry," she said from the other side of the door. "I just thought…."

"What? Tell me."

"I thought if I'd been so wrong about Trevor, well maybe I was wrong about you, too. I mean, what you did, Joe, was pretty amazing. Coming all this way to England just because a colleague is in trouble. Not your usual act of friendship."

Cass finally opened the door, and a towel was now around her body.

"So you *don't* want to sleep with me?" she asked.

He'd found Cass very attractive and had even fantasized about her at times. But after everything they'd been through, he wasn't the least aroused, even though saying so would hurt her feelings.

"Cass, you are by far one of the most beautiful women I know, and if I weren't married…well, let's just say, we would have gotten a room with one king-sized bed instead of two doubles."

She pushed past him and went to her bed, where—with her back to Joe—she let the towel fall while reaching into her suitcase. She pulled a long, black nightgown over her head and let it slide down over her body. Then she turned and looked at Joe.

"Is it because I'm black?"

Joe winced and took a step closer. "You know me better than that."

"Well, you *are* from the South."

"Not everyone from the South is a racist, Cass. Would I be here now if I felt that way?"

She shrugged, her eyes darkening.

"Have I ever done anything that would make you think that about me?"

Joe took another step closer. Part of him wanted to embrace

Cass again so she could believe his sincerity, but another part told him to keep his distance.

"I don't have that many friends, but I consider you one of my dearest. That's why I'm here for you now."

Cass watched Joe without speaking.

"And you're right about Sara and me. Our relationship is definitely up and down, and not in a good way. If things don't work out between us, then, believe me, you'll be the first lovely lady I'll look up. Okay?"

She smiled and nodded.

"My radar must really be out of whack," she said, then she climbed back into her own bed and rolled on her side facing Joe. "I'm sorry if I...if I embarrassed you, Joe."

Joe smiled, utterly relieved. He climbed back into his bed, sitting up against the headboard. "You didn't embarrass me. Surprised the heck out of me, but I wasn't embarrassed."

"Let's keep this little incident to ourselves, though, okay?"

Joe chuckled. "I will if you will." He reached over and turned off the light.

"Good night, Joe Conrad. Thanks for being a pal."

"Good night, beautiful Cassandra Johnson. Thanks for..."

"Letting you get to second base?" She laughed in the darkness. "Don't mention it. *Please*."

"Don't worry," he answered.

Joe lay in the darkness, his eyes adjusting to the lack of light, the edges of things blurred and unseen. Tears spilled from his eyes—he'd never missed his family more deeply.

CHAPTER 18

The next morning, Joe awoke groggy and a little hung over. The shower splashed in another room and the scent of coffee filled the air. Cass had already made a pot and there was certainly enough for two. With cup in hand, Joe strolled to the window. A fresh layer of snow powdered the sidewalks, cars and streets, but the sky was bright, clear, and blue. Whatever misgivings he'd had the night before evaporated as he sipped the coffee and admired the pure, clear sky over the rooftops across the lane.

Joe wanted to email Sara and ask her one question. Just one. *Do you still love me?*

If she said yes, they could work through their problems and continue to live together as a family. If she said no, they would have to get a divorce. The decision was that simple. No couples therapy, no begging. After all, he couldn't force Sara to love him. She either did or she didn't. He still loved her—that much was clear—even if it wasn't as deeply as it had been when they first married.

Staring at the blue sky, he recalled the days and nights when he and Sara had made love without using birth control because they wanted to have a baby. He'd never felt that close to another human being. Making love to Sara, holding her in his arms after they had joined together, knowing the two of them were coming together into one new human life—it was the most intense love he'd ever known.

The result had been Katie—precious Katie, the smartest, most precocious child in the world. She was a perfect blend of their best qualities, and he loved her more than he loved his own life. He felt a pang of regret about Brian. They hadn't been trying to conceive—they'd just had too much wine one night and had made love carelessly. Sara had kept the pregnancy a secret at first, when Joe had been accused of those brutal crimes. Sara had almost left him then, and she had planned to abort Brian. But then she was kidnapped and almost killed, and the meaning of life—every life— changed for both of them.

The bathroom door opened and steam rolled out. Cass peeked out and smiled.

"Good morning, sleepy head. You found the coffee?"

"Yeah. Thanks."

"You want to jump in the shower?"

"No, I'll just shave. Showered last night."

"Okay. Give me a few minutes."

She closed the door, so Joe took off his pajama bottoms and pulled on clean underwear and jeans. While he waited for Cass, he sat at the desk and turned on her laptop. After it booted up, he searched for an internet connection but couldn't get one.

"Were you able to get on the net?" he called.

Cass opened the bathroom door. "What?"

"Were you able to get on the internet?"

"No, there's no access in the rooms. We have to go to the lobby."

Joe started to close the laptop's lid.

"Leave that on. I want to show you something before we go for breakfast."

Thirty minutes later, Joe was clean-shaven and Cass was

dressed for the day. She'd pulled up her bed coverings and was sitting cross-legged in the middle of the mattress, her laptop on her legs and her journal beside her.

"Let me show you one of my other discoveries. This will blow your mind."

Joe sat on the edge of the bed, looking over Cass's shoulders. She had goose bumps on her neck, and her skin smelled of soap, her hair of shampoo.

"I found a previously unseen poem by Ted," Cass said. "It's titled 'Last Letter' and it describes what happened during the days leading up to Sylvia's so-called suicide, from Ted's point of view."

"Why's it significant?" Joe asked.

"Because it wasn't included in Ted's best-known work, *Birthday Letters*, a collection of poems about his relationship with Sylvia. Some of the poems do refer to Sylvia's suicide, but not one addresses the circumstances of her death directly. This is the missing link, so to speak."

"Where'd you find it?"

"In the British Library's Ted Hughes archives. It was in a little blue book that contains drafts of several poems that appeared in *Birthday Letters*. I found a revised draft in a hardback notebook. Check it out."

Cass leaned to the side so Joe could see. The scratchy, haphazard handwriting looked very different from Plath's.

"The last image is from the hardbound notebook. As far as I know, these images haven't been made public before, Joe. When I include them with my analysis of what really happened, I think people will have to take Sylvia's murder a little more seriously."

She pressed the arrow key and the next image popped up. It wasn't as exciting as the handwritten plays of William Shakespeare, but it was close.

"In a letter, Ted said he first started to write simple verse 'letters' to Sylvia in the early 1970s, writing them piecemeal. Then later he said he tried to write the letters in a more determined manner but found he couldn't, so he went back to writing them occasionally. Some of them appear in the 1995 book titled *New Selected Poems*, but he told friends that others were too personal to publish."

"Do you have a typed copy of the poem?" Joe asked.

"Here you go." She scrolled down and brought up the typed version. "It's long, but read the excerpts I've highlighted. They read like a confession to me."

Joe read only the stanzas Cassandra had highlighted, skipping over the rest, trying to see the evidence of murder she'd inferred.

> **"Last Letter"**
> **by Ted Hughes**
>
> **What happened that night? Your final night.**
> **Double, treble exposure**
> **Over everything. Late afternoon, Friday,**
> **My last sight of you alive.**
> **Burning your letter to me, in the ashtray,**
> **With that strange smile. Had I bungled your plan?**
> **Had it surprised me sooner than you purposed?**
> **Had I rushed it back to you too promptly?**
> **One hour later——you would have been gone**
> **Where I could not have traced you.**
> **I would have turned from your locked red door**
> **That nobody would open**

Joe glanced up. "That's interesting. Where he says he can't imagine how he would have gotten through that weekend." He continued to read. "'Your note reached me too soon?' Sounds like he was there, Cass, on the night she died." He continued reading quietly, until he came to another section, which he read aloud.

SYLVIA'S SECRET

My escape

Had become such a hunted thing
Sleepless, hopeless, all its dreams exhausted,
Only wanting to be recaptured, only
Wanting to drop, out of its vacuum.

"Wow, Cass. His 'escape' had become a 'hunted thing'? Sure sounds like a guilty conscience to me." He read on in silence until the end.

My room slept,
Already filled with the snowlit morning light.
I lit my fire. I had got out my papers.
And I had started to write when the telephone
Jerked awake, in a jabbering alarm,
Remembering everything. It recovered in my hand.
Then a voice like a selected weapon
Or a measured injection,
Coolly delivered its four words
Deep into my ear: 'Your wife is dead.'

"He practically admits he was there the night she died."

"The poem is evidence—evidence of murder," Cass said.

Joe rubbed his chin. "At least evidence of guilt—of a sense of guilt for Plath's death. Whether we can make a case for murder with this alone, I don't know."

"But it's the cumulative effect of the evidence. When you put it all together, Joe, it sure raises doubts about Sylvia's suicide."

Joe nodded. "Granted. But we'll need more."

"There *is* more," Cass said, leaning closer. "When you read Sylvia's final poems and see the events she was planning, it sure doesn't sound like a woman who's ready to throw it all away."

Joe suddenly became more aware of the way Cass smelled—fresh and musky and sweet as roses—her skin still glistening from the shower. She was not the hard, angry woman who'd leapt across the table the night before to throttle an enemy. Now she was soft and feminine, a woman yearning for affirmation. Her eyes glistened as she gazed at him, her lips parted slightly in an expectant grin.

Joe climbed off Cass's bed and sat on the edge of his own. "Well, at least we've solved one murder."

"What do you mean?"

"Trevor. He wasn't murdered. The poor guy just stumbled into traffic."

Cass closed her laptop. "You're basing that on what Diane told you, right? And Diane says they heard that explanation from the bartender."

"So?"

"What if the bartender is lying?"

Joe chuckled. "Why would he lie?"

"Because maybe someone paid him off."

"I don't know, Cass. Sounds a bit farfetched."

"There's one way to find out. We need to talk to that bartender."

He shook his head. "I don't want to go back to that place again. Not after what happened last night."

Cass laughed. "*That* pub isn't the bar where Trevor went the night he died. There's a tavern closer to the main thruway, near the train station. That's the place we used to hang out together most of the time."

"Maybe we can go there after breakfast. I'm getting hungry."

"The bartender won't come on 'til three. I want to take you to Court Green, the place where Sylvia and Ted lived together when Ted's mistress Assia came into the picture. It's where I found Sylvia's notebook."

SYLVIA'S SECRET

He nodded and stood up. "Okay, but can we eat first?"

"Sure," Cass answered, smiling. "First we feed our bodies. Then we feed our souls."

CHAPTER 19

Before going into the tiny dining room, Joe sat at one of only two computers in the lobby. He read a few emails from students asking for their grades and two more from Sara, asking where he was, but he ignored those and chose to send Sara a new email. It was the middle of the night in California and it would be hours before she could reply.

> I have one very important question to ask you. Do you still love me? Please answer honestly. Your response will help me determine where I go from here.

He read it over once—there were a thousand things to say—but he was satisfied this was all he needed to express. His stomach churned, perhaps only from hunger and too much alcohol the night before, but he put his finger on the SEND button and after a few seconds of second thoughts, pushed it down. Now his words with electronic wings were flying across the Atlantic, hurtling like a meteor across the American continent, only to land in some nebulous electronic wasteland until Sara's fingers danced delicately across a keyboard and brought them to life.

Cass was at a table next to the window, sipping coffee. She flashed that charming smile of hers and her eyes twinkled in the sunlight pouring through the window.

"Is everything okay?"

Joe nodded. "As far as I can tell. A few emails. Nothing urgent." He shook out his napkin and looked around. "Is it a buffet, or will someone take our order?"

"A waitress stopped by and poured my coffee. She should be back in a moment. Hungry?"

"Yeah, I think so. Anyway, I need something on my stomach."

The waitress—a young dark-haired girl with tattoos covering her neck—came to the table, her eyes glazed with indifference.

"What would you like?" she asked flatly.

Cass tried to win her over by flashing that smile. "Are the buttermilk pancakes good?"

"Good 'nough, I guess. People that order 'em, finish 'em, and no one's died of 'em yet, far as I know."

"That's a ringing endorsement," Cass said, grinning at Joe. "Can I have them with yogurt on top instead of butter and syrup?"

The girl nodded. "I'll bring the yogurt separate and you can apply it as you like it."

"She's quoting Shakespeare, Joe. Did you hear?"

"What?"

Cass smiled. "Shakespeare. She said 'as you like it'!"

"Oh." He put the menu down. "I'll have pancakes, too, but I want the butter and maple syrup, okay?"

The waitress jotted down their orders. "Anything else? Orange juice? Bloody Mary?"

"Don't tempt me," Cass answered.

Joe shook his head and the waitress rushed off.

Cass reached across the table. "I'm sorry about last night. Hope I didn't ruin our friendship."

SYLVIA'S SECRET

He took her hand and gave it a squeeze. "Not at all. Our friendship is stronger than ever."

"Don't tell Sara, okay? I don't want her looking at me differently when we all get together."

He wasn't sure how to answer. If his marriage survived, he'd have to be honest with Sara, just as he'd expect her to be honest with him. Still, right now Cass needed reassurance. "Consider it forgotten."

Cass smiled and pulled her hand away.

"So, off to see Court Green this morning, right?" he asked.

"You know, Ted lived there for years, on and off, after Sylvia's death. It's a haunted place. Sylvia wrote most of the *Ariel* poems there, and Ted wrote most of his later stuff there, including *Crow*."

"Did he die there?"

"No," she answered. "He died in a London hospital of a heart attack while being treated for colon cancer." She let out a wry chuckle. "Colon cancer! Served the *asshole* right, right?"

Joe grinned uneasily. "I guess."

The waitress arrived and placed their plates in front of them, along with a bowl of white yogurt.

After inspecting the yogurt, Cass asked, "Do you have any honey?"

The waitress rolled her eyes and stepped away, returning in seconds with a jar of golden honey.

After they had put their respective toppings on the pancakes, Joe asked, "Is someone living there now? At Court Green?"

Cass nodded while chewing her first bite of food. "A middle-aged couple. They seemed nice enough in the fall when I went there. Gave me the grand tour as though they'd done it dozens of times."

"I'm sure the place is visited by tourists all the time."

"Yes, especially in the summer when teachers are on vacation. Not so much this time of year, I suspect."

Their conversation lulled as they ate, and a change crept across Cass's face. She'd been cheerful and filled with energy before breakfast, but now she grew sullen, her eyes blank.

Joe paid the bill and walked Cass to the sidewalk in front of the hotel, where he hired a cab to drive them to Court Green. From the town center, the cab rumbled up the street and turned right onto Essington Road. Joe was surprised by the narrowness of the lanes. A dead brown rabbit lay on the road, the rear of its body obliterated, but the head and front paws were remarkably untouched. He turned away in disgust. Cass sulked.

"You're certainly quiet all of a sudden," he said.

"It always makes me sad to imagine her at that place, thinking her marriage to Ted was safe, that their relationship was somehow exalted, only to find out that he was like every other horny jerk. It's the place where her world crumbled, Joe. For Ted, it was just a piece of real estate, a piece of property, like Sylvia's poems and notebooks. Something he owned. His *possession*."

She said the word "possession" with such contempt that even the cabbie glanced in the rearview mirror.

Small square cottages dotted the landscape, their thatched roofs covered with a layer of snow and their chimneys billowing white smoke that rose gracefully against the open sky. A hedgerow separated part of the property from the road, and a sturdy stone wall separated another section of land from a cemetery. Beyond, through the trees draped with snow, the land opened up to fairly flat snow-covered fields and rolling hills in the far distance.

The cab stopped, and Joe and Cass climbed out.

"Should I wait, then?" the cabbie asked after Joe had paid him.

"No," said Cass, "but come back in about an hour, please."

"Will do," he said. He turned the car around and it chugged by them and disappeared down the lane.

"It's like a postcard, Cass. Beautiful."

SYLVIA'S SECRET

"Isn't it, though?"

They walked side-by-side up the muddy driveway beside a green hedge topped with the whipped cream of snow.

"Where'd you find the notebook?"

Cass stared straight ahead, as if in a trance.

"You can almost feel them here—Ted, Sylvia and the babies. Happy, loving, caring for each other. Until Assia seduced Ted, and he allowed himself to be taken from them."

They walked on together, as if they were neighbors coming to call. When they reached the front door, Cass knocked confidently and waited. Joe worried that the occupants would be less than pleased to have visitors before noon.

No one came to the door, so Cass knocked again, louder this time. They waited.

"They're either very late sleepers," said Joe, "or very hard of hearing."

"Let's go around to the kitchen."

Joe followed as Cass led him to the back of the square house. She peeked into each window they passed. The kitchen sat dark and empty, nonetheless, Cass knocked again. Joe peered through the window into a small narrow kitchen and a little living room beyond, also dark and apparently uninhabited.

"I don't think anyone's home," Joe said.

"Oh, that's too bad. I really wanted you to get a feel for this place, on the inside. I mean, yes, it's kind of cramped, but you have to see the views from inside to see how inspired they both must have been. Especially in the spring when the daffodils were blooming."

"Like something out of *Doctor Zhivago*, huh?"

"Let's peek inside—I'm sure they wouldn't mind."

They crept from window to window like burglars plotting a heist. At each window Cass sighed or exclaimed with emotion and awe. To Joe, the rooms were cluttered with old-fashioned furniture and over-stuffed shelves, the walls adorned with pictures that could have come from a Goodwill store.

But electricity radiated from Cass. Joe imagined that she could see Sylvia Plath holding baby Nicholas in her arms, Frieda playing on the carpet at her feet, Ted sitting across from them, stoic and proud.

When they had gone full circle—or full square, to be more accurate—Cass lowered her head toward the muddy ground as if viewing a fresh grave. It would be half an hour at least before the cab returned, and Joe didn't want to hang around the front of the house—a neighbor might call the police. It wouldn't be a long walk back to town.

"I'd like to rent this place myself," Cass said. "I'd love to pull up the floor boards and check the attic for more journals."

"You think more are hidden here somewhere?"

Cass had a sort of sad intensity in her eyes. "Who knows? I asked them when I was here before if they'd found anything from Sylvia or Ted. They said they hadn't, but you wonder if they'd really say if they had."

"Don't you suppose we would have heard something? Finding one of the lost notebooks would be pretty big news, wouldn't it?"

Cass nodded. "Yes, if they went public. But I found one of her journals nearly a month ago and no one knows about it but you, so...."

"You didn't answer me before. Where'd you find Plath's journal?"

"The Yew Tree in St. Peter's Churchyard. Let's go there."

They crunched through the snow toward the church and easily found the massive tree. To Joe, it looked like an array of dark green castle turrets or grain elevators clumped together. Snow weighed down some of the higher boughs. Stopping ten or so yards away, Cass smiled up at it.

"I climbed up into its loving arms, up and up, and there it was, nestled in the crook of a branch, hugging the main trunk, a dirty brown canvas sack with the leather-bound notebook wrapped in layers of waxed paper, waiting like an Egyptian mummy to be discovered."

"What on earth compelled you to climb it?"

"Feeling too earthbound, I suppose. I wanted to get a new perspective on the landscape. And I loved Sylvia's poem, The Moon and the Yew Tree. Do you know it?"

Joe shook his head. "I may have read it years ago."

"A few lines in particular resonated with me when I was thinking about climbing the tree, as if a voice inside was urging me on. It was eerie and wonderful."

"Can you recall the lines?" Joe asked.

Cass closed her eyes and began to recite the poem: "'This is the light of the mind, cold and planetary / The trees of the mind are black. The light is blue.' The rest of the stanza escapes me, but the third stanza goes like this—'The yew tree points up, it has a Gothic shape. / The eyes lift after it and find the moon. / The moon is my mother.'"

"That's lovely," Joe said.

"Yes. It was the last few lines that haunted me and sent me up into her arms. Listen—'Inside the church, the saints will all be blue, / Floating on their delicate feet over the cold pews, / Their hands and faces stiff with holiness. / The moon sees nothing of this. She is bald and wild. / And the message of the yew tree is blackness—blackness and silence.'"

She stared up like a child straining to see the star or the angel at the top of a Christmas tree.

"Blackness and silence," Joe repeated. The air was frozen, quiet. He followed Cass's gaze up at the tree, losing himself within its dark branches.

"Yes. There was something about that line and the reference to the moon as Sylvia's mother image that made me climb. I swear,

Joe, it was as if I was inside Sylvia herself, not her physical body, maybe not even her mind, but her spirit."

Joe watched Cass's face in profile as she stared up into the shadowy boughs..

"Or maybe," she whispered, as if forgetting he was there, "Sylvia's spirit entered me."

The way she said it sent a chill through Joe.

Chapter 20

By the time they'd reached the road in front of the house at Court Green, the taxi waited, the engine at an idle, and the driver leaned against the door finishing a cigarette. When Joe and Cass approached, he crushed the cigarette under his heel and opened the back door.

"Right, then. Have a good time, did we?"

"It was something of a disappointment, I'm afraid," said Cass as she climbed in. "The renters weren't home."

"Oh, I could have told you that. Went on holiday, didn't they? To Spain, I think. Or was it Portugal? Anyway, I took them to the train station myself only two days ago. Coming home the day after Christmas."

"You might have told us that before you dropped us off," Joe said. He climbed into the back seat behind Cass.

The cabbie grinned. "You didn't ask, though, did you?"

Joe chuckled. "No, I guess you're right."

Once he'd climbed into the front seat, the cabbie leaned back and asked, "Where to now? Back to the hotel?"

"No," answered Cass. "Take us to the tavern by the train

station."

"Having lunch there, are we?"

"Yes," said Cass. "And maybe a few drinks afterward. Do you know any of the bartenders who work there?"

"Only one bartender works there, besides the manager. A bloke named Roland."

"Roland," Cass repeated. "Does he work nights?"

"Sure. Either him or the manager, as I said."

"What's the manager's name?"

The cabbie glanced back with an impish grin. "Winston. As in Churchill."

The Old Railway Tavern was half a block from the train station where Joe and Cass had arrived just twenty-four hours before. Though it wasn't quite noon, the tavern was already half-filled, the dark interior abuzz with people grabbing a meal before catching the train.

Joe and Cass took a small table in the back and waited. Eventually, a slender, dark-haired young man came and took their orders.

"Tell me more about Ted's second wife, Assia," Joe said.

"Oh, they never married."

Joe almost choked on his water. "Ted never married the woman he left Sylvia for? That seems odd."

Cass snorted. "Their whole relationship was bizarre. Assia Esther Gutmann was a German Jew born in Berlin, and she and her family escaped Nazi Germany by going to British Palestine. Her father was a doctor. She met her first husband, John Steel, at a dance at the British soldier's club in Tel Aviv. They moved to London, lived there awhile, and then relocated to Vancouver, British Columbia, where she attended the university. That's where she met husband number two, some Canadian economist named

Lipsey."

"Wow," Joe chuckled. "That girl got around."

"Oh, I'm just getting started. Assia and her husband were sailing back to England when she met David Wevill, a twenty-one-year-old poet. She was twenty-nine. The two of them had an affair, and she divorced Lipsey shortly after to marry David."

Joe nodded. "I know that Ted and Sylvia met the two of them when they rented their house in London, right?"

"Yes. Ted and Sylvia needed to rent their flat in Chalcot Square so they could afford the place here. Assia and David Wevill responded to their ad, and Sylvia liked the idea of renting the flat to a fellow poet. There was probably a spark of attraction at that first meeting, but it turned red hot when David and Assia visited Ted and Sylvia here at Court Green. After that visit, Ted found excuses to visit London."

The waiter came with their sandwiches and sodas. The room was almost full now, the chatter of holiday travelers filling the space. One young couple sitting at a table close to the window with their two small children reminded Joe of Sara, Katie and Brian.

"Did you know," Cass asked, "that Assia was pregnant with Ted's child when Sylvia killed herself?"

Joe, taking his first bite of sandwich, shook his head. He chewed and swallowed. "Was that the daughter Assia killed when she committed suicide?"

"No. I mean, she *did* kill that baby, too—she had an abortion—but that wasn't the daughter she murdered. Assia never divorced David Wevill, but she and Ted moved back here to Court Green. Can you imagine? The two of them living together at that lovely little cottage, just as he and Sylvia had? It's obscene. Absolutely obscene."

After chewing another bite, Joe asked, "What was the daughter's name again?"

"Her real name was Alexandra Tatiana Elise, but they called

her Shura. Don't ask me why."

"You're not *sure, huh!*"

Cass groaned. "Oh, Joe, I'd forgotten how bad your puns can be."

Joe shrugged innocently. "Sorry. Just trying to lighten the mood."

"Then you don't want to hear about Assia's death, do you?"

"Didn't she basically do the same thing Plath did?"

"Yes. In late-March of 1969, she dragged a mattress into the kitchen, sealed the window and door with tape, just like Sylvia supposedly did. Then she took sleeping pills, turned on the gas, and lay down on the mattress with her daughter for a nap. She was forty-one and her daughter was only four."

Joe shook his head, remembering Katie at four, smiling and full of life. "Too sad," he said.

"Now I'm wondering if maybe Ted didn't do the same thing with Assia that he did with Sylvia."

"You think Hughes might have killed Assia and their four-year-old daughter, too? But why?"

Cass laughed sarcastically. "For the same reason he murdered Sylvia. To be free of the burden. He was already seeing at least two other women, the wife of a friend and some twenty-year-old hottie."

"I had no idea he was such a ladies' man."

"Assia bragged to friends that he was an animal in the bedroom—a ferocious lover, as she put it, who smelled like a butcher in bed."

"Too much information, especially in those days."

"Yeah. But I don't think he wanted to be saddled with another child. Besides, he never really admitted that Shura was his daughter, so...."

"What a sordid mess."

"Want to know the cherry on top?" asked Cass. "When Ted's

mother learned about Assia and Shura's deaths, she was so upset that she went into a coma and died a few days later."

Joe frowned. "That seems strange. Did she care for Assia and Shura that deeply?"

Cass shook her head. "Not really. In fact, I don't think Ted's family cared for them anymore than they had cared for Sylvia. They'd never liked Sylvia, you know. And Ted's father wouldn't sit at the same table with Assia."

"I didn't know that."

"They thought both women were bad for Ted's career. Can you believe that?"

"Then why the extreme reaction from Ted's mother when Shura and Assia died?"

Cass leaned across the table. "Maybe she knew Ted had murdered them both, the same way he'd murdered Sylvia."

Joe—starting to take another bite of his sandwich—put it back down. "It *is* pretty suspicious. Two wives die the same way within, what, six years of each other? You'd think the police would investigate their deaths more thoroughly."

"Oh, Joe, you don't know the half of it. Not much was made of their deaths at all! The London newspapers didn't even report it. You search the crime columns for that week in March, and you'll read about a woman who was strangled by her husband and a girl who set fire to herself in Paris, but no mention of Assia murdering the daughter of Ted Hughes. It was covered up."

"Covered up?" Joe asked. "Unbelievable."

"One small local paper ran a tiny blurb on like page 13, but didn't mention anything about Ted Hughes, who by then had made quite a name for himself."

Joe pushed his plate away, a partially eaten sandwich resting on it like road kill.

"Cass, that's a lot of dead bodies to lug around in your conscience, Sylvia, Assia, Shura, and then his mother."

"Not to mention Sylvia's miscarriage and Assia's abortion."

"The body count in the life of Ted Hughes is almost as high as in *Hamlet*."

Joe grew sullen. The room had emptied out, people left to catch the early afternoon train to London, probably on the first leg of a Christmas holiday trip. The depleted dining room depleted Joe, too. Their talk of so many deaths had reminded him of the close calls he'd suffered with Sara. He took a long, deep breath and blew it out slowly. He desperately longed for his family.

"I need a drink," Joe said. He waved the waiter over.

"I could use a beer myself," Cass answered.

They ordered a couple of pints of Guinness and fell into a comfortable silence. After their glasses came, they sat together, sipping them quietly.

Joe's mind filled with questions. Had Sara replied to his email yet? It wasn't just the habit of being married to her. *I love Sara and the kids. I know I do.* Joe sipped his beer. *Can we work through what had happened?* It made him sick to think about another man being inside her. He drained his glass. *Can I ever forgive her?*

Cass interrupted his thoughts. "Are you going to have another?"

"What's that?"

"Do you want another Guinness?"

Her glass was empty, too, with just a layer of suds at the bottom.

"Sure. I guess. What's the plan? You really want to question the bartenders?"

Cass nodded and waved the waiter back over. He'd made it halfway to the table when Cass held up two fingers and pointed to the glasses.

"Yeah, I do," she answered. "I'd just like to hear the witness's first-hand account of that night."

"You're turning into Sherlock Holmes."

Cass chuckled. "Does that make you Watson? Because I think of you more like Jason Bourne than Dr. Watson."

Joe smiled. "Wow. Thanks."

"You look a little like him, you know. I'm sure you've been told that before, haven't you?"

Joe nodded. "I don't see it, but thanks."

Two more pints of Guinness arrived.

"Excuse me," Cass said. "Who's tending the bar?"

The waiter glanced over his shoulder. "That's Winston, the manager. Why? Something not right with your drinks?"

"No, no. The beer is fine. Wish it were served cold, like in America, but it's fine. Does Roland work today?"

The waiter cocked an eyebrow at her. "Yeah, but he won't be in 'til nearer to dinner. About half past four, I should think. Why you asking?"

"We just have a couple of questions," Cass answered. "Nothing serious."

"Well, like I said, Roland should be here in about an hour." Then the waiter carried off the old glasses on a tray.

Cass sipped her beer and smiled at Joe. "Should we pretend to be cops?"

"What?" Joe asked, then laughed.

"You know, when we question the bartenders, should we say we're cops or something."

Joe smiled. "If we say we're cops, we'd have to show them a badge."

"Oh, yeah. I just thought they'd answer more truthfully if we said we were here in an official capacity."

"I've got an idea." Joe pulled his wallet out and fished through some business cards. Finding the one he wanted, he handed it to Cass. "You could show them this and say you're an attorney investigating the hit and run for an insurance company."

Cass took the card and read it aloud: "*Susan Taylor, J.D. Attorney-at-Law*. Who's this?"

"My sister-in-law. She's an attorney in Sacramento."

"Yes, I see that." Cass smiled. "I'll use this only if they refuse to talk to us, okay?"

"Sure. I could show them Ryan Dunn's card, too. He's my police detective friend."

"Wouldn't that be impersonating an officer?"

Joe slurped his beer, smiling. "Yeah. Bad idea, I guess."

At four forty-five, a tall, dark-haired man, thirtyish or so, meandered in the front door of the tavern and walked to the end of the bar. He lifted a section of the bar surface and slipped behind it, nodding at the other bartender, the shorter, plumper man Joe guessed to be Winston.

"I think Roland's here. Ready to go to work?"

Cass grinned sheepishly. "No. Now I'm not so sure."

Joe drained his glass and stood. "C'mon. It'll be fun."

Reluctantly, Cass stood, too, and stepped behind Joe, nudging him. "You start the conversation, okay?"

He laughed. "Okay."

The place was almost empty. Two couples who were probably tourists were sitting near the stone fireplace, which had held a steady fire all afternoon, the waiter feeding it a fresh log every half hour or so. Joe approached the end of the bar where the older, heavier bartender was bent over a newspaper, reading intently. He looked up when Joe reached the barstool and took a seat.

"What'll it be?" the man asked, his voice gravelly.

"Two more, please," Joe answered. Cass sat down next to him.

The man went to work immediately, pulling the tap and filling two pint glasses. When he placed them down in front of Cass, flashing her a smile, Joe handed him a twenty pound note.

"You're Winston, aren't you?"

"Yes, sir. Glad to meet you." He held out his hand and Joe

shook it.

"Can I ask you a couple of questions?"

Winston pulled his hand away. "I dunno. What about?"

"We're investigating that hit-and-run accident that happened a few nights back."

The bartender wiped his hands on his apron and glanced around the room.

"Who are you?" he asked.

Cass reached over and touched Winston's forearm. "I was Trevor's girlfriend. Trevor is the one who was killed."

"Oh, I see. Well, you have my deepest condolences."

"Can you help us?" Joe asked.

"No, not me. It was Roland that saw the accident. I'd already gone to bed."

"Is it okay if we talk to him about it then?" Cass asked, her voice soft and pleading.

"Sure." Winston walked over to Roland, who was doing something at the cash register. He glanced at Joe and Cass while Winston filled him in. Then he nodded and approached them.

"What can I do for you?"

Joe held out his hand, saying, "I'm Joe Conrad and this is Cassandra Johnson. She knew the man who was killed outside your bar and wanted to hear more about that night."

Cass started to tear up.

After letting go of Joe's hand, Roland shook Cass's, saying, "I'm sorry for your loss. He seemed like a decent guy."

"He was," Cass said. She dabbed her eyes with one of the paper napkins on the bar. "Tell me what happened that night."

Roland shrugged and stared over Cass's head, as if trying to conjure up that fateful night in his mind's eyes.

"Not much to tell, really. He was the last to leave. He and his friends had been here since about ten or so. I could see they were trying to cheer him up about something, but one by one they gave up and left. Once the other customers left, I cut him off. It was close to closing time anyway and he'd had enough to drink."

"Was he angry about being cut off?" Joe asked.

Roland squinted. "Not angry exactly. More like, I dunno...."

"Betrayed?" Cass asked.

Roland nodded. "Yeah, I guess. Betrayed. Like, *you, too, Bartender?*"

"So tell us what happened," Joe said. "He got up to leave and how did he seem?"

Roland chuckled. "Oh, he was tipsy. But not so drunk he was stumbling or falling over. Just sort of weaving, you know?"

"Tell me about the accident," Cass pleaded.

"Well, before he walked out the door, I asked him if he wanted me to call for a cab. He said he already had a ride."

"Really?" Joe asked. "Did you tell the police that?"

"Come to think of it, no."

"So, Trevor was expecting someone to come for him, you think?"

"Maybe. He had been texting someone right before I kicked him out."

Joe turned to Cass. "I wonder if the police ever checked Trevor's cell phone."

"They asked me about the car," Roland said, "and what the driver looked like, but they didn't give a sod about what he was up to before leaving the bar. Funny, that, now you mention it."

"So what happened?" asked Joe. "What did you see?"

"I saw your man Trevor walk down the sidewalk toward the city center, and then before I realized what was happening, he stepped into the street as a car came up behind him."

"He didn't see the car?" Cass asked.

"No. Had his back to it. In fact, he was facing the snicket, like somebody was in there he didn't want to see."

"Snicket?" asked Joe.

"Alley. That's right. Had his head turned one way whilst walking the other and stepped right out in front of that car. Come to think of it, the driver didn't seem to be watching where she was going either."

"The driver was a woman?" Cass asked.

"From the brief glance I got of her, yeah, but she was looking toward the snicket, er, alleyway, too."

"You told this to the police?" Joe quizzed.

"More or less. They wanted to know the make and model of the car, mostly. Wanted to know if I wrote down the license plate number, but I was too stunned to notice. His body flew onto the bonnet and then hit the windshield, which spun him right round. Landed headfirst on the sidewalk."

Cass put her face in her hands and cried.

Joe scooted closer and wrapped an arm around her shoulders. "What make of car was it?" he asked the bartender.

"A Rover. Older model. Gray, I think. Least that's what I told the constable."

"Did you recognize the driver at all?"

Roland shook his head. "Naw. All happened too fast. But you know...."

"What?" Joe asked.

"Mind you, I didn't get a great look at her face, but from what I saw, she could be a twin of hers." He pointed to Cass. "Except, well, you know...white."

Cass stepped back. "She looked like *me*?"

Joe and Cass said in unison, "*Diane*."

CHAPTER 21

A young couple came in and sat at the bar close to Cass, so Roland excused himself and stepped over to take their orders.

Cass dabbed her eyes, shaking her head. "Why wouldn't Diane confess, if she was the one who hit Trevor? And why wouldn't she have stopped?"

"I don't know. Maybe she panicked."

"I can't believe they laid that guilt trip on *me* about Trevor."

"They were obviously trying to deflect blame."

"I was sure it had something to do with Sylvia's journal. Do you think Diane could be working for Ted's law firm?"

Joe sipped his beer and mulled over Cass's question. "I don't think so, but who knows? If my past brushes with criminals have taught me anything, it's that you can't trust anyone."

"What should we do now?" asked Cass.

"Do you know where the police station is?"

Cass nodded. "Just down the street."

Joe checked his watch. "Let's go. It's a little after five."

They climbed off the barstools, waved at Roland, who nodded, and left. The sky was still clear, but the air was turning colder a evening fell. The police station was just past the town clock—an odd red brick structure with a high-pitched green-shingled roof.

To Joe, the police station looked like a small, refurbished drugstore. The inside reeked of cigarette smoke, and on one wall was a map of Devon County while on the other hung a picture of Queen Elizabeth II. One unmanned gray metal desk met them just inside the door, its surface barren but for a calendar blotter, a stapler, and a matching cup to hold pens and pencils. One gray metal chair with worn green cushions sat in front of it and a matching chair sat beside the desk. A similar chair with arms was behind the desk.

The command center was in the rear of the building, behind a counter and a glass wall with a circular hole in the center— probably where the druggist had worked in the building's former life. A uniformed officer sat behind the glass.

"Can I help you?" He was about Joe's age, in his mid-thirties, with very short hair and nervous, darting eyes.

Joe put his hand on Cass's back and guided her to the window. He leaned down to speak through the hole in the glass window.

"We're here to talk to someone about the hit-and-run accident that happened a few days ago. Should we speak to you, or is there a detective we should talk to?"

The policeman chuckled. "*Detective!* We're lucky to have any police here at all."

Joe smiled, trying to put the officer at ease. "Well, should we speak to you then, or is there someone else?"

"Constable Davies is the one you want, but he's gone home. Can you come back in the morning?"

Cass fidgeted and her lips stretched into a thin line.

"I suppose so," he said. "We think we know who might have hit the man who was killed, though. Should we tell you right now or wait?"

The officer picked up a cigarette that had been resting in an ashtray, took a drag, then blew out the smoke toward the ceiling.

"Let me ring up the Constable."

Joe and Cass waited while the officer dialed a number.

"It's ringing. Why don't you have a seat in the waiting area."

The "waiting area" was two chairs by the desk. Joe grinned, led Cass to the chairs and took a seat.

"This suddenly seems silly," Cass whispered. "I mean, we can't really be sure it was Diane, can we?"

"No, but we can share what we know and let the police figure it out."

The officer waved them back to the window.

"The Constable says to write down your contact information and leave it with me. He'll be in touch in the morning."

"But we were going back to London in the morning," Cass whined.

The young officer chuckled again. "No you aren't. There's no train to London until noon." He opened a drawer in the counter and slid through a yellow legal pad. "Jot down your names, mobile numbers and where you're staying. Constable Davies will ring you up first thing in the morning."

Joe complied and then handed the notepad to Cass.

"Do you want me to write down the name of the person we think drove the car?"

The man shook his head. "No. Wait until the interview with Davies."

Cass wrote down her information and then put the pad of paper back inside the tray. "Is that it?"

He closed the drawer, took out the pad, checked it over, and then nodded. "Unless there's something else I can help you with."

Cass snorted. "Don't you want to go arrest the hit-and-run driver right now?"

"There's only the two of us in town, aren't there? I've got to man the station and the Constable is home having dinner with his family. It can wait 'til morning."

"What if the person gets away?" Cass pleaded. "What then?"

With as serious an expression as the young officer could muster, he said, "In that case, we'll go after the bugger with all the forces at our disposal, which would be me and Constable Davies, and maybe his bulldog named Prime Minister Thatcher, or Thatch, for short."

Joe smiled at the officer's sarcasm but placed his hand gently on Cass's shoulder.

"C'mon," Joe said. "We'll have to wait until morning." He held the door open for Cass, and the two stepped onto the sidewalk.

"Well, *that* was frustrating as hell," Cass huffed.

"Not nearly as satisfying as an episode of *Criminal Minds*."

"Let's go back to the pub and see if Diane's there. I want to see what she has to say about all this."

Zipping up his jacket against the cold, Joe frowned. "I don't think that's a good idea. Not after what happened last night."

"I'm going to the pub, Joe," Cass said, and started walking. Joe caught up.

"We should go back to our room and cool our jets, Cass."

"My jets are cool enough. If Diane killed Trevor, I want to find out why."

Joe had to quicken his pace to keep up. "I'm sure she didn't mean to. It was just an accident. A horrible accident."

Cass stopped suddenly. "If it was an accident, then why didn't she stop and try to help? Or wait for an ambulance and the cops?"

"I don't know. Maybe she panicked, like I said."

"I'm mad as hell and I want some answers." Cass stomped on, and against his better judgment, Joe followed.

The pub was all but empty, but there at the back table sat the same crew as had been there the night before. Diane's back was to the door, but Zenon watched Joe hold the door open for Cass. He scowled.

Cass stormed across the room and rushed up behind Diane, poking her shoulder hard. "Listen, you pasty *Twilight*-loving bitch, why'd you murder Trevor?"

"What the hell!" Zenon yelled.

Diane tried to stand, but Cass pushed her down.

"You heard me—why'd you run down Trevor like a dog?"

"I don't know what the hell you're talking about!"Diane yelled.

Zenon pushed his chair back and raced around the table, but Joe put his hands on the tall Spaniard's chest.

"Let Diane answer."

Hearing Joe, Diane glanced over. "I have no idea what you two insane Americans think you're doing, but if you don't leave now, I'm calling the police."

Still holding Zenon back, Joe addressed Diane. "We talked to the bartender who saw the accident. He saw *you* behind the wheel."

"How could he have? *He* doesn't know me or what I look like."

"He described you to us," Cass explained. "*We* know what you look like."

Diane shook her head, her hair tossing about violently. "He's mistaken. Besides, there must be a hundred women who look like me."

Zenon tried to push by Joe, but Joe held a finger up in front of his face.

"Just answer a question," Joe said to Diane. "What kind of car do you drive?"

"I, I don't own a car."

The woman sitting next to her said, "But you drive your dad's old Rover, don't you?"

Diane cringed and her face reddened.

Zenon squirmed in Joe's hands. "The bartender said the car he saw was an older model gray Rover," Joe said.

"A *gray* Rover?" Diane repeated. "My dad's car is green— British green."

Joe said to Zenon, "I wonder what British green looks like night under a street lamp?"

"I'll bet it looks gray," Cass answered.

"Oh, bloody hell," Zenon said, "you'd better come clean."

Diane burst into tears, grabbed her hair and screamed, "Oh, Christ! I didn't mean to! It was just a horrible accident!"

The others gasped with surprise.

Diane twisted free of Cass, and leapt to her feet, knocking over her chair. She ran to the back exit—the others lagging behind, shocked expressions on their faces.

"Oh, no you don't," Cass screamed. She ran after Diane, with Joe, Zenon and the rest following.

When Joe got out to the alley behind the pub, he saw Diane starting the engine inside a green Rover with damage to the front. The car made a piercing whine as it backed away from Cass into the street, where it turned and sped away.

"Where would she go?" Joe asked Zenon.

"I have no idea."

"I do," Cass said. "C'mon."

Joe followed Cass back through the pub and then out to the street. She ran to the hotel where the same taxi they'd taken that morning was sitting. Joe jumped into the back seat next to Cass.

"Take us to the cemetery," Cass ordered.

Zenon jumped in the front seat next to the driver.

In a few minutes, the cab was racing down Fore Street.

"There!" Zenon yelled.

Joe squinted. Small red taillights raced into the distance.

"Can you catch her?" Joe asked the driver.

"Oh, blimey, I don't know. She's drivin' like a bat out of hell!"

"Please try," Zenon pleaded.

The cab increased its speed, but so did the car in front of them. Both were hurtling down the narrow lane. Joe clutched a handle above the door as the car careened around a corner and Cass mashed into his side. On both sides of the narrow road, rows of snow-capped hedges undulated by like Chinese parade dragons.

SYLVIA'S SECRET

"Where the blazes is she going?" the cabbie asked.

"I told you," said Cass. "The cemetery."

"Well, she's going to stay there permanently if she doesn't slow down."

Slowing for a narrow bridge, the cab fell too far back and the car in front disappeared into the darkness. They drove on. Suddenly, another car flew right toward them, its horn blaring. The cabbie moved abruptly to the left, branches of the hedges slapping the window next to Joe's face. The two cars barely missed each other.

"Jesus, that was close," Joe said to Cass.

After rounding another bend and climbing a hill, they saw the Rover—it had crashed into a tree just outside the cemetery gate, its engine steaming and its left headlight still on. The driver's door hung open.

After the cab came to an abrupt stop behind Diane's car, Zenon addressed the driver. "Would you phone the police, please? We've got to set this right."

The cabbie was already punching numbers into his phone when Joe, Cass and Zenon climbed out and inspected the car.

Zenon gasped. "Oh my God, there's blood."

Joe leaned inside. "She must have hit the steering wheel or the windshield frame. There's no blood on the glass and the windshield isn't cracked."

The trio jogged into the cemetery. Rows of grave stones and stone crosses stood like dark, silent guards amid the snowy lawns. The farther they ran, the darker the graveyard became, lights from the two parked cars fading into the distance.

Joe shivered, partly from the cold, partly from the memory of running like this in the dark from a killer with Sara clutching his hand in terror. As his eyes adjusted to the lack of light, he followed Zenon who led them up a moonlit hill to the fresh grave. They found Diane, bleeding from the forehead, on her knees crying, slumped across the mound of earth. Zenon knelt down and put hi arm around her.

"Are you hurt?" he asked.

She shook her head, but blood was still seeping from a wound over her right eyebrow.

"But you're bleeding," he whispered.

"It isn't that bad—just a bump to the head. I'll be fine, fine. Fine! Not like Trevor!"

He wrapped his arms around her and let her bury her bleeding face in his shoulder.

Cass, still in a rage, lurched toward the couple, but Joe grabbed her. "Give her a few minutes, Cass. Please."

Cass's eyes were filled with anger, and her nostrils flared, but she slowly calmed down as Joe held onto her.

"It *was* an accident. You have to believe that." It was Zenon.

"Then why cover it up?" asked Joe.

"It was my idea," admitted Zenon. "Diane's had two other accidents while driving after drinking. She panicked. Look, I'm partly to blame, too."

"How?" asked Cass. "Were you in the car with her?"

"No, no. I was just coming out of the alley when Diane saw me. She didn't want me to know she'd gone to get Trevor."

"Oh, God!" Diane screamed. "We were seeing each other again behind Z's back, and I didn't want Z to know I'd gone to get him."

"He'd texted her, you see," Zenon explained. "She thought I was still asleep. The room was pitch black and she didn't want to disturb me, so she sneaked out of bed to come for him, not realizing that I'd left ten minutes earlier to walk Trevor back. He'd texted me, too."

Cass shook her head, saying to Joe, "Trevor and Diane had been together last year, but she broke it off to be with Z."

Diane sat back on her heels and watched Cass. Even in the dim light, Joe could see the dried blood and black mascara smeared across Diane's face like Marine camouflage.

Sylvia's Secret

"He was just so sad," she said. "After you left him, Cass, he wasn't himself. I felt so sorry for him, it broke my heart."

From the distance came the wailing of a police siren, the weird *wee-woo wee-woo* scream piercing the cold and silent night.

Cass began to weep. "But why didn't you stop? Why?"

Diane shook her head. "I don't know. I just panicked when I saw Z step out of the alley. Trevor saw him, too. I didn't want Z to know that Trevor and I were…*seeing* each other again. Besides, I was still a little drunk and I knew I'd lose my license, so I just stepped on the gas."

Cass nodded, and frowned. "Leaving him to die on that frozen sidewalk."

Joe grabbed Zenon by the shoulder. "What about you? Why didn't *you* stay?"

Its lights flashing blue, the police car rolled up and parked beside the Rover.

"I don't know," Zenon answered. "Maybe guilt. You see, I'd called to Trevor from the alley and he turned to look at me just as he stepped out in front of the car. He never saw it coming."

From the distance, a car door slammed shut.

"Maybe," Cass said, her voice dropping, "maybe you were glad to get rid of the competition."

Joe squeezed her arm. "Jesus, Cass, that's a horrible thing to say."

"No," said Zenon, "she might be right. At least partly. You see, I love this woman. He cupped Diane's face in his hands, whispering, I love her with all my heart, and I was losing her to Trevor. I knew I was. So I admit it—part of me was relieved that Trevor was gone."

Cass pulled away from Joe and stepped closer, then slapped Zenon across the face. "So why the hell did you lay that guilt on me?"

"But you *are* to blame, Cass," he answered. "At least, partly. Don't you see? If Trevor hadn't fallen so badly for you, he could have moved on, but he was drowning in drink over you."

Soon they heard voices, and then a flashlight beam shone in their direction.

"Still," said Joe, "you should've stayed with him that night. Both of you."

Diane wiped her face. "Don't you think we know that?"

The light grew steadily brighter until whoever was holding the flashlight stopped and shone it on Joe's face.

"Constable Davies, I presume?" Joe asked.

"Yes," answered a deep voice from behind the light. "Would someone please tell me what in God's name is going on?"

Joe smiled sadly into the light and turned Cass around so the Constable could see her. "Agatha Christie here has solved your hit-and-run case for you. Hope you didn't miss dessert."

CHAPTER 22

Joe knew the drill all too well. He and Cass, along with Zenon, Diane and the taxi driver, sat inside the stale-smelling, garishly-lit police station, writing their statements and answering questions for an hour. Constable Davies focused his anger on Zenon in particular.

"You two should have come forward sooner," Davies said, the veins in his forehead bulging. "Especially you, young man. I know you *think* you were trying to protect your girlfriend, but you might've gotten her into more trouble. She was obviously shaken up badly by the accident, so even more reason to think straight for both of you. Now she'll be charged not only with a hit and run, but also with not coming forward with information about the crime. And you? You may be charged as an accessory after the fact."

"Are you arresting me?" Z asked, his voice cracking.

Joe pitied him—it reminded him of the times he'd been questioned about the murders in California, the weight of it all, like his world was collapsing in on him.

But the Constable finally shook his head. "No, I'm not arresting you. Not tonight. The case will need to go before a magistrate, and I'm quite sure you'll be brought back for more questioning at later date. But for now, you're free to go. All of you except Lady Diane there."

He jerked his thumb over his shoulder to the small jail cell behind him. Diane sat inside the tiny cell on an army cot, her forehead bandaged and her head hanging down.

Before they left, Z walked over and spoke gently to her through the bars. Without looking up, she nodded a few times.

"Get some sleep," Z told her. "I'll come back for you in the morning."

Diane stretched out on the cot and laid her arm over her eyes, but then rolled onto her side with her back to Zenon.

It was time to go home.

Joe, Cass, and Zenon walked back to the pub together in silence. The cold air was biting Joe's face and exhaustion overwhelmed him. The adrenaline from the chase had evaporated, and the hour or so of questioning in the dismal little police station had taken a toll.

Zenon unexpectedly turned to Cass. "I'm so sorry, Cassandra. I know you were good for Trevor, at least at first. He called you his queen—his African Queen—like that old film with Humphrey Bogart and Katherine Hepburn."

Cass shook her head. "He never called me that to my face."

"Well, these past few weeks, that's what he called you when he was crying on our shoulders." Zenon put his hand on Cass's arm. She visibly tensed. "What happened anyway, Cass? Why'd you leave?"

Ever so slowly, Cass reached over and pulled Zenon's hand away. "He got too jealous after the party."

"Well, you *did* give him some reasons to *be* jealous, didn't you? You were all over us at that party."

Like a traffic cop stopping cars, Cass put her hand up to Zenon's face. "I was a little drunk, okay? I mean, put yourself in my shoes.

SYLVIA'S SECRET

Trevor was introducing me to all his old chums, folks he'd known all his life. I was nervous and had had too much to drink."

"Well," Zenon answered sadly, "I'm truly sorry for how this turned out."

They continued walking, but Zenon stopped again. "You know, I still feel Trevor's presence, like his spirit is still in the air. It's as if he's watching over you now, Cass. I can't help but feel he had a hand in bringing it all out into the open. Even in death, his love for you is strong."

Joe was afraid Cass might cry, so he tried to put his arm around her shoulders, but she stepped out from under his embrace.

"To quote Sylvia," she said, "'the word of a snail on the plate of a leaf? It is not mine. Do not accept it. Lies. Lies and a grief.'"

Zenon shrugged. "Not sure what that means, never really understood poetry, not like Trevor, anyway, but if you think what I'm saying is a lie, then I'm sad for you." With that, he turned and walked away.

"Let's get back to our hotel," said Joe. "I'm exhausted."

"Do you believe that jerk? Invoking Trevor's ghost like that?"

"He was trying to make amends, I think."

They walked side by side for a while, passing the pub without looking in. If Trevor's spirit was hovering over them, it was a quiet ghost. The only thing hovering over Joe at the moment was the damp, cold air seeping into his bones. The darkness drew a blanket of depression around him. Again he thought of the life he'd left behind—his wife of almost ten years and his two children. Was this to be his new life, living like a vagabond with no permanent home? Jumping from one friendship to another, making weak connections with people like Cass, people he knew but really didn't? Was he to be dragged into one drama after another like a secondary character in a soap opera?

With Cass lost in her own world beside him, Joe again ached for what he was missing. Years ago when he was suspected of mur

Sara had said that she didn't know whether or not she still loved him. He recalled feeling like an astronaut doing a space walk, surrounded by the freezing blackness of space, the tether being stretched to its limit as he floated farther and farther from the spaceship that was a home in the void. He could still remember floating away from Sara, her receding into the dark distance, worrying that the tether would snap and he'd be lost forever.

Now that tenuous connection between him and his wife may have finally snapped and he was adrift in the dark void. A thought occurred to him that made him chuckle, though he wanted to cry.

"You find something funny in this?" Cass asked, unable to mask the bitterness in her voice.

"No, not funny. Ironic, maybe."

"Do share."

"Well, I was just remembering that line from Donne's poem. 'No man is an island unto himself. We're all part of the continent.' You know the poem."

"Of course. And?"

"Donne was wrong. We *are* islands, all of us. Little islands alone in a dark ocean of despair."

"Wow. That's a pretty bleak view, coming from you, Joe."

"It's just how I'm feeling right now."

"I don't understand. You didn't even know Trevor."

He shrugged. "Guess I'm just missing my family."

"Oh," Cass replied. She stayed quiet for a few minutes, but as they turned toward the hotel, she said, "But you'll head back soon, and your kids will be so happy to see you that they'll jump into your arms like you were Father Christmas."

He wanted to tell Cass about Sara cheating on him and how he'd left without telling her where he was going, but he also didn't want to start crying, so he didn't.

After a good night's sleep, he'd tell Cass everything. Maybe owing about his plight would somehow ease her feelings of insecurity. Perhaps she'd even have some advice for him, a way back to Sara. Of course, the depressing story could also add to the burden Cass was already carrying.

Walking into the quiet warmth of the hotel lobby, he debated the wisdom of confessing to Cass, but decided to push the whole affair out of his mind until morning.

The little hotel lobby was more claustrophobic than before. Sometime during the day, the staff had put up a Christmas tree and decorated it. The scent of pine permeated the lobby, and once again Joe longed to be home. While Cass visited the front desk to check for messages, Joe walked into the little gift shop and bought a bottle of wine—the only alcohol in the store.

On the ride up to their room in the elevator, Joe asked, "What you quoted to Zenon about lies, what poem is that from?"

"One of the very first poems in *Ariel*, Joe. Christ, have you ever actually read *Ariel*?"

He was taken aback by Cass's hostility. "Yeah, but I don't have all her poems memorized like you do."

"Do you know even *one* of her poems by heart?"

"I'm not a Plath scholar, Cass. I teach a couple of her poems every semester, along with works from dozens of other authors."

"I'm sorry. You're right."

"It's been a long day," he responded.

"And an even longer night."

The doors to the elevator opened, and they walked side by side down the poorly lit little hallway to their room. Joe unlocked the door and smiled. "You'll be pleased to know that I *did* quote the first stanza of her poem 'Morning Song' when Katie was born."

Cass stepped inside and flicked on the light. "Oh? That's appropriate." She walked between the beds and put her purse down on the nightstand before turning on the lamp. "Don't you just love hotels? They change your sheets and make your bed while you're away."

Joe set the wine bottle down on the dresser and turned to Cass, with hopes that her mood was improving. "I still remember those lines. 'Love set you going like a fat gold watch. The doctor slapped your foot soles, and your bald cry took its place among the elements.' Are you impressed?"

"Midwife," Cass said, "not doctor. 'The midwife slapped your foot soles.' You blew that line."

Joe shrugged and grinned. "Cut me some slack. We had a doctor, not a midwife."

Later, after they both had showered and changed into pajamas, Joe poured himself a glass of wine—a bland, French chardonnay—and offered some to Cass. She moved away from the nightstand, her silky purple pajamas hanging loosely off her shoulders and hips. He tried not to notice the way her breasts swayed under the loose-fitting top.

"Is it cold?" she asked him.

Joe took a sip. "Not really."

"Do you mind putting some ice in it? I mean, you won't be offended, will you? I know how you NorCal wine snobs can be sometimes."

"No, I won't be offended." He picked up the ice bucket, grabbed his room key and went down the hall to the machine, somewhat self-conscious in his white v-neck tee-shirt and dark blue pajama bottoms. With the bucket filled, he returned and poured wine into a full glass of ice for Cass. Holding his up, he said, "To a mystery solved."

Cass touched her glass to his and then drained it, as if trying to wash away a bitter taste.

Joe sipped his—it was room temperature and very dry, not exactly to his taste.

"Want another?" he asked.

"Sure. Maybe it will help me sleep."

"Are you feeling restless?"

She nodded when she took the glass. "Nervous, like the police are going to break down the door any minute and arrest us." Cass's eyes flitted from the door to him and then back to the door.

"Really, Cass, I think everything's okay now. The police have their man—or their woman, in this case—so I think we're out of the woods."

Cass drank half the glass of wine, then shook her head. "*Out of the woods?* What's that mean?"

"Out of danger," answered Joe softly. "You don't have to be concerned that someone from Ted's law firm is out to get you now."

She burst into laughter. "Oh, you think they're just going to let it go? I mean, knowing I've got one of Sylvia's journals, they're just going to 'go gentle into that good night,' to quote one of your favorite poets?"

She drained her glass and held it out. He refilled it, adding a few more ice cubes. She drank half the glass immediately.

"You might want to slow down. This wine can still get you tipsy."

She laughed. "*Tipsy?* Did you really just say 'tipsy'? Damn, Joe. Sometimes you sound so damn...*white.*"

Joe wasn't sure how to respond. She was likely lashing out at him because he happened to be standing in front of her, when in reality she had other demons threatening her. Her eyes flared with anger, and for a moment he was afraid she might hit him, so he turned away and plopped a few ice cubes into his own wine glass before refilling it. Then he turned back toward Cass, smiled and held up his glass.

"Here's to Cassandra Johnson, the hero of the hour and finder of truths both big and small."

For several seconds, Cass stared up at him with a bewildered look on her face. Then her facial muscles relaxed and her lips opened into a grin.

"I swear, Joe," she said, touching her glass to his, "your wife is lucky to have you."

Joe strained to hold the smile, though the sudden flash of Sara's stunned face when Joe woke her up that day stabbed his heart again. He took a long drink of the chilled, watery wine and said, "Hey, it's much better cold."

Cass nodded as she swallowed. "It reminds me of the wine coolers we used to drink in college. Stupid, cheap wine mixed with Seven-up."

Joe laughed. "You mean you didn't buy Boones' Farms?"

"No, we bought wine by the jug and Seven-up by the liter, and mixed it ourselves. I got so sick once, I threw up all over my desk. Almost ruined my laptop."

Joe chuckled. "The truth comes out."

"What about you Southern boys down there in Baton Rouge? I bet you did your share of drinking."

"Drinking was a way of life in Louisiana. On game days at LSU, half the people in Tiger Stadium were plastered."

They both drained their drinks, and smiled at each other's memories. Then Joe refilled their glasses and reached into the ice bucket for the few remaining cubes of ice.

After taking a sip, Cass looked over the rim at Joe. "*Is* Sara really okay with you being here like this?"

"Sure," Joe said. But he'd replied too quickly and it sounded false to him as well.

"She isn't afraid I might jump you?"

Joe chuckled. "She knows we're just friends."

She stepped closer. "Just friends? You guys don't have an open marriage, do you?"

Joe explored Cass's sleepy eyes, examined her full lips, slightly parted in a smile, and he imagined for a moment what it would be like to kiss her—really kiss her, deeply, sensually. But once he started, he wouldn't be able to stop until they had dragged each other into one of the beds and made love. He imagined himself on top of her, kissing her mouth and then…what? What would they do afterward? Go on as if nothing had happened?

Sara would have no room to criticize him, if he ever told her about it. In a way, he had a pass. *What's good for the goose…*

"No, Cass, we don't have an open marriage, but if we did, you'd be the first one I'd call for a date."

She laughed. "What makes you think I'd go on a date with *you?*"

CHAPTER 23

Cass rattled her ice cubes, so Joe grabbed the wine bottle and poured the final drops into her glass. Seeing the empty bottle, she pouted.

"Want me to get another?"

"I could use more," she answered. "Couldn't you?"

Her drowsy eyes told him it would be much harder to resist her tonight. She'd put on perfume and hadn't been smoking, and her skin was still glistening from the warm shower. *I need to get a little drunk anyway.*

"Think it's okay to go downstairs dressed like this?"

Cass laughed. "Hell, yeah. Half of our students come to class in pajama bottoms. My only concern is, some girl's going to see how hot you look in that tight t-shirt, with that little tuft of chest hair sticking out, and she's going to drag you back to her room before you bring the wine back to me."

"Yeah, that kind of thing happens to me all the time." He grabbed his wallet and the room key. "Back in a flash."

The hallway was empty, and so was the elevator, but when the doors opened on the ground floor, an older, very staid-looking couple raised their eyebrows at Joe's casual appearance.

"Excuse me," he said, stepping around them.

One bottle of the same chardonnay awaited him in the gift shop cooler. The plump fifty-something woman at the counter, wearing heavy eye shadow and thick red lipstick, looked him up and down and smiled as she made change.

Feeling naked, he said, "Thanks," and grabbed the bottle before she could bag it.

"My pleasure," the woman answered, trying to make her voice husky and seductive.

Joe rushed to the elevator, pressed the button, and waited as it rattled to the ground floor.

Back in the room, Cass was sitting against the pillows propped up on the headboard of her bed. She smiled dreamily and held out her glass.

"Please, sir, may I have more?"

Joe chuckled as he pulled the cork.

He answered in a deep voice, trying to sound like Mr. Bumble from *Oliver Twist*. "More?!"

"Oh, yes, please, sir," Cass replied using a child's voice. "I'm ever so thirsty."

He filled her glass before filling his own, and then set the bottle on the nightstand between the beds. Cass looked up at him as she sipped her wine. *This is getting dangerous.*

What's worse, he was getting aroused, so he turned quickly and walked back to the ice bucket, grabbing a few cubes and plopping them into his glass. "Need more ice?" he asked, looking at Cass over his shoulder.

She smiled and nodded. It was a dangerous smile and an even more dangerous nod—slow and sexy. He grabbed a few ice cubes and carried them over to her, dropping them into her glass as she held it up. Then she glanced down at his pajamas and grinned.

Joe turned away and grabbed the remote for the TV.

"Should we find something to watch?"

Cass didn't answer until Joe looked at her over his shoulder again. She shrugged, grinning. "I'm okay with just...talking." She stirred the wine with her finger and then put the wet finger between her lips.

Uh-oh. I'm in trouble. Joe swallowed the rest of the wine in his glass and added more ice before setting the glass down on the dresser.

"Excuse me," he said. "Need to use the facilities."

Once in the bathroom, Joe locked the door, and spoke to himself in the mirror. "What are you doing, man?" He shook his head, whispering, "You're going to ruin a friendship and put the last nail in the coffin of your marriage."

Joe splashed cold water on his face, then dried it off. Would he have the strength to resist Cass if she really tried to seduce him?

Feigning a British accent, he whispered to his reflection, "Keep a stiff upper lip, old chap, and not a stiff you-know-what!"

When he came out of the bathroom, Cass was giggling on the bed, her hand to her mouth as if she were trying to contain her laughter.

"I can't help it," she blurted, laughing. "I could hear every word!"

Joe's face burned with embarrassment, but soon he was laughing as well.

"I'm sorry, Cass, I'm just not used to being around other women like this."

"Obviously," she said. She pointed toward his crotch and then rolled onto her side, laughing again.

Joe glanced down, then scurried to his bed after grabbing his glass, and climbed under the covers. Then he poured himself more wine from the bedside stand, took a sip and said, "We'll look back at this one day and laugh, right?"

Cass rolled over, nodding. "Why wait?" She burst into another round of laughter, and there was nothing Joe could do but laugh with her.

◊ ◊ ◊

In the morning, Joe awoke in a sweat. The room was stiflingly hot. Cass wasn't in her bed, so he threw off the covers and went to the thermostat. The heater had been turned up to 80 degrees. He lowered it, then went to the window and drew open the curtains.

It was raining, a steady downpour from heavy gray clouds. Joe cranked the window open a few inches and enjoyed the cold air as it rushed in on his chest and face. But then the wind shifted, blowing rain in through the opening, so he reluctantly closed the window again. A dull headache throbbed at his temples and forehead. They had finished the second bottle of wine, each in their own bed, talking about the day, remarking at Zenon and Diane's duplicity.

Joe couldn't recall when he'd fallen asleep, only that he'd slipped down into the covers while Cass told him stories about her time with Trevor. He must have nodded off while listening to her.

Cass came out of the bathroom wrapped in a towel. She neither smiled nor frowned when she saw him. "You finally woke up."

"Guess I drifted off while you were talking."

She shrugged. "Sorry if my tales of woe are so boring."

"Tales of woe? What do you mean?"

She shook her head, clearly annoyed. "It doesn't matter."

"No, please tell me."

She reached into her suitcase and pulled out some clothes. "It doesn't matter. I was just telling you how I felt about Trevor, how I almost thought he might be the one, and then you're snoring. Real nice."

"I'm sorry, Cass. We had a pretty rough day yesterday. And then the wine…"

"Yeah, the wine." She turned and walked back into the bathroom.

Cass's mood swing put him on edge. If he hadn't been so

sweaty, he would have dressed without showering, but his t-shirt was drenched. Joe was still groggy, and hoped Cass had made coffee, but she hadn't. And with her now locked in the bathroom, he couldn't get water to make his own.

Then he had an idea. He checked the ice bucket. The ice had melted, so it was about a third full. Joe poured that water into the coffee maker, tore open a packet of coffee and got the little machine started. He grabbed the remote and turned on CNN. An ice storm had coated the eastern U. S. north of New York—power lines down, airports closed, interstates all but undrivable. California, on the other hand, was having warmer than normal weather, sunny with temperatures in the mid-60s. The screen showed sailboats on the San Francisco Bay.

At the window again, with the drizzle and gray skies, Joe was suddenly very homesick.

Cass's mood didn't improve during breakfast in the dismal, little hotel cafe, nor when Joe suggested they take another drive out to Court Green before taking the train back to London.

"What's the point?" she said. "We can't get inside to look around, so all we could do is muck around in the mud. Waste of time."

"What should we do, then, before the train arrives?"

Cass shrugged. "I'm going back up to the room to work on my laptop. I don't care what *you* do."

Cass's eyes had been so sparkling and full of life the night before; now they were dark and empty. Maybe he was still feeling the effects of the wine, but the scrambled eggs and greasy undercooked bacon he'd just eaten had turned his stomach.

"I guess I'll stay down here and use the computer. I can check flight schedules."

"So you're going to leave?"

He was surprised by the intensity of her objection. "Yeah. Why not?"

Cass turned away—she was angry, but it didn't seem to fit with her morning mood.

"No reason."

"We solved the mystery of Trevor's death, haven't we? That's what had you so spooked, right?"

The anger in Cass's eyes frightened him.

"*Spooked!* You did *not* just use that word in front of *me*, did you?"

"Oh my God, Cass. You know I didn't mean it like that."

Cass seethed and shook with anger.

"I didn't mean it that way," he repeated. "You know I didn't."

She closed her eyes and took a few deep breaths. "I'm going upstairs to work. The train leaves at 12:30. Come upstairs and get your bag at 11:30 or so, okay?"

Afraid of saying something that would only make her angrier, Joe nodded and waited for her to leave. He'd seen her dramatic mood swings several times in the last few days, but he'd never seen such hatred. It was irrational. The earlier episodes could be blamed on her sadness over the loss of Trevor and her fear that his death was somehow connected to her work, but now he was convinced that something else was going on. *What can I do? I'm stuck here. At least for the time being.*

After paying the bill for their breakfast, Joe went to the computer and checked email. Several students wanted to know their grades, but without his grade book, he had to ignore those. There was an email from Sara sent the day before yesterday. He was afraid to open it. This day had started so badly, he was sure Sara would tell him she wanted a divorce. He couldn't take that.

His stomach churned with worry, yet he opened the email.

I'm sick about what happened. I don't love him. It was just a

stupid fling. I don't know why I did it. I guess I was flattered by the
attention. These past few days without you have made me realize
how much I love you and only you. I want you back and I want
you back in Katie and Brian's lives. Please, please, please come
home. I'll do anything. Counseling. I'm so ashamed. Can you ever
forgive me? I'll never cheat on you again. I promise.

Her words were so welcomed that Joe could barely contain
himself. He didn't want to cry, not in public, but he couldn't help
allowing a few tears to fall. He wrote a hurried reply, wanting to
book his return flight as soon as possible.

Sara, yes, I can forgive you. Being away from you and the kids
has made me realize how much I love you, too. I'll try to book a
flight home asap.

Next, he checked the airlines for flights back to California.
Every flight on American and United was booked until after
Christmas. He checked British Airlines, Virgin, even Quantas, but
nothing was available.

*You're kidding! Am I going to have to stay here for another
week?*

The idea of being stuck in London made him sick. He knew
he couldn't stay at Cass's flat—he'd have to find a hotel—so he
began a search. Nothing near her flat was available. Even when he
widened the search, he couldn't find a vacancy.

Just my luck. No room at the inn. Merry Christmas, Joe.

SYLVIA'S SECRET

CHAPTER 24

On the train to London, Cass's face reflected in the glass as the landscape, darkened by the downpour outside, made a mirror of the window. Joe was being ignored so he dozed for a while and then read one of the books Cass had given him, Ronald Hayman's *The Death and Life of Sylvia Plath*. He had been absorbed in it for about an hour when he came to the chapter on infidelity.

"Listen to this," he said without thinking. "You were telling me about this radio play titled 'Difficulties of a Bridegroom' that Ted wrote. It was performed on the BBC. The one about a guy named Sullivan who runs down a rabbit while driving to London to meet his mistress."

Cass glowered at him.

Hoping to break her mood, Joe continued as if they were still on good terms. "But listen to the way Hayman describes it. Ted's character Sullivan accelerates to run over the hare and then stops to pick it up. After arriving in London, he sells it to buy flowers for the, and I quote, 'irresistible woman.' Hayman writes, 'If Sylvia, who was a keen listener to the Third Programme, heard the play, she'd have been forcefully reminded of Assia by the character's provocative way of talking and by the line, "Here she comes, her perfumes before her." Sylvia knew how aware Ted was of Assia's perfumes and he says that Sylvia 'identified with the hare.' Not only that, but the play was repeated on the radio just two days before Sylvia committed suicide."

Cass rolled her eyes. "I know all about that. We talked about it before, didn't we?"

Joe nodded. "It's too much of a coincidence. Ted's practically telling everyone beforehand that he's going to kill Sylvia and use the money he makes from her writings to buy nice things for Assia."

"That's what I've been trying to tell you."

Joe fell into deep reflection. "Hughes was like John Edwards—charming, charismatic, and very manipulative. Completely self-serving and egotistical. Like he just expected women to sacrifice themselves for him."

She nodded. "Exactly. He was a user of women and regarded them as little more than pets and playthings provided for his amusement."

"Now I see why you were so interested in Trevor's research on Ted's psychological profile."

"Trevor was convinced that Hughes fit the profile of a psychopath or at least a sociopath."

"Is there a difference?"

"I think so. A subtle one."

"I wonder what happened to Trevor's notes?"

Her eyes widened. "I didn't even think to ask. How stupid of me."

The cover of Hayman's book showed a photo of Ted and Sylvia bundled up on the beach on a chilly, windy day. Ted is holding a walking stick in his right hand and Sylvia is holding Ted's left arm. The smile on her face is pure joy and pride, while the smirk on Ted's face makes him look like a cad.

"I imagine Trevor's parents have his notes," Joe said.

"Yeah, and his laptop, but I doubt they'd be willing to give me his work."

"It could really complement what you're doing."

"Don't I know it. But, Joe, then I'd be guilty of robbing the dead, just like Ted robbed Sylvia."

"No, it's not the same. You didn't intend for Trevor to die." They rode on in silence, the damp hillsides now giving way to the outskirts of London. "What do you suppose will happen to Trevor's research?"

Cass shook her head. "I don't know."

"Is there anyone else in his family who's doing that kind of work?"

"No. He didn't have any siblings, and I know his parents didn't go to college."

"So there's no one else who might pick up where Trevor left off?"

Cass sighed. "You met his friends. None of them is interested in literature. They're all up and coming yuppies."

"All his work will be lost then?"

"Yes, I suppose so."

"We can't let that happen, Cass. Give it a week or so, and then write to Trevor's parents."

"But you saw them at the funeral. They hate me."

Joe clutched Cass's arms, turning her toward him. "But that's when they thought you were responsible for his death. Once the truth about Diane comes out, they'll know you had nothing to do with it."

"That's true."

"Of course it is, Cass. In a couple of weeks, their wounds will have healed somewhat, and you can write to them, telling them how you really felt about their son and how it would be tragic if his work never saw the light of day."

She nodded. "It *would* be tragic."

"Absolutely. You've at least got to try, Cass. By citing him and quoting from his work, you'll keep Trevor's memory alive."

She nodded as a tear spilled from her eye. Then a faint grin tugged at her lips. "Thanks, Joe. You're right. It's the least I can do for Trevor." She turned toward the window, wiping tears from her cheeks.

The flat on Fitzroy was cold and dreary when they walked through the door, and a foul odor assaulted them.

Cass held her nose. "Ooo, I must have forgotten to take out the garbage before we left."

Setting his bag down, Joe covered his mouth and nose. "I'll get it." He tugged the plastic garbage can out from under the kitchen sink.

Cass scurried over and opened the window.

"Where do I take this?" Joe asked.

"There's a rubbish chute at the end of the hall."

Joe hustled down the hall with the bag at arm's reach and found the door in the wall marked TRASH. Cass was lighting scented candles when he returned. Already the flat smelled better.

"Problem solved," Joe said, closing the door.

"Oh, please leave the door open for a while, just until the room airs out."

Joe complied and then waited to see what Cass's next instructions would be. Since leaving the train, she'd given one curt order after another, first on the best way to find the subway and then on the best route back to her apartment building. He'd followed each directive without question, hoping Cass's mood would improve if she met no resistance. This was *her* city, after all, and he was *her* guest—as uncomfortable as that made him.

"I'm going to unpack," she said, picking up her suitcase. "Can you put some water on for tea?"

"Sure," he answered.

After Cass left the room, he filled the teapot with water, put it on the stove and turned on the gas. A box of matches was on the counter, so he lit one and the hissing gas whooshed to life in a sudden circular blue flame that made Joe step back.

With the water on, he went down the hall to the bathroom. Cass had her back to him, pulling clothes out of the suitcase on her bed.

"Mind if I use the facilities?" he asked.

Without turning around, she said, "Of course not."

Joe looked at himself in the mirror and shook his head. *This is going to be awkward.*

He found Cass pouring water into two cups when he came back.

"Some nice hot tea will warm us up," she said, forcing a smile. "I've turned up the heater, too."

"Should I close the window then?"

Dipping her teabag, Cass nodded. "Sure. The place has aired out enough."

"The candles help."

He closed the window. Low and gray, laden with rain, the clouds looked like an armada of battleships floating overhead.

"It stopped raining."

"Perfect. Just when we get inside."

Cass held up his cup, inviting him to the counter.

"You take cream and sugar, right?"

Joe nodded, and climbed onto a barstool.

She took a carton out of the refrigerator and sniffed it. "Still good." Then she poured a splash of cream in and stirred in two spoons of sugar. Holding the cup out, she said, "Hot, sweet, and white, just like your women, right?"

He took the cup. "Can you let that go?"

Feigning ignorance, she shrugged. "Let what go?"

"My stupid choice of words, Cass. I wasn't thinking."

"It just sort of slipped out, huh?"

"Yes. A slip of the tongue."

She sipped her tea. "A Freudian slip maybe?"

"No, it wasn't sexual. Freud was all about sex." He took a sip of the tea, even though it was very hot. "Tastes good. Thanks."

"You're welcome."

Cass moved near the heater. Joe grabbed his cup and joined her, sitting on the sofa. The warmth from the fake electric fire took the chill out of the air, and Cass's expression. "Let me treat you to dinner tonight to make amends, okay?"

Cass sipped her steaming tea, the moisture glistening on her face, and nodded. "Sounds good, especially since I don't have anything for dinner anyway."

Joe reached up to shake hands. "Friends?"

Cass took his hand, nodding. "Friends."

"You were there for me when I needed someone, so I wanted to be here for you."

Still holding his hand, she said, "I knew you couldn't have killed those girls."

"Well, you were about the only one who believed me at the time."

She released his hand and wrapped her fingers around the cup. "Of course, a few years later, you *did* kill that guy who was after the Shakespeare manuscripts."

"That was an accident. I was defending myself."

"Still, Joe. Trouble has a way of finding you."

He sipped the sweet tea and nodded, resigned to the truth of Cass's observation.

"You aren't the first person who's told me that."

"Well," she responded, "let's hope I'm the last."

The tension between them had broken, and the rest of the afternoon passed pleasantly. Cass worked at her desk and Joe drowsed in front of the heater while finishing Hayman's biography on Plath. After freshening up, they strolled down to a place on the corner, The Queen's Pub & Dining Room. It was quaint, dark, and smelled of stale ale, and they served meat and potatoes. Joe found that adding loads of salt, pepper and brown mustard gave flavor to the overdone beef. But the Guinness was good, and food and drink seemed to relax Cassandra.

When the dishes were cleared and they were working on their second pints of stout, Joe broached a topic he'd been reluctant to bring up earlier.

"I should be getting back to Sara and the kids, so can I use your laptop tonight to look for flights?"

"Oh? I thought that's what you were doing at the hotel this morning."

He nodded. "Didn't have much luck."

"Which airlines did you check?"

"All of them. United, American, British Air, Virgin, even Qantas."

"Try KLM."

Joe chuckled. "K-L-M? Who names an airline Kill-em?"

Cass laughed politely.

"So can I get on your computer tonight, or will you be working?"

"No, that's fine. I have some other reading to do."

He smiled, hoping to keep the mood friendly. "Thanks."

They sat together, quietly sipping their beer as the place emptied out. Hoping not to sound too eager, Joe asked, "Should we get back?"

Cass shrugged. "I could use another drink, but if you're anxious to get back, we can go."

"No, let's have another round."

Joe sensed that Cass wanted to talk about something, but he was worried where the conversation could go, so instead of waiting for the waiter, he grabbed the two mugs and walked over to the bar.

The waiter took the mugs and told him he'd be right over with fresh glasses of Guinness.

"I have one more favor to ask," Cass said when he sat down. "Don't leave tomorrow. If it's possible, book your flight for the day after."

"Why?"

"I made an appointment to see Ted's attorneys. I want you to come with me when I confront them."

"Confront them? About what?"

The waiter came with the drinks, and Cass stayed quiet until he had gone.

"I need a witness, Joe. I want to ask them again in front of another person to allow me to see Sylvia's notebooks and journals, the ones they've kept locked away from the public for all these years."

Might be interesting. Joe took a sip and then wiped the froth off his upper lip. "What makes you think that having me along will make them change their minds?"

"I don't know that it will, but it's worth a chance. Besides, you can look kind of intimidating when you want to."

Joe chuckled. "Should I dress like a gangster or a lawyer?"

Cass smiled. "Is there a difference?"

Back inside the warm flat, Joe sat on the sofa in front of the heater, and searched for a seat on a plane—any plane—back to the states. Christmas was in a week. The only thing he could find was a first-class seat on Japan Air to San Francisco, leaving on December 20th. It was over two grand, but he booked it anyway.

A sense of relief washed over him.

Cass was reading and taking notes at her desk. Her eyes flashed black and darted from book to paper and back again. Her work had no doubt led her further into the secret world of Sylvia Plath and

Ted Hughes than she'd ever expected, deeper into their darkness than she had wanted to descend.

"I could use a nightcap," he said. "How about you?"

She continued to write, ignoring his question, so he approached her at the desk. She seemed to be writing lines of poetry while reading one of the books on Plath, but her penmanship was so scribbled that he couldn't make out the words.

Touching her shoulder, he asked again, "Want a nightcap?"

Cass flinched. "Oh, sure. I guess. There's a little sherry left."

"You were a million miles away, weren't you?"

"Guess I was. Sometimes I get so caught up in the work, I just space out."

He found the bottle of sherry and poured some into two wine glasses.

"Want it over there?"

She closed the notebook and turned off the lamp. "Let's sit by the heater. I'm a little cold."

Joe and Cass faced each other on the little sofa, and raised their glasses and toasted. The sherry burned Joe's throat going down, but then it warmed and relaxed him. The low light from the lamp behind Cass illuminated the edges of her hair and put her face in darkness. Only the orange glow from the heater underlit her features, so he couldn't read her expression. *Hope this sherry relaxes her. No drama tonight, please.*

"So what do you hope will happen tomorrow at the law offices?" he asked.

"They have at least one of Sylvia's journals locked up in a safe. They may have more—who knows? I mean, there might be dozens of notebooks. With Ted gone, I just don't see what good it could do to keep them locked away from the public."

"It has to be about money," Joe said. "There must be something in the notebooks that the lawyers feel will hurt the Hughes estate somehow."

"With their son Nicholas out of the way, only Frieda and Ted's widow, Carol, have any financial interest."

"What about Sylvia's relatives? Could they cause trouble for the Hughes descendants?"

"I don't see how," Cass said. She took a sip of the sweet red wine, swished it around in her mouth and then swallowed. "They've been cut out since the beginning."

"How'd that happen?"

"Sylvia left no will behind, so Ted got everything."

"Why didn't her mother step in?"

"She was in America. Ted was here, in London, and he was the children's father, so…" She stopped speaking and her eyes teared up.

"You really empathize with her, don't you?"

Even in the dreamy dim light, he could see her expression darken. She swirled the sherry in her glass before finishing it. "I feel like I've gotten inside her skin, inside her heart." She closed her eyes, whispering, "Inside her very soul."

Cass's low, husky voice raised goose bumps on Joe's arms. "Maybe…maybe you're too close. You've been at this nonstop for weeks."

She titled her head back and laughed bitterly. "*Weeks?* No, for months. Hell, it feels like years. It feels like all the years of my life, all my studies have led me here. Sometimes I feel as if…." She put the glass down on the floor and stared into the heater's orange glow.

"What?"

Cass leaned toward him, searching his eyes, for what, he wasn't sure.

"Do you believe in life after death, Joe?"

He would have laughed but for the seriousness of her tone. "I was raised Catholic, Cass, so I guess I do. I'm not very religious now. Haven't felt very connected to God since my parents…"

"Since your parents were killed," she stated flatly. "Lost your faith then, didn't you?"

He nodded. "I suppose so."

Cass grinned. It was an odd grin, as though she held a secret that was too important to share.

"Joe, you've gone up against killers. Nearly killed by the I-5 Strangler, you fought a hired mercenary and won, and other people have tried to kill you, too."

He chuckled, a little nervous. "When you put it all together like that, it seems so… unreal."

"Are you Superman?"

"What?" *Where's she going with this?*

"Do you have superhuman strength or supernatural abilities that the rest of us don't have?"

"Of course not."

"Then how is it you're still alive?"

Confused, he shook his head. "What are you getting at?"

"Your parents have been watching over you, Joe. Their spirits have influenced events in your favor."

He laughed again half-heartedly, but a chill crept up his spine. "I'd love to believe that, Cass, but—"

"How else can you explain your incredible good luck surviving those attacks? And your good fortune? Think about it. Of all the people in the world, why did *you* end up with the Shakespeare papers?"

He detected the jealousy in her voice. "Because Jack Claire sent them to me before he was murdered."

"Don't you sometimes feel them, Joe? I used to see my mother all the time, after she died. Daddy told me she was in heaven watching over me, but I'd been to church enough to know that your soul doesn't go to heaven if you commit suicide. I think a troubled soul has to redeem itself here on earth before it's able to be at peace. That's how I know Lydia's spirit was with me when I was younger and still needed her. Don't *you* feel your parents watching over you, too?"

He recalled vividly the cold, damp night when, wounded and bleeding, with the I-5 Strangler on top of him, he'd felt sure he was about to die. Had he felt his parents watching over him then? *No. A police detective saved me, not some guardian angel.*

"Honestly, Cass, I haven't felt their presence—not since they were buried."

She leaned closer still. "Sometimes I feel Sylvia's presence, Joe. I know she's with me." Cass held Joe's face between her hands. "I feel she's possessed me."

"Possessed?"

"It isn't a demonic possession," she whispered. "It's as if her spirit is inside me, using me, guiding me. There's unfinished business in her life, and she's chosen me—*me*—to help the world learn the truth."

Cass let go of his face and sat back. If she was smiling, it was a strange smile—one side of her face stretched into a weird, crooked grin. Or maybe it was just the odd way the shadows fell.

He finished his glass of sherry and shivered again, but it wasn't ghosts he feared. *Just how disturbed is she?* For the first time since he arrived, he was seriously worried about his friend.

CHAPTER 25

Cass could tell Joe didn't believe her. The way he looked at her, like she was crazy, helped her realize he had led a shallow existence. *Everything he's been through, so many brushes with death, and he's learned nothing. Nothing.*

The dead are all around us, Joe. You should know that better than most.

Part of her wanted to yell at him or slap him, to make him understand. But it would do no good. Instead, she'd show him concern. *Flattery and concern—that'll keep him on my side.*

"You look tired," she said. "I'd better let you get some rest. We've got a big day tomorrow, and I want my knight in shining armor to be well-rested."

She didn't even hug him good night, the way she had a couple of times before. *He had his chance to have me, but he blew it.*

She stood and said, "Good night, Joe."

He answered ever so sweetly, so politely, as though everything was fine, just fine, but he was afraid. *Of what? Of her?*

She went to the bathroom, dropped her pants and sat on the toilet. *Maybe he's worried about going to the lawyer's office. Maybe*

SCOTT EVANS

Joe Conrad isn't as brave as I thought he was.

When she'd finished, she washed her hands at the sink and looked at herself in the mirror. Sometimes she could almost see Sylvia's aura hovering around her, not a physical presence, nothing like she'd seen in movies, but like a vapor or a sheer veil enveloping her, like her silk robe. Then entering her, filling her emotions, taking control of her mind, working through her.

Even if Joe doesn't understand, I still need him. Now that the lawyer knows who he is, he'll take me more seriously.

Joe Conrad had become famous in England only a few years earlier. The events had been all over the news—the woman who fell to her death on the giant Ferris wheel on the River Thames, the damage to the statue of Shakespeare in Stratford-upon-Avon, and the arrest of a murderess fugitive.

With Joe Conrad standing beside me, I'll rattle that bastard's cage. Even if Joe is a reluctant protector, he'll make an impression on that slimy snake.

She went into her bedroom, turned on the bedside lamp, and closed the door. Stripping off her clothes, she kicked them into the corner with the other dirty laundry and began to dance—slowly at first, her arms stretched upward, her hips swaying back and forth. It felt good to dance—she heard the music playing in her mind and hummed Adele's song "Turning Tables" as she gyrated around her bed.

I'm going to turn the tables on you, you slimy bastards! All of you!

It wasn't just that smug attorney—it was all of them, everyone who'd doubted her, questioned her, betrayed her. Zenon, Diane and all of Trevor's other stuck up prep-school chums. The whole lot.

It was odd, though. Trevor's presence wasn't here. His spirit *must* be unable to rest—his death was too terrible—but even in Devon, she hadn't felt him.

SYLVIA'S SECRET

He must be hovering around Diane. I bet she feels his presence but doesn't even know how to recognize it.

That would explain why they'd tried to blame her. Trevor's presence was troubling Z and Diane, but they weren't in tune enough to understand how to deal with him.

She slowed her dance and watched her glowing body in the mirror on the back of her bedroom door. Her ribs were showing—she'd never been this thin—but she was filled with energy. And her breasts!

Have they gotten larger? Firmer? Or is it just that I've lost weight?

She smiled at her body in the mirror. What did it matter? She was glorious! *Poor Joe doesn't know what he's missing!*

His silly wife doesn't know what she's got. She should take better care of that man. I would never let him leave me like this to spend Christmas with another woman! What the hell is she thinking? And the kids! What's up with that? Leaving his kids behind?

She had an inkling then that Joe was more torn than he'd admitted. Part of him wanted her—badly. But he was so straight, sometimes ... so uptight.

He wants me. I know he wants me. I can almost sense his desire seeping under the door.

She opened the door ever so slowly. No lights were on and the hall was dark. *He must be asleep.*

Opening the door all the way, she stepped into the hall. It was only her now. Sylvia was gone—nearby, but not inside her or around her. She strode toward the sofa with confidence, knowing Joe was waiting for her. She would have to make the move.

I'll take matters in hand.

The heater's orange glow warmed the back of her legs as she stood over Joe. He was curled up under the afghan, breathing in the steady, heavy rhythm of sleep. She knelt down next to his peaceful face.

Are you dreaming about me, Joe? Dreaming of making love to me over and over again? We could make each other so happy!

She stroked his temple lightly, then pressed her lips against his forehead. He smelled good—his cologne mixed with the sweet sherry—and the salty flavor of his skin made her tingle. She could imagine him on top of her. Her hand slid under the blanket and found his thigh.

Still dressed? My God, why's he still dressed?

He squirmed, and his breathing changed.

Then without opening his eyes, he whispered a word, a name, but it wasn't hers, it was Sara's.

She pulled her hand away and leaned closer to his face, trying to hear his thoughts. He whimpered in his sleep.

Cass drew back, all the inner warmth draining from her body. Now the heater's glow against her bare back irritated her.

What a child he is. A silly, silly little boy who sleeps the night away instead of grabbing life by both hands. And dancing, dancing, dancing!

She stretched her arms to the ceiling, waved her hands in circles, as if summoning Sylvia's spirit again, and then spun away. Away from sleeping Joe Conrad, away from the little love seat that hadn't yet known love. She danced in circles around the desk. Like a belly dancer, she moved into the middle of the living room, dancing on the carpet in her bare feet, tilting up on the balls of her feet, spinning like a ballerina, turning and turning, her dizziness feeling wonderful, wonderful. Until suddenly it didn't.

Something stopped her. Some dark force placed a cold hand on her shoulder. She opened her eyes, expecting to see Joe standing in front of her, a bewildered look on his face, his normal, cold hands clutching her shoulders. Was it Death that had grabbed her instead?

Death took many forms. Sometimes it came like a tornado sweeping across the landscape, destroying everything in its path. Sometimes it was a tidal wave, a tsunami that washed over everyone, drowning them in waves of despair. But sometimes Death came as a man. A sick, crazed, desperate, foul man. She could almost smell his foul presence. Who was it?

Charles Manson? Jeffrey Dahmer? Ted Bundy?

Ted Hughes?

Is that you, Mister Hughes? I should have expected you to show up eventually. Is that your hand on my shoulder, Ted? Are you looking for Sylvia? Or have you come to stop me? You don't want the world to know the truth, do you, Ted? Are you still there?

Whatever cold, bony hand had clutched her bare shoulder, it had retreated as quickly as it had arrived. Knowing its name was enough to send it back to hell.

Exhaustion swept over Cass. She dropped her head and walked slowly to her room, closing the door to whatever evil force her sensations had aroused.

CHAPTER 26

After a fitful night's sleep, Joe awoke to bustling noises from the kitchen. He sat up to see Cass wearing a silky robe, her hair in rollers.

"Good," she said. "You're awake. Are you hungry?"

"No, not yet. Too early."

"Me neither," Cass said. "Feeling a little queasy, in fact."

"You're so nervous about this meeting, you're making yourself sick."

She waved her hand in the air, dismissing Joe's comment. "I've made you coffee and I've already gotten my shower, so…"

"So I should get a move on, is what you're saying."

"Well, yes, if you don't mind."

He stretched, glad that Cass's demons from the previous night disappeared with the daylight.

Joe showered, shaved, and dressed in record time, only to find himself standing at the mantle, waiting for Cass. He smiled, thinking about Sara. *What takes women so damn long to get ready?*

Dressed in a tailored light-gray suit, Cass clopped down the hall in high heels, spilling coffee from her cup.

"Christ, I wish I had a cigarette. By the way, Joe, do you have a tie?"

"Do I need one?"

"I want us to look like professionals when we go into that law office. Did you bring a tie or not?"

"Actually, I didn't."

Cass huffed. "Well, Harrod's is on the way."

"Fine. That will be my memento from the trip."

Cass fretted on the subway during the ride to the heart of London, brushing lint from her clothes repeatedly and checking her face in a makeup mirror half a dozen times. Instead of the purse she had carried on their previous trip, she held only a thin black briefcase, the kind that a laptop might fit into, its long leather strap draped over her shoulder. It was as if she were going to a job interview.

Joe patted her knee. "Relax. You look great."

They'd been lucky to find seats. The subway car was packed with men and women dressed in business clothes and a few holiday travelers—the business folks serious and preoccupied, and the folks on holiday laughing and distracted.

Joe was a man alone, in London neither on business nor on holiday, just a stranger on a strange mission, aiding a friend whose emotional well-being was in question. Cass's anxiety was infecting him too. If he or someone else said the wrong thing or made a wrong gesture, Cass might erupt in a violent outburst. He could only hope that whatever happened at the law offices would finally satisfy her so she could finish her research and publish her work.

She had a lot riding on this Fulbright. While a well-respected minor poet in her own right, she was hardly a scholar. If she didn't publish something significant—and soon—her chances of being granted tenure, at CLU or any other university, were very slim.

Joe had two books to his name—the story of being falsely accused of murder, and the collaboration with Drs. Smythe and

SYLVIA'S SECRET

Williamson on the Shakespeare manuscripts—as well as a few minor newspaper and journal articles. Yet he had not been granted tenure because, like Cass, he lacked a doctorate. Of course, in her case, her MFA was considered a terminal degree for poets, but without a scholarly work to her name, she was unlikely to get tenure.

For him, it didn't matter that much. Not really. Because of the Shakespeare manuscripts, he was financially independent now. The denial of tenure at CLU was insulting, but it wasn't the end of the world. Not the way it would be for Cass. Once you'd been denied tenure at one institution, it was almost impossible to earn it elsewhere. Cass had to be thinking about that, too, the pressure obvious. That helped explain some of her nervousness: a single woman alone in the world, trying to make it on her own. It made Joe think of his daughter Katie, and that he must always be there for her, no matter what happened with his marriage.

The train slowed at Kensington Station, and Cass pushed through the exiting crowd and scurried up the steps like a woman possessed. The clouds had moved on and the sky was clear, the air smelling fresh and clean as they hurried along the crowded sidewalk. Joe'd been to London before, but not this part of it, so all he could do was trust that Cass knew where she was going.

Soon they were outside Harrod's—an enormous building more like a palace than a department store. The eight or nine story structure seemed to take up an entire city block. Despite its brown facade, its windows decorated for Christmas with cheery red bows and green wreaths gave Joe a moment of joy.

"C'mon," Cass said, grabbing his sleeve. "I know right where the men's clothes are located. I bought a tie for Trevor here once."

They pushed between shoppers whose various perfumes and colognes filled the air.

"Jeez, Cass," he said. "Slow down."

They finally reached the men's section, and the ties lay

displayed across a large rectangular table. All were priced at around sixty pounds. A clerk who could have been Michael Caine's double stepped forward.

"May I help you?"

"You have any less expensive ties?"

The salesman smirked, but pointed to another display nearby before turning away.

The second table was cluttered with merchandise, and a SALE sign poked up from the middle of the pile. After digging through the stack, Joe grabbed a raspberry-colored one and held it up to his neck. "What do you think?"

Cass inspected it closely, and then nodded. "Very nice."

He put the tie on at the counter while paying for it and checked himself in the mirror. Turning to Cass, he said, "Satisfied?"

"You wouldn't want to trade in that ski jacket for a new overcoat, would you?"

"Uh, no." Joe tugged Cass's arm and they stepped away from the counter. He was getting claustrophobic and wanted to go. "I don't think the way we're dressed is going to make that much difference."

"You don't know these people," Cass said. "They're stuck on formality and protocol. You should have seen the way they looked at me—like I was some kind of insect."

"They have no reason to help you. I know something about lawyers, Cass. My sister-in-law is an attorney. They're only interested if they can make money off you."

"*That's* pretty cynical."

They'd reached the revolving door and stepped into a space together, rotating until they hit the chilly air.

"Which way?" Joe asked.

Cass pointed east, and they started walking side by side through

SYLVIA'S SECRET

the throngs of Christmas shoppers.

🕯 🕯 🕯

The law offices *were* intimidating—Joe had to admit. On the twentieth floor of a building several blocks from Harrod's, the spacious outer office was as silent as a tomb. Its dark wood-paneled walls and dark leather couches suggested centuries of tradition. The receptionist—dressed like an undertaker's daughter in a black suit and white blouse—watched them as if they were shoplifters as they walked from the elevator to her desk.

"Hello, Ms. Johnson," she said, expressionless. "Mr. Parker will see you shortly. *Please*, take a seat."

There was something about the woman's voice that grated on Joe. So damn condescending. Cass turned to sit down, but he lingered.

"Could we get some coffee?" he asked, still standing at the woman's desk.

"Coffee?" she asked, her voice going up an octave.

"Yes," he said. "Unless—," he turned to Cass, "unless you'd prefer tea. I know how fond you've become of these silly British customs."

The receptionist glared at him.

Cass eased into a chair, and fidgeted with the handle of her briefcase, trying to hide her nervousness. "No, coffee would be great." She put the briefcase on her lap and clutched it tightly.

Joe said to the receptionist, "Two cups, please—as long as it's fresh. I can't stomach old, stale stuff."

The lady glared at Joe, then pushed her chair back and stood. "Cream and sugar?" she growled.

"Do you have Equal? I really prefer Equal."

"I'll check. And for Ms. Johnson?"

"Cream and sugar, Cass, or just black?"

Cass smiled, her lips thin and tight. "Black is fine."

Joe grinned at the receptionist. "Got that?"

"I'll be just a moment." The woman stalked through a nearby door.

"Actually," Cass whispered, "if I drink any more coffee, I think I'll throw up."

"Then don't drink it," he whispered. "Tell her you don't like it. That it's stale and bitter, like her." Joe smiled. "The coffee isn't important anyway. It's about putting these people in their place and reminding them that they're no better than we are."

The woman came back carrying two expensive-looking teacups on saucers. "Mr. Parker will see you now."

Parker's office had a bank of windows on the right and bookshelves filled with law books on the left wall. It took a moment for Joe's eyes to adjust to the brightness of the room. A massive mahogany desk had two neat stacks of files on one side and a large, flat computer screen on the other. A tall, portly man with thick gray hair walked around his desk and held out his hand to Joe.

"We haven't met formally, Mr. Conrad, but I know who you are."

Joe eyes widened. "Oh?" He transferred the coffee cup from his right hand to his left and shook hands. "How do you know *me*?"

Parker's grip was like a vice. "Aren't you the brash American who knocked England's greatest writer off his pedestal? The man who caused a young Asian woman to fall to her death from the London Eye?"

Joe swallowed hard.

"Yes, indeed," Parker said, finally releasing Joe's hand. "You're rather famous, Mr. Conrad." He gestured to the chairs in front of his desk. "Please, have a seat."

Joe waited until Cass sank into her plush, leather chair before sitting. Parker reminded him of James Mason's character in *The Verdict*, the movie with Paul Newman playing the underdog. Unable to think of something to say, Joe took a sip from the China cup.

SYLVIA'S SECRET

"How's the coffee?" Parker asked.

"It has a stale bitterness the sweetener can't mask," Joe replied. He smiled at the older man, and then toward Cass. She looked nervous as hell—her eyes wide and her hands shaking.

"Shall we get down to brass tacks?" Parker asked. "I assume you're here once again to ask to see Plath's notebook, and if that's the case, then once again we have to decline your request."

"Why?" asked Cass, her voice breaking. "If I can just have an hour with that notebook, I'm sure it will answer all my questions."

"If it were up to me alone, Ms. Johnson, I'd be ever so happy to comply. But Mr. Hughes left very clear instructions that no one was to see the last notebook until well after his death."

"He died years ago," Cass whined. "What are you people hiding?"

"I can assure you, the directives my client left are in everyone's best interest."

Cass huffed. "I'm sure they're in Ted's interest, but I'm not so sure about Sylvia's."

Parker looked to something over their heads—at what exactly Joe wasn't sure. A row of law books on the top shelf?

"I know you imagine that the notebook contains some deep, dark secret. That it's filled with new, wondrous poems that will become masterpieces." He turned his gaze back to Cass. "Or that it reveals evidence that Ted murdered his wife and staged the whole affair, as you've intimated before."

Cass leaned forward with anticipation.

"Try to imagine just the opposite, Ms. Johnson."

"What…what do you mean?"

Joe studied Parker's face, which softened, along with his voice. Was he feigning it—this grandfatherly earnestness? *Lawyers know how to fake sincerity.*

"Without being specific, I can tell you that you'd be quite disappointed."

"How is that possible?" Cass asked.

"Don't you see, Ms. Johnson? Off the record, I'll tell you that Ted was trying to protect Sylvia's reputation as a poet. You may not quote me and I'll deny ever telling you this, but the stuff in that journal is...well, it's dreadful. Amateurish. Some of it is childish, the ravings of a jealous teenager who couldn't get her way. Releasing it would diminish Plath's reputation as a writer, not enhance it. That's why Ted made us keep it locked up. He wanted his wife's work to be respected."

"So he could make more money off it, I assume," Cass snarled.

"Indeed." Parker admitted. "I'm sure that was part of his reasoning. But I can assure you, he also cared about her."

"What about the journal Ted burned?" she asked. "I mean, he admitted to destroying one of her other notebooks. Why'd he do that, if it didn't contain something that incriminated him?"

Parker held up his hands. "When I asked Ted, he hinted that it contained disgusting, pornographic writings and drawings that he wouldn't allow his own mother to see, let alone Sylvia's mum. Or their children."

"I don't believe it."

"But as a Plath scholar, you *must* be aware of the many sexual innuendos and the sexual symbolism in some of her work. For God sake, how Freudian is that poem 'Daddy'? She talks about his *root!*"

Cass sank into her chair, and her cup tipped, almost spilling coffee onto her lap. Joe took Cass's cup and saucer and placed them on the edge of Parker's desk.

"What about the journal Cass found?" Joe asked. "I've read it. It's filled with good writing. Some of it in the form of poetry, some of it straight diary-style writing."

Parker gestured to the thin briefcase on Cass's lap. "Did you bring it?"

"Yes," admitted Cass. "I was hoping we could work out a deal.

SYLVIA'S SECRET

I could make copies of the journal you're holding and you could make copies of the one I found."

Parker shook his head. "That isn't possible. I can't show it to you yet. Because of the clause in Ted's will, I cannot share it with anyone for another twenty years."

"I don't see what difference it could make," Joe said.

"It would be a breach of legal ethics, Mr. Conrad. I don't expect someone like you to understand."

"What do you mean, someone like me?"

"Someone who profited from stolen property. Those Shakespeare manuscripts you received—they belong to England, not to you."

"The courts ruled differently. Besides, I've shared them with lots of places. Cambridge and Oxford, for example."

"For a price, Mr. Conrad. For a price."

"And I gave the bound copy of the *First Folio* to the Earl of Oxford's descendent, for free, I might add. It was worth a fortune."

"You did nothing more than return the *Folio* to its rightful owner. Now you're encouraging Ms. Johnson to follow your example and keep something that doesn't belong to her."

"Oh, please," Joe answered. But he could hear the anger in the lawyer's voice.

"If that journal really was written by Sylvia Plath, then it belongs to the Hughes estate, not to some fourth-rate *American* poet who only wishes she had half the talent Ms. Plath possessed."

Joe wanted to say, *finders, keepers, losers, weepers*, but instead, he asked, "Isn't possession ninety percent of the law, Mr. Parker?"

Cass screamed a piercing, shrill scream, like something out of a horror movie, startling both men. She jumped to her feet and slapped the porcelain cup off Parker's desk. It flew through the air, coffee splashing on everything in its wake. The cup broke against the bookcase, and pieces dropped to the dark red carpet. "SHOW ME THAT DAMN JOURNAL, YOU BASTARD!"

Joe's first instinct was to grab Cass, and hold her down. He was afraid she would climb across the desk and strangle Parker, who had pushed his chair back and leapt to his feet. Instead of grabbing Cass, though, he lightly touched her arm. She snarled before pulling away.

She yelled again at the solicitor. "I DON'T BELIEVE YOUR LIES!"

"That is quite enough!" Parker said, his face bright red. "Please escort this woman out of my office, Mr. Conrad, before I have you both arrested."

Joe grabbed Cass's wrist. "We need to leave. Right now!"

Cass tried to pull away, but he tightened his grip.

"LET GO OF ME!"

"No, Cass. You need to calm down."

She struggled, but instead of releasing her, Joe wrapped his arms around her and tried to stop her from squirming away.

Cass began to cry hysterically. "LET GO OF ME, LET GO OF ME!"

Holding her even closer, Joe whispered, "Shh. It's going to be alright. Shh." Her body went limp and she collapsed in his arms, tears spilling from her eyes.

Joe turned to Parker. "I'm sorry. I had no idea she was this… emotional."

"Just get her out," the old lawyer said, his voice trembling.

Cass struggled again to break free and Joe was tempted to let her go so she could pummel the old fart, but the door opened, and Parker's secretary rushed in with a security guard close behind.

Seeing the guard, Cass composed herself, and Joe released her. She picked up her briefcase and walked toward the door. The secretary stepped aside to let her pass.

"Your coffee tasted like piss," she told the woman. Then, holding her head up, Cass stomped out of the room.

Joe quickly followed, flashing an apologetic look at the security guard who seemed eager to have them both leave.

In the elevator going down, Joe started to relax. He glanced at Cass and gave her a nervous smile. "*That* could have gone better."

As if coming out of a trance, Cass shook her head. "I don't believe a word that bastard said. Not one word of that bullshit. I just know Sylvia's last notebook holds the truth about Ted murdering her. *That's* why that old bastard doesn't want anyone to see it."

"Maybe," Joe said softly. "Or maybe he was telling the truth. We need to consider that possibility."

"We need to break into that office."

"What?"

"You know how to do stuff like that, don't you, Joe?"

He laughed. "What makes you think I know how to burgle a lawyer's office?"

"You did all that stuff before, didn't you?"

He shook his head. "I never broke into any place."

Cass watched the numbers change above the door of the elevator. "You leave tomorrow, so we have to do it tonight."

"Are you insane?"

"We can do this, Joe. I know we can."

"No, Cass, I'm not breaking into Parker's office. We're lucky he didn't have us arrested. I don't want to spend Christmas in the Tower of London."

"We'll come back right after dinner when the building should still be open, but most of the people will be gone by then."

The elevator reached the ground floor and the doors opened. A gaggle of people were waiting to board, and Joe and Cass rushed through them.

On the sidewalk just outside, Joe stepped in front of her. "You aren't serious, Cass. You can't be."

"It won't be that hard. We need a big screwdriver and a hammer. I've got those at the flat. Maybe a pair of pliers, just to play it safe."

"Nothing about this half-baked plan is playing it safe."

"Don't tell me that Mighty Joe Conrad is afraid of a little breaking and entering, after all your previous run-ins with the criminal justice system."

Joe gestured toward the buildings across the street, saying, "Here I am in the heart of London. Can we just take a little break from all this drama and do some sightseeing?"

"Well, Joe," she asked sarcastically, "what would you like to see? The Tower of London? You know, just in case?"

He nodded, hoping she wouldn't suspect that it was a ploy to calm her down. "Actually, yeah. We aren't far from Parliament, are we?"

"Are you serious? We've got to plan this thing. No, there's too much to think about."

Mustering a sympathetic look, he put his hand on Cass's shoulder. "Maybe a walk and some fresh air will help us sort out our thoughts."

"You're just stalling, hoping I'll change my mind."

"Maybe I am, or maybe I'm trying to talk myself into helping you. Either way, if I get arrested, I'll hate myself for not taking an opportunity to see the sights before heading to the dungeon for a year."

Cass sighed. "Sure, Joe. We can do a little sightseeing." She craned her neck to get her bearings and then hooked Joe's arm and led him to the crosswalk.

They were ten blocks from Parliament, and as they strolled the streets, heavy, gray clouds lumbered across the sky, plunging them into shadow at times.

The government offices were closed, even to tourists, so Cass guided Joe toward the Thames. They stood at a retaining wall looking down at the river, at the dark, slow-moving water. The temperature near the water had plummeted and the air was frigid and stagnant.

"The river's usually so muddy," Cass said. "It's almost black now."

SYLVIA'S SECRET

Joe shivered. "That water must be freezing cold. I'd hate to fall in."

She stared, trance-like. "There'd be no getting out. You'd sink to the silty bottom like Ophelia and be dragged ever so slowly out to sea."

Cass's voice sent a chill down Joe's back again, and he vividly recalled splashing into the cold, dark water of Lost Slough the night he'd almost lost Sara.

"Feels like it might snow again," he said. "Let's get back."

Cass wore a strange smile Joe couldn't figure out. "We'll go back to my place and plan exactly how we'll get inside that damn lawyer's office, and then we'll come back downtown after dinner." Then she winked, saying, "C'mon, Joe. It'll be fun." With that, she turned and strode toward the subway station.

Unsure if he could find his way back to the flat without her, Joe had no choice but to tag along.

CHAPTER 27

Cass was unusually animated on the subway back to Fitzroy Road. Every few minutes, she leaned over and whispered in Joe's ear.

"We'll eat a late lunch so we can skip dinner to get back to Parker's office around six."

A few minutes later, she said, "I don't have a crowbar. We'll need a crowbar, don't you think?"

Joe didn't answer; she couldn't be serious.

"There's a hardware store near Regents Park. We can get one there."

By the time they reached Great Portland Street, the sky had clouded over and the air had cooled, and Cass strode down the sidewalk so fast Joe had to jog to keep up.

"Cass," he called, "slow down. I need a cup of coffee or a beer."

She ignored him at first, but when he stopped walking, she finally looked back.

"What's the matter?" she called to him.

"Can we go somewhere and talk about this, please?"

She grinned and nodded like a hyperactive poodle while Joe caught up. "Sure, sure. Plan it out. Good idea. Where should we go?"

"I like that pub we went to last night."

"The Princess of Wales? Sure, sure." She leaned closer and whispered in his ear, "Let's get a beer and plan the heist."

The main dining room was almost full, but there was a little table by the fireplace. Joe rushed to grab it before someone else got it—it was almost noon and the lunch crowd was coming in.

Cass followed and sat facing the fireplace. "Cozy. I feel like getting coffee, not a beer. What about you?"

Before he could answer, she added, "I wish it was warmer. We could sit in the little courtyard in back. We'd have more privacy." She pronounced "privacy" with a British accent and smiled at him as if it was some sort of inside joke.

Joe grabbed a menu. "I know you said we'd have a late lunch, but mind if I get something now? We didn't have much breakfast."

Cass waved her hand regally, as if granting a servant's wish. "Go ahead, if you must. I'm not in the least hungry."

A thin, young waitress with crooked yellow teeth came to their table. Smiling at Joe, she asked, "Take your order, dear?"

"Is the coffee fresh?" Cass asked.

She glanced at Cass as if insulted by the question. "It's fresh enough."

"If it's good and fresh, I'll have a cup, but if it's old and stale, then give me tea."

The waitress moved closer to Joe, and smiled. "And you, sir, what can I provide for you?"

Embarrassed by the waitress's obvious flirtation, Joe answered curtly: "The corned beef sandwich and a beer."

She took their menus and left. Outside, a few snowflakes were drifting down, landing on the roof of a black car parked nearby.

"She couldn't have been less subtle," Cass said. "Jeez, Joe, everywhere we go the waitresses come on to you."

Joe blushed. "That's not true."

"I don't know how Sara puts up with it."

"Let's change the subject."

"Yes. Back to the plan." Cass leaned across the little table. "I'll bet there's a safe in the wall behind Parker's desk. What do you think?"

Joe shrugged.

"I bet one of those rows of law books is fake. Anyway, we'll find it. Or maybe he keeps the notebook in his desk. What do you think?"

The waitress came back with a cup of coffee and a mug of beer. Joe waited until she'd left to speak.

"We need to think this through."

Ignoring him, Cass sipped her coffee, grimaced, and then added four cubes of sugar, stirring the swill so rapidly some of it spilled over the edge of the cup. The image reminded Joe of the expensive-looking porcelain cup breaking against the law books in Parker's office.

"If the notebook's in a safe, we won't be able to get at it," he said. "Not with a crowbar and a hammer."

Cass nodded, and then glanced around the room. "Right, right. We'll need a drill, won't we, with drill bits that can go through metal. The hardware store should have one, shouldn't they? I wonder if they have one of those big electric saws, you know, the kind the firemen use to cut people out of wrecked cars."

Cass's conversation turned Joe's stomach. He almost hoped someone else had heard her.

"Look, Cass," he whispered, "even if we could break into Parker's office and steal the notebook, who do you think the police will question first?"

She smiled. "Me, of course. But I'll just deny it, and without any proof, they can't do a thing."

SCOTT EVANS

"Then what good will having the notebook do you? You won't be able to admit you have it without giving the police the proof they'll need to arrest you."

"At least I'll know what's really in it, Joe. And in time, I can admit I have it. Once I'm back in the States."

"But then you'd be admitting your guilt."

She grinned and shook her head. "No, no. I'll say someone else stole the notebook, some burglar looking for money or something, and then heard that I was looking for it, so he found me and sold it to me. At worst, I'll be guilty of receiving stolen property. But by then, I will have made copies of the notebook and I can just give the original back to Parker. Don't you see, Joe? It's a win, win situation."

Joe took a long pull from his beer. The amount of thought Cass had already put into her plan surprised him. She must have been thinking about it for weeks.

"What if we get caught during the break in?"

She sat back, annoyed. "Well, then, at least we can say we tried."

The waitress arrived with Joe's plate. Beside the sandwich was a stack of chips—greasy pieces of fried potato. Cass reached over and grabbed one as the waitress was placing the food in front of Joe.

He picked up his sandwich and took a bite, self-conscious as Cass watched him chew with a disgusted look on her face. After swallowing, he washed the food down with a gulp of beer and then asked, "Is something wrong?"

"I thought you'd be more helpful, that's all. You've had all those amazing experiences with killers and cops and mercenaries. Even that arse Parker knows about your...adventures."

Joe shrugged. "Half the time, I didn't know any of those *adventures*, as you call them, were going to happen. I certainly didn't plan them."

"I thought you'd be braver, Joe, and more...heroic. But you're just a lame coward, aren't you?"

Anger rose in Joe's chest. "If not wanting to be arrested for breaking and entering makes me a coward, then, yes, I guess I'm a coward."

Cass pushed her chair back and stood. "I'm going to the bathroom. You won't be afraid, will you, if I leave you all by yourself?"

He shook his head, afraid that if he answered, he'd say something that would destroy any friendship that remained. Once Cass had gone, he drained his mug and motioned to the waitress for another.

Outside, the snow was falling steadily, a thin sheet of white covering everything in sight. It should have been a beautiful afternoon.

Joe had finished eating and had paid the bill by the time Cass came back. She scowled and remained quiet as they walked back toward the flat in the falling snow.

"Just a minute," Cass said. "I want to pick up a few tools."

They were in front of a small hardware store, and before Joe could stop her, Cass pushed inside. He followed reluctantly.

The store's four narrow aisles were crammed floor to ceiling with every tool, part, and piece of equipment imaginable. Two cash registers stood near the door, and only one was manned—by a heavy-set, dark-haired gentleman who looked to be in his mid-forties. He smiled at Joe and Cass, apparently happy to have any customers at all.

Cass grabbed a shopping basket and wandered up one aisle and down another, touching objects as she went. She lingered in front of a display of screwdrivers, grinning deviously at Joe. She picked out the largest flathead screwdriver hanging on the wall and stuck it in Joe's face. Then she dropped it into her basket. "In case my old one breaks. Now, for a good pair of pliers."

Joe worried that a security camera was recording their movements. None in sight.

Cass stopped in front of a rack displaying simple pliers, channel locks and clamp grip pliers. She grabbed the largest pair of adjustable clamp grips on the rack and held them up to Joe. "These look absolutely vicious, don't they? Should do the trick." She dropped the chrome tool into the basket and they made a sound like a single bell strike as they hit the metal end of the screwdriver.

Cass moved to another display. Several crowbars of various lengths lay on a table in front of her.

"What do you think? The longest one?"

"This is your show, Cass. You decide."

Fondling the longest crowbar while smiling at Joe, she shook her head. "No. This one will be too hard to hide. The shorter one, I think." She grabbed a black iron crowbar that was about a foot long and placed it in her shopping basket. "Now where are the saws?"

He followed her around a corner, glancing about to see if anyone was watching them. *Maybe this seems perfectly innocent.*

"Ah, here we go," Cass announced. She stood in front of a wall adorned by various types of saws hanging on brackets. She ran her fingers across the handles of several different hacksaws before choosing the sturdiest-looking one. "This should do nicely." She dropped that too into her basket. "What do you think, Joe? Should we get extra blades, just in case?"

"Whatever you say."

"Have you used hacksaws before? I mean, do the blades break easily? They look awfully thin."

Joe shrugged. "Depends how you use them. I doubt you'll be able to cut open a safe with a hacksaw, if *that's* what you were thinking."

"What tool would *you* use, then?"

SYLVIA'S SECRET

Joe couldn't help chuckling, but stopped himself when he saw the serious expression on Cass's face.

"This is crazy, Cass. You can't be serious."

"I thought I'd made myself clear. Now tell me, what tools will work?"

Joe shook his head and sighed. "Well, if we're to believe the movies, than you'll need a high-powered drill with drill bits that can cut into metal. I doubt they ever carry something like that here. You have to go to Burglars-R-Us, I think."

"Very funny. Let's just check."

The power tools were in the rear of the store. Cass's eyes went wide and she smiled like a child in a toy store. "Merry Christmas to *me*!" She hurried to a table cluttered with electric saws. Pointing to one, she glanced at Joe. "What kind of saw is this? It looks absolutely wicked!"

"That's a reciprocating saw, otherwise known as a saws-all."

"Looks like a little jackhammer with a saw blade."

"Essentially, yes," Joe answered. "Some folks say you could take down the Empire State Building with one of those."

Cass winked at him. "Or the Tower of London, maybe?" She checked the price tag. "Good, God. It's over two-hundred pounds!"

Joe nodded. "Power tools are expensive."

She turned toward the display of drills. "That one looks pretty powerful," she said, reaching toward the largest drill on the table.

With its distinctive yellow casing and black letters, Joe recognized it as a heavy-duty DeWalt. In addition to the pistol-grip handle, it had an additional handle on the side, reminding Joe of a type of machine gun used by the French resistance in older films.

"*This* is what we need." Cass held up the price tag. "Cricky, it's as expensive as the jackhammer saw."

Joe nodded. "But, remember, it won't do you any good if you don't have the right drill bits."

Under the table were gray-metal drawers. Cass pulled one open and found packages of drill bits. As she inspected one package after another, Joe again glanced around to see if they were being watched.

"Here we are," Cass said, holding up a long cardboard box. "For metal."

"Can you afford all this?" he asked. "You're going to spend almost four hundred pounds. What is that in American money, about six hundred dollars?"

Cass nodded. "It's worth it. Besides, tools last forever, right? These will be my Christmas presents to myself." On the shelf over the display table perched a large gray-plastic case that held a new DeWalt drill. "Will you grab that for me, Joe? I can't get it with this heavy basket in my other hand."

Joe hesitated—he didn't want his fingerprints on the handle of that plastic case or any of the other tools, either. But he caved and tugged the heavy case off the shelf.

"Now can we pay and get the hell out of here?"

Cass smirked. "Sure. If we can't retrieve Sylvia's notebook with all this equipment, then…"

"Then, what? You'll give up, right?"

Cass smiled. "No. I'll come back with dynamite."

By the time they got back to Cass's flat with all the tools, it was late afternoon. They set the packages down on the carpet under the coat stand and Joe took off his jacket and hung it up.

"I'll make some good strong coffee," Cass said. "We can organize the equipment and do some planning."

"Fine," he replied. He went into the bathroom and closed the door. For some reason, he felt compelled to wash his hands. Then he whispered to himself in the mirror, "What are you doing, Joe? Get the hell out of here."

Two cups with steam rising from them sat on the counter. Cass was spreading the tools in a row on the floor, starting with the smallest tool at one end and the heavy-duty drill at the other end. She'd added her old screwdriver and a ball-peen hammer.

She stepped over next to Joe, grabbed the two cups and handed one to him. After blowing on her coffee, she took a sip.

"What do you think? Do we have everything we'll need?"

Joe sipped his coffee to avoid answering.

"I think I can carry everything but the drill in my backpack. I think I have an old satchel in the closet that's big enough for the drill. Can you carry that?"

He shook his head slowly, worried about Cass's reaction. "I'm not going with you tonight, Cass. If you go to Parker's office, you're going alone."

"WHAT! I knew you weren't thrilled about the idea, but are you really going to abandon me now?" When he didn't answer, she added, "Just like Ted, leaving Sylvia to do the dirty work." Still he offered no reply. "That's fine. I'll wait a few days. You can go back to your safe little wife and kids."

"Cass, I hope you'll reconsider your plan. I'd hate to hear about you being arrested. And you'll lose your job at CLU if you get caught. You know that, don't you?"

"It's worth it. If I get my hands on that notebook, I'll be in a position to negotiate a better position at most any university."

"Are you sure about that, Cass?"

"Yes. I'll be like you were a few years ago when you had all those Shakespeare manuscripts. You could have gone anywhere, to any big name university, but you chose to stick around that little hellhole of a school."

"I thought you liked it there."

She shrugged. "It's a stepping stone, Joe. I'm moving on once I publish this book. Getting that notebook will be a coup."

"I didn't know you were that ambitious."

"There's a lot about me you don't know."

He nodded. "Yeah, I'm beginning to realize that."

"So fly back to your safe little life, Joe, and I'll get on with my career. I don't plan to stay in Stucktown my whole life."

With that, she stomped down the hall to her bedroom and slammed the door.

Joe ambled to the window and watched the snow scatter over the road. Night had fallen and the street lights had come on. The sidewalks and cars by the curb were already covered. Only the occasional car driving down the lane kept the snow from completely obscuring the pavement.

Stucktown. That was a nickname the students at CLU had given Stockton. Maybe Cass was right. *Forbes* had described Stockton as one of America's most miserable cities. Maybe he should move on, too. They didn't want him at CLU—hadn't given him tenure. And he really didn't need the money.

But he liked teaching. He enjoyed working with the students, especially when they got something he was trying to teach them—really got it. There was something so rewarding about knowing you had passed on a piece of knowledge or wisdom that would be a part of a person's intellect for the rest of their life.

He didn't have to make a decision now. He'd have the spring and summer to think about his career. The first priority when he got home would be to repair his marriage. He still loved Sara, but he'd have to work through forgiving her. It would be easy to hold her cheating over her and browbeat her into being some kind of Stepford wife. But that's not what he wanted either. He wanted her to be the strong, bright, independent woman she'd always been, in love with him the way she had been when they first met. Somehow, they'd have to get back to that kind of love.

Besides, there was no way he'd leave Katie and Brian. Even if he didn't love Sara, it would be important to try to make the marriage work for their sakes. Thinking about everything made him long to fly home. For a moment, he considered packing up right away and getting a taxi to Heathrow. His flight wasn't until tomorrow afternoon, but maybe he could get an earlier flight if he was actually at the airport. And spending another night with Cass with the way she was behaving now would be miserable.

He would wait a little while to see how she acted once she came out of the bedroom. Her mood swings were so dramatic now there was a good chance she'd be back to her old, pleasant self and they could have one last night together. His relationship with Cass wasn't nearly as important as his relationship with Sara—not even close—but it was still worth fighting for. He'd rather leave tomorrow on good terms. And maybe he could talk some sense into her, if she really was serious about stealing the Plath notebook.

Joe walked to the heater and kicked off his shoes. He curled up on the small sofa, pulling the afghan over him and, resting against a pillow, began to read. He read for several hours, expecting Cass to come out of her room and join him. Maybe offer to cook dinner. He wasn't the least bit hungry, but he thought she might use the opportunity of a home-cooked meal to try to persuade him to help her.

Cass's coffee hadn't worked. He was tired. Cass's antics had exhausted him emotionally. The sandwich and the two pints of beer had made him drowsy as well. Besides, by this time tomorrow, he'd be on a plane flying back to California, back to his wife and children. *And, yes, Cass, back to my safe little life.*

CHAPTER 28

In her room, Cass paced the floor. *What a coward Joe Conrad has turned out to be!* It was all going to hell. She needed that last notebook! It was absolutely crucial that she have it! How could she convince Joe to help her? Maybe if she had seduced him back in Devon, he'd be more willing, more loyal.

Should I sleep with him now? He's leaving tomorrow. This is my only chance. Maybe if I let him sleep with me, he'll help me.

She went to her nightstand and found a stray cigarette and the matches. Lighting up, she inhaled deeply, filling her lungs with smoke. Something about smoking aroused her. She could do it. She'd undress—take everything off except her blouse and panties. Then she'd go to the bathroom, douse herself with perfume, paint her lips and put on eye shadow. Joe Conrad wouldn't know what hit him. She could be a lioness in bed—he wouldn't stand a chance.

Give him a few minutes to calm down. Then go out and tear his clothes off.

When she finished her cigarette, she crushed it out in the ashtray by her bed and undressed. She took everything off except her panties, and then, with her bra removed, put her blouse back on without buttoning it. She wanted Joe to have easy access.

She opened the door a crack and peeked down the hall, unable to see Joe. She tiptoed to the bathroom and quietly closed the door. First the lipstick—a bright red glossy shade that she wore when she went out to clubs. Next, eyeliner and pink eye shadow. Then she sprayed perfume into her hair, on both sides of her neck, on both breasts and into her panties. All of these little rituals excited her. It would be so good to feel a man again. It had been weeks since she and Trevor had made love. Thinking about it made her tingle.

I wonder what kind of lover Joe will be.

She hoped he'd be generous. Either way, she'd have him. Once a man made love to a woman, he was obligated. He'd want to please her, especially if he wanted to come back for more.

As she had the previous night, Cass opened the bathroom door slowly and peered out. She padded down the hall and peeked around the corner to the kitchen. The smell of burned coffee filled her nostrils.

Shit! I forgot about the coffee!

The little gas flame was still hissing under the pot, but the coffee must have all but evaporated. She turned off the gas and, grinning expectantly, tiptoed to the couch. There he was, curled up under the afghan, asleep again.

Then she felt it, the cold presence of Death. It was in the room now, but how? When they had opened the window to air out the flat, had it crept in then? Studying Joe's face, she saw the transformation—oh so subtle but unmistakable. Ted.

Just as Sylvia sometimes possessed her, Ted now infected Joe Conrad. She should have seen it coming. Joe was a ladies' man, just like Ted Hughes. Women threw themselves at him, ordinary women, perfect strangers—waitresses, even Trevor's old lover Diane!

And hadn't *she* thrown herself at him, too?

It was like a disease, this power Ted had over women. And now it had found a receptive soul to possess in Joe. If he had been a stronger soul, Ted wouldn't have been able to infect him. But Joe, the Coward, had appeal, and women had died in his wake.

Sure, the I-5 Strangler was the killer of those women six years ago, but what about Autumn Smith? Poor, beautiful Autumn. Had it not been for Joe Conrad, Autumn would never have been targeted by that madman.

How could I have ever sympathized with him, when all those women died?

Dead Ted must stay dead.

This will not do, it will not do, black shoe!

Cass knew what she must do—summon Sylvia and the strength to do what she should do.

Rhymes. Rhymes are chants, and chants are rituals
That bridge this realm to the other,
The realm of my mother.

Clutching her blouse and buttoning it, Cass stared at the ceiling, as if some invisible thing had entered.

"Sylvia?"

Her whispered voice did not disturb the lump of demon-possessed clay curled up at her knees. Turning her back to it, she stared at the strange, false fire at her feet. It was too hot. *She* was too hot. Her skin sizzled. The weird orange glow of the fake birch logs inspired her, infected her, infused her mind with the entity she'd come to know, giving it voice.

Sylvia's voice leaves no choice,
Her rhymes fill my mind.

She shut her eyes and reveled in the feeling of Sylvia's spirit inhabiting her, an empty carafe, and Sylvia, the warm, blood-red wine....

SCOTT EVANS

Rhymes are chants, and chants are rituals
That bridge this realm to the other
The realm of my poor, dead mother
And the other, the poet who dwells
Between two hells,
This hell of men, men, men
Who pry and spy and lie and die,
Who lay and betray and never stay.

Cass bent down and turned off the heater. Then she wandered to the window in a trance. Snow fell heavily and had darkened the fading day. Knowing night was inevitable, Cass drew the curtains closed, sat at her desk, turned on the lamp, and opened her notebook.

Sylvia was inside her now, possessing her, guiding her to write one final poem. *The snow. The falling snow. Little pieces of death.*

She picked up a pen and wrote furiously, knowing it would be the last time Sylvia guided her hand.

Snowflakes fall like ash from Auschwitz ovens
Covering all with gray-white death.
Spirits fall from a witch's coven
Filling my soul with white-hot dread
It is the season, it is the season,
But there is no savior, no redeemer,
Only the ash and the Mein Kampf moustache
And the hard, black boots
Stomping, stomping, stomping
On my pretty, black heart...

She continued to write for an hour, until suddenly it stopped. Whatever force had gripped her hand was gone. It had evaporated like cooked coffee left on too long.

She knew what she had to do.

SYLVIA'S SECRET

When she turned off the lamp, the rooms were almost pitch black. But she knew her way in the dark, back to her room for the comforter and pillow. She clutched the pillow like a baby and dragged the comforter down the hall to the kitchen, arranging a nice little bed on the floor in front of the oven door.

Before turning on the gas, she opened the door, leaned in, pursed her lips and blew out the pilot light. Then she turned on the gas as high as it would go, the little whisper saying, *shhhh*.

Now it was time to sleep. Cass wrapped herself in the comforter and curled up, her head resting comfortably on the cool pillow. The smells that filled her nostrils made her smile—the old coffee, the new gas, and her own perfume.

Soon, Sylvia, soon, we'll be with you.

CHAPTER 29

From darkness Cassandra's face emerged, as large as a swelling balloon, a weird smile and crazed eyes glowing like flames as the face metamorphosed into Sylvia Plath, smiling, then crying, then changing into Sara, but Sara's face was cold, stoic, the eyes dull and flat, the mouth closed, neither smiling, nor frowning. Yet her voice echoed from some distant place behind her head, as if her living soul was somewhere behind her, but floating closer, and he knew that once Sara's soul re-entered the shell of her body, she'd be whole again, whole and alive. Now her voice was near, and it was saying his name over and over again in the darkness, but Sara's face remained as still as stone. But her voice—her weird, panicked voice was smothering him...

"Joe? Wake up, Joe. Can you hear me? Joe?"

He opened his eyes slowly, his body tingling all over, his vision blurry. He couldn't move and it felt as if his chest had been crushed, or he was under water.

"Joseph Lawrence Conrad, wake up right now!"

Joe's eyes were open, but still his vision was fuzzy and he couldn't breathe. His legs and arms were numb, or asleep. Waking up was too hard, too painful. He just wanted to go back to sleep.

"Damn it, Joe! Open your eyes!"

He forced his eyes open. The face hovering over his was Sara's. The voice was Sara's, too. *But how is that possible?*

"Sit up, Joe. Can you sit up?"

The woman who looked like Sara pulled him into a sitting position. His body still tingled and his chest still felt compressed, like a bag of cement sat atop of it.

"Where, where am I?"

"You're in Cassandra Johnson's apartment, remember? In London."

He shook his head. "Sara? You aren't here, are you?"

"Yes, I'm here. I came to London to get you."

The heater was off. Joe rubbed his face and looked around. Cass's flat was cold. The window was open, the drapes pulled back.

"Why is it so cold in here?"

"We had to open the window, Joe, to let the gas out."

"Gas?" He tried to stand, but his legs buckled and he dropped back down. "What happened?"

"When I got here, I could smell the gas, so I ran to the neighbor's and we broke Cass's door down. We found her on the floor in the kitchen, dragged her into the hallway, and then I came back and found you. The neighbor turned off the gas and opened the window."

The *wee-woo wee-woo* of a siren grew louder and then stopped on the street below.

"Wait. How did the gas get turned on in the first place? I don't understand."

"It looks like Cassandra was trying to kill herself, and she didn't mind taking you with her."

His vision finally cleared and he could see that it really was

Sara on the couch beside him.

"You're here?"

"Yes, I'm here."

"You came to London?"

She smiled. "Yes, I came to bring you home."

Joe shook his head in disbelief. "How did you know where to find me?"

"I called the English Department. The secretary gave me Cass's address."

"Molly?" Joe shook his head again, saying, "I swear, that woman knows everything about everybody."

"She's very concerned about you. She told me she didn't agree with the tenure committee's decision."

Joe chuckled. "I wish she'd had a vote."

His mind was still fuzzy. "What time is it anyway?"

"A little after midnight."

He stared at Sara in disbelief. "How'd you get from the airport?"

"I rented a car. It has GPS."

"You *drove*? In *England*? At *night*? On the wrong side of the road?" He rubbed his face once more. "Am I dreaming this?"

Sara smiled and kissed his cheek. "No, you're not dreaming."

He threw his arms around her and kissed her hard on the lips. "I'm so happy you're here. You came for me, Sara. You *do* still love me, then, right?"

She laughed and nodded. "Yes, Joe. I still love you. And I want you to come home so we can be a family again."

"Wait. Where are the kids?"

"I left them with my sister."

"Oh, great. She'll probably blame me for *this*, too."

"No. She was the one who told me I should come here and get you. She said I should crawl on my hands and knees, if that's what it takes to bring you home."

"*That* doesn't sound like Suzy."

Sara put her arm around Joe's shoulders and kissed his cheek. "Well, maybe I made up that last part, but it's how I feel."

"Is Cass alright?"

"I don't know. She looked pretty bad when we dragged her out."

Joe tried to get to his feet again, and this time with some effort and help from Sara, he was able to stand. But he wobbled, drunklike. Sara helped him walk around the sofa toward the front door. The door was hanging at a slant, its top hinge jangling.

Cassandra's body was already on the stretcher, an oxygen mask on her face and a medic in white pumping her chest.

The other medic rushed over and placed a stethoscope to Joe's chest, and fingers to his wrist.

"How do you feel, sir? Do you know where you are and who you're with?"

Joe nodded and smiled at Sara. "Yes, I know I'm in London at my friend's apartment with my wife Sara."

"Follow my finger," the medic instructed. He watched Joe's eyes as he moved his index finger back and forth in front of Joe's face. "You seem alright, but I want you to follow us to hospital and get checked out, okay?"

Sara nodded, saying, "We'll be right along."

The medic stepped back to the stretcher and joined his partner. They wheeled Cass down the hall to the elevator while Joe, still woozy, watched from the broken door. The neighbor he recognized from the next apartment came over.

"How's he doing?" he asked Sara.

"Better," she answered, tightening her grip around his waist.

"You're a lucky chap, aren't you? Your wife showed up just in the nick of time, didn't she?"

Joe nodded and looked into Sara's tear-filled eyes. "Yes, I guess I *am* lucky. You saved my life, Sara."

She smiled up at him and nodded. "Now we're even."

SYLVIA'S SECRET

He kissed her then, a full and deep kiss filled with longing, and her body trembled.

"Why are you shivering, Sara?"

"I don't know exactly. I've been so worried, so frightened that I'd lose you. Now I'm just glad you're holding me."

Joe tried to smile, but grew dizzy again and swayed to one side. Sara held him steady.

"We'd better get you to hospital," the neighbor said. "Let me throw on some clothes and I'll drive you there."

"Thank you," Joe said. "Thank you very much."

A plastic mask on his face, breathing pure oxygen, Joe sat on a narrow bed in the Emergency Room while a dark young doctor named Fahad Hayat examined him. Sara was standing behind the man, biting her lip.

"How do you pronounce your last name?" Joe asked, trying to show he was okay.

"Hi-yat. Like the hotel."

The doctor thumped Joe's chest while listening through a stethoscope and then pulled the earpieces from his ear.

"You appear to be fine, but I want you to stay on the oxygen for another hour or so before I release you."

Joe lifted the mask off his mouth. "How's my friend Cass?"

The doctor frowned. "Not so good as you, I'm afraid. The next few hours will tell the story."

"Can I see her?"

Dr. Hayat shook his head. "No, I'm afraid not. The police have arrived. They want to question the two of you separately."

"*Why?*" Sara whined. "My husband did nothing wrong. If anything, he's the victim here."

"So it would seem," said the doctor. "But the police, they have their own procedures. We are obliged to follow their orders."

"It's okay, Sara. We've been through this before. Let them investigate."

An attractive, if somewhat plump, red-headed nurse pushed through the white curtains. She smiled broadly and carried a plastic tray with a small plastic pitcher and a paper cup on it.

"This is Deb Rose, everyone's favorite nurse," the doctor said. "She'll take good care of you."

With that, Dr. Hayat turned and left.

Nurse Rose set the tray down on the nightstand and grabbed Joe's wrist firmly. In a Scottish accent, she asked, "How are we feeling, Mr. Conrad?"

"Much better, Nurse. How are you?"

Silent while counting Joe's heartbeats, the nurse nodded. Her smile and outgoing manner put Joe at ease.

She released Joe's wrist and patted his forearm. "You seem like a healthy young lad. Your color's coming back." She turned to Sara. "And married to this lovely young lass, too. Tell me, do you have children?"

Sara nodded. "Two. A boy and a girl."

"Lovely, lovely," Nurse Rose repeated. "You have everything in the world to live for, then, don't you?"

"Hey," Joe said, "it wasn't my idea to turn on the gas."

She poured water into the small cup and handed it to him while flashing a sympathetic smile. "Drink up, please. You'll drink lots of fluids for me over the next few days, won't you?"

Holding the plastic mask away from his mouth again, he said, "Yes, just for you, Nurse Rose."

She grinned. "There's a good lad. The fluids will flush the poisons from your system." Turning to Sara, she said, "You'll see to it, won't you?"

"Yes, of course."

"Do you need anything else, then, Mr. Conrad? Another blanket?"

SYLVIA'S SECRET

"I'm fine, but can you tell me how Cassandra Johnson is doing?"

Her face tensed slightly, but she maintained her cheerful smile. "She's in good hands. The doctors are doing what they can." The nurse positioned Joe's oxygen mask back over his mouth and nose. "I shouldn't worry about her right now. Your job, young man, is to get well for your lovely wife and beautiful children." Looking back at Sara, she added, "Isn't that right, dear?"

Sara nodded bravely, but then her face crumbled. "It's all my fault," she blurted. Then she burst into tears, collapsing into the nurse's arms.

"There, there, lass. Let it out."

Nurse Rose held Sara while she cried and cried, and Joe felt helpless. He took a deep breath of the oxygen, held it in his lungs and then exhaled. The nurse seemed so caring and compassionate that, for the first time in years, he missed his mother. *Thirty-three years old and I want to be cradled in my mom's arms like a baby. Come on, Joe, grow up.*

He was almost asleep half an hour later when two police investigators, dressed in dark gray suits, came into the room. Both were clean-shaven, tall and fit, though one looked a few years older. They might have been brothers. Short dark hair parted on the left, bushy eyebrows, and thin lips. Neither man smiled.

One handed Joe a business card, saying, "I'm Detective Russell and this is Detective Golding. We need to ask you a few questions about tonight's events."

Joe raised the bed and tried to wake up.

"Should I leave?" asked Sara.

The younger detective named Golding shook his head. "You were the one who found them, weren't you?"

"Yes. Along with one of the neighbors."

"We've already questioned him at the scene," said Detective

Russell, "so we have his statement. Now we just need to dot the *i*'s, as it were."

The man named Golding asked, "What's the first thing you recall about the incident?"

Joe smiled at Sara. "My lovely wife shaking me awake."

"How did the evening begin?" asked the other detective.

"Well, Cass was upset because...."

"Go on, Mr. Conrad," Golding instructed.

"Look," said Joe, "she's been doing research on Sylvia Plath, the American poet who was married to Ted Hughes. Do you know who I'm talking about?"

Golding grinned. "Of course. Mr. Hughes was England's Poet Laureate."

"Well Cass was obsessed with the idea of reading one of the journals Plath left behind, but the attorneys for the Hughes estate wouldn't let her. We'd had a meeting with a lawyer earlier today. Or was that yesterday?"

"Go on," instructed the older detective.

"Anyway, Cass had this hair-brained scheme to break into the lawyer's office and somehow steal the journal. I told her she was crazy and I wouldn't go along with it."

Golding was typing notes on a Blackberry. "How'd she react to your telling her that?"

"She was angry. She said a few nasty things—I can't recall exactly what—and then stormed into her bedroom."

"And what did you do next?" Detective Russell asked.

"Me? I went to the couch and lay down. I was exhausted. Being around Cass the past few days has been...stressful, to say the least."

Detective Russell put his strong hand on Joe's shoulder and gripped it tightly, saying, "I'm going to ask you something now that will be difficult to answer in front of your wife, but we need the absolute truth. Understand?"

Joe's heart bounced inside his chest and he swallowed,

wondering what they were about to ask.

"Were you and Miss Johnson having an affair?"

Sara glanced away.

"No, absolutely not."

"That's not exactly how Miss Johnson answered," Golding said.

Joe laughed. "What? Well, then, she's lying. If she said we were sleeping together, she's lying."

"Didn't the two of you share a hotel room in Devon?" It was Russell.

The blood drained from Joe's face. "Yes, but we did *not* share a bed. The room had two beds." A tear rolled down Sara's cheek. "I'm telling you the truth. We're friends, colleagues. I came here to help her, but we are not romantically or sexually involved."

"She tells it a little differently," Golding said. "Says she climbed into bed with you."

Joe slumped back against the pillow and closed his eyes. "Yes, that's true. One night she *did* climb into my bed, but I was already asleep. She was drunk. Once I woke up and realized what was happening, I stopped her and made her go back to her own bed."

Detective Russell drew his hand away and chuckled. "You had an attractive woman in your bed and you *didn't* have sex with her?"

"You're a stronger man than I," said Golding. "You were never tempted?"

"Of course, I was tempted. Cass is an attractive woman. But she's troubled—I could see that shortly after I got here. And, besides, I'm married."

Russell scratched his head. "You've been with this woman almost a week, and the two of you never once had intercourse. That's hard to believe."

"Should I step out?" Sara asked again, her voice cracking.

Golding turned to her. "Would your husband's answers be different if you left?"

"NO!" Joe said. "Sara, I'm telling the truth and you've got to believe me."

The two detectives exchanged glances, then Golding turned off his Blackberry and slipped it into his coat pocket.

"Actually, Mr. Conrad, that's precisely what Miss Johnson told us. Said you were a perfect gentleman."

Detective Golding patted Sara's shoulder. "You've got a keeper there, Mrs. Conrad."

The other man stepped away from Joe's bed and spoke to Sara. "Miss Johnson said she goaded him quite a lot and teased him badly, but your husband held his ground."

Sara smiled and wiped the tears from her eyes.

"Sorry to put you through it like that," Golding said, "but we thought it might be wiser for you to hear everything yourself, in case you had any questions about what happened."

"How is she?" Joe asked. "Miss Johnson, is she doing okay?"

"I'm not a doctor, of course," said Russell, "but I think she's doing a little better than she was when they first brought her in."

"Right," Golding added. "The doctor refused to let us question her initially, but then he found us a little while ago and said it'd be alright."

"She's resting fairly comfortably now," the other detective said, "which is what the both of you can do once we've gone."

After Golding gave Joe a reassuring nod, the two detectives left.

Sara bent down next to Joe, and he held her as well as he could in the awkward bed. Her body was familiar and yet somehow foreign, as if she'd lost weight or grown smaller. Had it really only been a week since they'd been apart? It felt like a year.

SYLVIA'S SECRET

CHAPTER 30

Joe awoke in the morning to Nurse Rose touching the IV needle in his hand. He squirmed and sat up. "Have you been here all night?"

"Yes, dear. Working a double."

"I don't see how you can possibly still be awake."

"Oh, I managed a short break and a quick nap about an hour ago, before morning rounds. One gets used to the hours."

Sara, asleep in the easy chair beside his bed, woke with a startled look on her face. "Where am I?"

Joe smiled. "You're where you should be, in London with me."

She threw off a blanket and looked around the room. "I thought this was all a dream...a nightmare."

The nurse checked Joe's pulse, and Sara stretched and stood up. "Good morning, dear. How'd you sleep?"

"Don't ask. Groggy and stiff." She eyed the cup on Joe's breakfast tray. "Is that coffee?"

"Cold tea," answered Joe. "Help yourself. It was almost as bad as the rubbery eggs and bland yogurt."

Nurse Rose dropped Joe's wrist and patted him on the arm. "Well, we don't want our patients to get too comfortable here, do we?"

"Any news about my friend, Cassandra Johnson?" Joe asked.

"Greatly improved. At least physically. She'll be examined by Dr. Aimes later this morning."

"Dr. Aimes?"

Nurse Rose held a thermometer to Joe's ear. "The resident psychiatrist," she whispered.

"Oh," he said. "May I see her?"

"No, dear. Not for a few days. She'll need considerable care, I should think."

Joe nodded and ran the situation through his mind. As pleased as he was that Sara had come to London, he felt guilty about Cass, as if he'd let her down or failed her.

"I should have seen it coming."

The nurse wrote numbers on Joe's chart and said, "We can't possibly know what's in another person's heart, can we."

Joe shook his head. "Still, I should have known she'd try to, to…follow in Plath's footsteps." He hoped Sara could help lift the weight he was under.

"Where can I get some hot coffee?" Sara asked.

"There's a vending machine down the hall that puts out something akin to coffee, I'm told, or you can go downstairs to the cafeteria." The nurse pushed the papers in front of Joe and held out a pen. "Or you can wait a few minutes and hit the Starbucks on the corner after he's discharged."

Sara and Joe said in unison, "Starbucks."

With fresh coffee in their hands, they took a cab back to Cass's flat on Fitzroy. The sky had cleared and most of the snow had melted, leaving the streets and sidewalks wet. The door to Cass's apartment had been repaired, so they had to knock on the manager's door to be let in. He scowled and didn't ask how his tenant was doing.

"Let Miss Johnson know she'll be billed for the repairs," he said, letting them into her apartment.

Joe took the key from the man. "That's the least of her worries right now."

The little man left, and Joe and Sara stood together in the middle of Cass's living room. Some of Cass's papers had blown off her desk when the window had been opened and were strewn across the floor. With daylight streaming in through the open curtains, the dust on the furniture showed all the more.

"This place is filthy, Joe. I'm surprised you stayed here—you're such a neat freak."

He shrugged. "My mind was on other things, like whether or not I'd have a wife to go home to."

She put her hand on his shoulder. "I know. I'm sorry."

He grabbed her in his arms and kissed her, feeling her body relax in his grip. She returned his kiss with equal passion, and for a few seconds, he felt that everything would be alright. When he opened his eyes, tears were streaming down Sara's cheeks.

"I'm so sorry, Joe. I, I feel so ashamed."

He shook his head. "We've both done things we shouldn't have. One thing I've learned here is that people who love each other have to learn to forgive each other. If there's real love, there's got to be forgiveness. Without forgiveness, we die."

"Is our love real?"

"Mine is. You're the mother of my children. Whether or not your love for me is real, only you know that."

Sara continued to cry. "All I know is that I can't imagine my life without you in it. Having you gone, not knowing where you were—it felt like someone had cut out my heart. I just hurt so badly."

He held her head to his chest and closed his eyes, remembering how she had looked on their wedding day. Though her mother had begged her to wear a traditional white dress, she'd chosen a somewhat revealing off-white gown, saying, "I'm not going to be a hypocrite, Mother. I'm certainly no virgin!" He'd laughed out loud in the store, despite her mother's chagrined expression.

At the altar just before the priest began the ceremony, he had leaned over and whispered, "You're the sexiest math teacher I've ever seen." The flirtatious way she'd smiled up at him that morning had always been one of his favorite memories.

Sara stood on her toes and whispered, "I want to make love to you, Joe, but not here. Not now."

He pulled away and smiled. "I understand completely. This place is..."

"It's a pig sty."

"Yes, but it's also, I don't know, haunted somehow."

Sara shivered. "You're giving me the creeps."

Joe glanced around the room. "I've got to cancel my flight and book our return trip for the day after tomorrow, right?"

Sara nodded. "If we want to be back in time for Christmas, then we must leave then."

"Then I want to go through Cass's research. Maybe there's a clue as to why she wanted to end her life."

"And yours, don't forget."

"I don't think she cared whether or not I was here. I was... incidental."

"Well, while you're doing that, do you think it would be okay if I cleaned up the kitchen? Cass wouldn't be angry if I cleaned up a little, would she?"

He shrugged. "Honestly, I don't know. In the last few days, she was so unpredictable. I didn't know what to say or how to act."

Sara stepped away, put her hands on her hips and scanned the room. "Well, I'm here to fix things, and right now it seems like the best way I can help is by tidying up this filthy place. That way, when

Cass comes back, she'll have a nice, clean apartment to recover in."

With that, Sara marched into the kitchen and began clearing the counters. Joe turned on Cass's laptop and waited for all the programs to boot up. He made the internet connection and miraculously booked their flights back to Sacramento. Only a few days earlier, he'd found it nearly impossible to find a flight. Was a higher power at work? They'd arrive on Christmas Eve.

Then he scooped up the papers from the floor and returned them to Cass's desk. After turning on the lamp, he was caught by a red-highlighted line in one of her books.

"Oh my God," he said.

"Find something interesting?"

"Yes. I just read a line from *The Unabridged Journals of Sylvia Plath.* Listen to this: 'Ted dreams about killing animals: bears, donkeys, kittens. Me or the baby?' Plath wrote that on November 1, 1959. Jesus, that was years before she died, and she already suspected that Ted wanted to kill her."

"Wait," Sara said. "I thought Plath committed suicide."

"That's the official verdict, but Cass was convinced that Ted murdered her and staged it to look like suicide."

"Is there any proof?"

Joe chuckled. "Just lines like this one, I guess. And the journal Cass discovered. It contains even more accusations, and closer to the time of Sylvia's death."

"Great. You've stumbled your way into another murder investigation."

He nodded. "It would appear so."

Sara shook her head and smiled. "How do you manage it? I mean, really, who goes from leaving his family to finding an unsolved murder?"

Returning her smile, he held up his hands. "I guess I do."

"Can we make this your last murder case, Dick Tracy? Please?"

"*Dick Tracy?* I prefer to think of myself as Phillip Marlowe or

Sherlock Holmes."

"Sherlock Holmes? Really? Maybe Inspector Clouseau."

Feigning a scowl, he said, "Hey, Cass compared me to James Bond. The Daniel Craig version."

She smiled seductively, the same smile she'd given him on their wedding day. "Well, you've got the body for it, that's true."

Maybe everything would be alright after all.

Sara went back to cleaning and Joe continued with the page that Cass had marked. Reading further, he was surprised by something that sounded familiar. The more he read, the more concerned he grew, until finally he searched the desk drawers. In the bottom drawer under some loose papers he found the old leather-bound journal, which he pulled out and opened on Cass's desk next to the other book.

Back and forth he went, comparing pages from the book to pages from the so-called "missing" journal. The words were Plath's, it was true, but they'd been copied, it seemed, from the book. The more he read, the more his suspicions were confirmed. Cass had copied randomly chosen lines from Plath's published journals and re-organized them in an attempt to construct a narrative of Sylvia showing her growing suspicions that Ted was planning her death.

He compared the handwriting of Cass's notes on the loose papers to the handwriting in the old-looking journal. Cass had changed her penmanship so it mimicked Sylvia's. *Oh my God. If she had tried to pass this off as Sylvia's, she would have been a laughing stock.*

The entire journal was a hoax, a forgery. *No wonder she didn't want to show it to the Hughes lawyers. They would have immediately spotted it as a forgery.*

Sara was hard at work, and though Joe wanted to share his discovery with her, he could tell she needed to be doing something productive.

Poor Cass. She was much sicker than anyone realized.

SYLVIA'S SECRET

Joe continued to pour through Cass's notes, as well as articles she'd collected. Her early notes from September and October were cogent and well-documented, and she'd been on to something very interesting—a discovery about Sylvia's death that might take scholars in an entirely new direction. But in November, her writing style and tone changed. Her thinking devolved and grew more disorganized. Then it became a series of rants against Ted. *What in God's name had happened to Cass? How could a woman of her intellect and talent descend into such a grandiose delusion?*

CHAPTER 31

The next day at around noon, Joe sat solemnly beside Sara in the doctor's office, listening to the diagnosis from Dr. Aimes, the psychiatrist who had been treating Cass for the past few days.

"Miss Johnson has listed you, Mr. Conrad, as her advocate."

Joe glanced at Sara and then back at the doctor. "What's that mean?"

He shrugged. "Only that, while she's hospitalized, you will be informed about her condition and asked to confer with her about any treatments or medications we prescribe. It's just a way to make sure that a patient who might not be fully competent has someone to offer advice."

"Shouldn't her parents do that?" Joe asked.

"Yes, yes. But since they aren't here yet, she's requested you."

"I guess that'll be okay. Do I need to sign anything?"

The doctor nodded, and pushed a form across the desk to Joe.

Joe took it and began to read.

Sara leaned forward. "I don't want to sound insensitive, but does that mean Joe might be responsible for her medical bills?"

"No, no, no. She has excellent insurance."

Joe took a pen off the doctor's desk and signed the form, handing it back afterward. "So can you tell us what's wrong with her, Doctor? What's your prognosis?"

The older man took the form, glanced at the signature, and then placed it into a manila file before speaking.

"Your friend suffers from severe manic-depressive illness and schizophrenia," Aimes said. He looked like a Freud wannabe—gray goatee and prominent forehead, wrinkled with concern—his British voice tainted with a slight Vienna accent that Joe assumed was an affectation. He would have found the good doctor amusing and silly, if he hadn't been so concerned about Cass. "Those illnesses had been kept in check by prescription drugs until her stay in London, but then she ran out of her medications. Elated to be here doing the research that she found so inspiring, she failed to recognize the danger of going off her meds until it was too late."

"Her dramatic mood swings?" asked Joe.

"Classic manic-depressive symptoms. And the paranoia resulted from her schizophrenia."

Joe glanced at Sara, saying, "Which probably explains why she believed people from the Hughes estate were after her. What about her claim that Plath's spirit was working through her, enabling her to write Plath's so-called missing journals?"

Dr. Aimes nodded. "Ms. Johnson's hallucinations also resulted from paranoia."

Sara leaned forward again. "So what's your prognosis?"

The doctor grinned. "She's already showing remarkable improvement now that she's back on her medications."

Sara smiled at Joe. "*That's* good news!"

"One more thing," the doctor added. "She's pregnant."

Sara looked at Joe. "What?"

"Don't look at me," he said. "It must be Trevor's, the boyfriend I told you about, the guy who was killed in the hit and run accident in Devon."

Sylvia's Secret

"At any rate," the doctor added, "her pregnancy also explains some of her mood swings. Her hormones are fluctuating."

"What about the medicines she's taking now for her depression? Will they hurt the baby?"

The doctor shook his head. "We're using drugs we know are safe for the fetus."

"Cass is quite well-respected at our campus, Doctor," Joe added. "We're very fond of her back in the states."

"Good, good. That affection and admiration will aid her recovery and help her stay vigilant in her fight against her illnesses. So long as she stays on her meds and receives regular check-ups from a good psychiatrist, I see no reason why she can't have a long and fruitful career."

"Have her stepmother and father been notified?" Joe asked.

"Yes, yes. I spoke to them only this morning. They're on their way. Once Ms. Johnson is well enough to travel, they plan to take her back to the States. They live in California, I understand, like you."

"In southern California," Joe explained, "about three hundred miles from us. California is a big state."

"Having the patient return to her family to be cared for and loved will be the best therapy. She'll need lots of care if she is to bring a new life into the world."

"When can we see her?" Joe asked.

Dr. Aimes checked his notes. "Let's give her another day. Come back tomorrow. By then, I believe she will be ready to chat."

Joe and Sara came back to the hospital the next day and found Cass sitting up in bed, reading the *London Times*. Though her hair was disheveled, her face looked more relaxed than he'd seen it since he had first arrived in England. She seemed to have gained a little weight, too, and didn't resemble an anemic heroin-addicted model anymore.

"How are you feeling?" Joe asked her.

She lowered the newspaper and smiled. "Almost back to my crazy old self."

Sara stepped over to the bed and gave Cass a hug and a kiss on her check. "Glad you're okay."

"I am, thanks to you. I understand we have you to thank for getting to us before it was too late."

"Well, I wouldn't have come to London in the first place if Joe hadn't been here."

"So," Cass said, "Joe Conrad saves the day again?"

Joe laughed. "No, not this time. Sara's the hero in this story."

"But also the villain," Sara said. She stepped away from Cass and closer to Joe. "I assume you told Cass why you came here."

Cass looked from Sara to Joe and back again. "To help me, right? To help a friend in need. Wait—am I missing something?"

Still looking at Joe, Sara said, "Joe caught me with another man."

Joe took her hand, saying, "Sara, don't. Cass doesn't need to hear about our problems."

"But I need to tell her, Joe. In case anything happened that she might feel guilty about—or you, for that matter."

Cass laughed. It was a good, hearty, normal-sounding laugh, but it startled Joe.

"Wait, *you* were unfaithful to *him*? Wow. And I thought *I* was screwed up."

Joe chuckled nervously. "I just needed some time away, to sort out what I was feeling. Your email came at the perfect time. It gave me a reason to leave."

"So, you and Sara were on a break, and you *still* didn't sleep with me?" She threw a pillow at Joe. "What am I, chopped liver?"

Joe caught the pillow and glanced at Sara nervously. She had forced a grin, but her eyes were filled with tears.

SYLVIA'S SECRET

"So nothing happened between you two?" Sara asked.

"No," Joe answered. "As I told the detectives, Cass is a good friend who needed my help, that's all."

"Tell the truth, Joe," Cass said. "Sara, you need to know. I tried to seduce your husband. More than once, I might add. He was a perfect gentleman, the rat."

"You were...not yourself," said Joe.

"Still, you had a hall pass, for all intents and purposes, and you *didn't* take it? That doesn't sound like the Joe Conrad I know."

"Well, maybe he's finally growing up." Sara smiled and wiped away tears that still found release.

"Yeah, maybe," Cass replied. "Or maybe he didn't want to get it on with a crazy-ass bee-otch."

Joe threw the pillow back at Cass, and she caught it, laughing. "You aren't crazy, Cass."

"If I go off my medications, I am. *That* won't happen again." She adjusted the pillows behind her back. "I've got to take better care of myself now that—" Cass caught herself and looked from Joe to Sara. "Now that I'm pregnant."

Sara stepped forward and took her hand. "I think it's wonderful, Cass. You'll be a great mom."

A tear leaked from the corner of Cass's eye and she swiped it away. "As long as I stay on my meds and get regular check-ups."

"You'll do fine," Sara said.

"And we'll be around to help out whenever you need us," Joe added. "We have a little experience."

"I'm worried about my father," Cass admitted. "Samantha— she's my stepmom, Sara—she'll be fine with it, but I'm not sure how my dad will feel about me being a single mother."

Joe tried to imagine his own daughter Katie coming to him in the future with news she was pregnant. *Geez, that's going to happen one day.* "You know, as the father of a daughter, I'd have to say that he'll probably be a little shocked at first, but then he'll be overjoyed. If he loves you as much as I love Katie, he'll love your child, too."

"I hope you're right," Cass said.

"Have you given any thought to names?" asked Sara.

Cass smiled. "Actually, I was doing that earlier this morning. I don't know the gender yet, but I think I've picked out a couple of good names."

"Can you share?" Sara asked.

"Well, if it's a boy, I want to name it after your husband, if you two don't mind, since he helped me through all this. But I don't care for Joe or Joseph."

"Conrad can be a boy's name," Joe chimed in.

"Yeah, but then he might get called Connie. No, I really like your middle name, so if it's a boy, I'm naming him Lawrence. Besides, I've always liked Lawrence Fishburne. He reminds me of my dad."

"And if it's a girl?" asked Sara.

"Sylvia, I bet," said Joe.

"No, not Sylvia. Too tragic. But you're on the right track. I'm thinking Ariel would be a good name."

"After Sylvia's mother," noted Joe.

"Yes, and in honor of Sylvia's poems."

"Ariel Johnson," Sara said. "Sounds beautiful and, I don't know, somehow inspirational."

"I have a favor to ask, Joe." She turned from Joe to Sara and back to Joe. "Would you be my baby's godfather?"

Joe tried to read Sara's face. She smiled and nodded.

"Sure, Cass. I guess so. If that's what you really want."

"I do. You're a good father, so I know you'd be a good person to look after my child if something ever happened to me."

Sara examined Joe's bleary eyes. "You know what that means, don't you?"

"I guess so. Why?"

SYLVIA'S SECRET

"You'll have to go to church for the baptism. You haven't been to church since Jack Claire's funeral. That was three years ago."

"I have, too, been to church. I went with Cass to Trevor's—" He stopped abruptly, not wishing to remind Cass. "Anyway, I don't mind going back to church. It will be good to go for something happy and wonderful—like the baptism of Cass's baby."

Cass nodded, looking very satisfied. "I'm still foggy on a couple of things. Trevor's death—that really was an accident, right? I mean, there's no way anyone from the Hughes estate arranged that?"

"I don't think so," Joe said. "Diane admitted everything, and I don't see any connection between her and the Hughes attorneys."

Cass nodded, accepting the reality. "About that missing Plath journal I found." She looked Joe square in the eyes. "That isn't real, is it? I mean, I wrote that, didn't I?"

"Let's just say, you made creative use of Plath's writings."

"God, Joe, what if I had tried to pass that off as authentic. I mean, my career in higher education would be ruined."

He nodded and touched her toes under the blanket. "You managed to cull all of the most damaging statements from Sylvia's actual journals to paint Ted Hughes in the most unflattering light, making him seem guilty as sin."

"I might as well burn that rubbish," she said. She shook her head, disappointment tugging at the corners of her mouth.

"I don't know. You might be able to publish it as long as you acknowledge that you're the one who edited it and rearranged Plath's own words. You might be able to market it as *The Case against Ted in Sylvia's Own Words*."

She nodded. "But there's no actual evidence that he staged her death, is there? I mean, that's all pure fantasy, right?"

"There's no tangible evidence Ted murdered Sylvia. Not that I can find in the materials you've collected, anyway. He had an alibi for the morning of her death, Cass. He was with Assia—she swears to it."

"But she could have been lying, right? I mean, she was in love with the great Ted Hughes, so she might have lied for him, right?"

"Yes," Joe responded, hoping their discussion wouldn't rekindle Cass's emotional tirade. "But there was other evidence, Cass. Evidence that will take your research in an entirely new direction."

"Well," Sara added, "he did drive her to suicide, didn't he?"

Joe shook his head. "Not exactly. What Cass's research has uncovered is the truth about Sylvia's suicide. That's why you've got to get better, to finish your work."

"I'm confused," Cass responded. "What did I uncover? What secret did I reveal?"

"Based on your notes, Cass, I'm convinced that Sylvia staged things to look like a suicide attempt, but she had planned it carefully so she would be found in time."

"What makes you think so?"

"It's all in your notes. Her timing was too precise. She had asked Mr. Thomas what time he was leaving. Then she left a note for him, asking him to call Dr. Horder. She turned on the gas at the time she figured Mr. Thomas would be waking up. Normally, his *au pair* girl arrived promptly at 9:00. If things had gone according to Sylvia's plan, she would have been rescued. But as the Scottish poet said, '*The best-laid schemes o' mice an' men. Gang aft agley…*'."

"What happened?" Cass asked.

"Basic physics. The gas didn't rise, as Sylvia assumed it would. That's why she sealed the kids' room and opened their window. She thought the gas would float up, but it didn't. The gas was heavier than the air, so it sank and seeped into Mr. Thomas's flat, knocking him out. She planned on him coming to her rescue, but he simply couldn't. When the *au pair* arrived, Mr. Thomas was unconscious, so he didn't answer the door."

"Wait," said Sara, "I don't understand. She figured she'd be found *before* the gas had taken her life? Is that what you're saying?"

SYLVIA'S SECRET

"Yes. If she had really wanted to die, she could have turned on the gas the night before, but instead she waited until the morning when she assumed she'd be found before she'd expired. Just like before, when she was a teenager and banged her head under the house. It's all described in *The Bell Jar*."

"And like her other so-called suicide attempt," Cass added.

Joe glanced at Sara, and then back at Cass. "There was another attempt?"

Cass nodded. "Yeah, in 1962. She drove her car off the road and told everyone she was trying to kill herself."

"What happened?" asked Sara.

"Nothing," Cass answered. "It wasn't like she drove off a cliff. The land was flat on both sides of the road. She rolled through the field and eventually stopped. It was obvious to everyone she was never in any real danger. It was just a ploy to get Ted's attention and sympathy from their friends."

"You need to tell the truth about her, Cass. Her suicide attempts were desperate attempts to get attention. I don't think she really wanted to die."

Cass let out an audible gasp of air. "She wanted to live, didn't she?"

Joe smiled. "Yes, I think so. She staged the suicide attempt to shine the spotlight of shame on Ted for his infidelity."

Cass nodded, her brown eyes clear. "She wanted him to feel the same level of guilt as her level of despair. She wanted the public to see how his actions had put her and the children at risk. After devoting so much of her life and energy to this man's career, she wanted to discredit him in the public eye."

"It's all in your notes," Joe said. "Her last poems show that. Her style and tone were less harsh, less angry. Softer. 'Sheep in the Fog,' 'Kindness,' 'Child,'—these are poems of hope more than despair. And when she wrote the sadder poems, it was as if she was weeping through her words, tears spilling from her pen as she wrote."

"Such a waste. Such a horrible waste of talent," Cass said.

"Exactly," said Joe. "Her death was accidental."

"So tragic," she muttered. "So damn tragic."

"That's why you've got to finish your research. Young women like Sylvia need to know the truth, especially if they're battling depression. They won't be able to use her death to justify their own. They'll have to see that despite everything, Sylvia Plath wanted to live. She wanted to go on being a mother and poet."

Sara added, "She wanted to be found in time and live to tell the world what an assho—what a jerk her husband was."

Cass giggled. "It's okay. You can say asshole in front of me. I won't flip out."

Cass's attitude told Joe she would be all right. "Your findings will give hope to people like Plath who suffer from depression. That hope will save lives, Cass."

"I hope you're right."

Sara clutched Cass's hand again. "And the fact that *you* did this work and *you* wrote about Plath's battle—someone who battled the same kinds of demons—that will give people hope, too."

"You mean because I suffer from the same illnesses, right?"

Sara touched her cheek. "Being honest about that will help remove the stigma associated with depression. Folks will see you as a role model. That will make it easier for them to get help."

A single tear escaped the corner of Cass's eye. "It's just so embarrassing."

Joe walked around to the other side of the bed and took Cass's free hand. "You once told me you thought I was brave because I'd gone up against people who were trying to kill me. Remember?"

She nodded, and closed her eyes.

"Well, I think you're much braver. You fought a terrible battle against the demons inside your own mind, Cass, and you won.

That's inspiring."

"The demons of the mind—that might be a good title." Cass opened her eyes and smiled at Joe.

"I like it," Sara said.

Cass nodded. "'The Demons of the Mind: How Creative People Battle Depression.' How's that sound, Joe?"

"Sounds good," he said, "with one revision. 'How Creative People *Overcome* Depression.'"

Cass pursed her lips. "Overcome," she repeated. "That's a good word, isn't it?"

Joe smiled. "Yes, Cass. It's a very good word."

THE END

SYLVIA'S SECRET
NOTES

Some of the "poems" in the "discovered" journal are actually sentences from the published journals of Sylvia Plath; others are this author's humble attempt to write something like Plath's poetry, a poor imitation of a great poet's style.

Some locations, such as the Old Railway Tavern, are fictitious. Passenger trains stopped running as far as North Tawton in 1973, so Cass and Joe would not have been able to ride the train all the way to the town. However, according to some sources, plans are in the works to restore passenger travel via train, so this author hopes the sleepy little town will be served soon.

Two characters' names were auctioned for charity. Those donors were Zenon Castillo and Diane Mousilina. Thanks to their generosity, as well as the generosity of others, over $5,000.00 was raised for the One Alternative Education Program in San Joaquin County. Thanks also to Debra Rose Nichols, whose name I borrowed for good nurse Rose, for helping to organize the fund raiser.

BIBLIOGRAPHY

Alverez, Al. *The Savage God: A Study of Suicide.* London: Weidenfelf & Nicolson, 1971.

Cooper, Brian. "Sylvia Plath and the Depression Continuum." *Journal of the Royal Society of Medicine,* 96.6 (2003). 296-301.

Hayman, Ronald. *The Death and Life of Sylvia Plath.* Great Britain: Sutton Publishing, 2003.

Kukil, Karen V., ed. *The Unabridged Journals of Sylvia Plath.* New York: Anchor Books, 2000.

Middlebrook, Diane. *Her Husband: Ted Hughes & Sylvia Plath—A Marriage.* New York: Penguin Books, 2003.

Moses, Kate. *Wintering: A Novel of Sylvia Plath.* New York: Anchor Books, 2003.

Plath, Aurelia Schober. *Letters Home by Sylvia Plath.* New York: HarperCollins, 1975.

Plath, Sylvia. *Ariel (The Restored Edition).* New York: HarperCollins, 2004.

Plath, Sylvia. *The Bell Jar.* New York: Harper Perennial Modern Classics edition, 2006.

Rose, Jacqueline. *The Haunting of Sylvia Plath.* Cambridge, Mass: Harvard U. Press, 1992.

Slater, Eliot. "*The Savage God: A Study of Suicide* (Review).": *Journal of the Royal Society of Medicine and British Journal of Psychiatry.,* 121 (1972). 100-1.

Wagner-Martin, Linda W. *Sylvia Plath: A Biography.* New York: St. Martin's, 1987.